I0555484

The
MESSAGE
on the
13 TH FLOOR

WINTER
LAWRENCE

THE MESSAGE ON THE 13TH FLOOR
Copyright © 2021 by Winter Lawrence

ISBN: 978-1-953735-71-3

Fire & Ice Young Adult Books
An Imprint of Melange Books, LLC
White Bear Lake, MN 55110
www.fireandiceya.com

Names, characters, and incidents depicted in this book are products of the author's imagination or are used fictitiously. Any resemblance to actual events, locales, organizations, or persons, living or dead, is entirely coincidental and beyond the intent of the author or the publisher. No part of this book may be reproduced or transmitted in any form or by any means, electronic or mechanical, including photocopying, recording, or by any information storage and retrieval system, without permission in writing from the publisher except for the use of brief quotations in a book review or scholarly journal.

Published in the United States of America.

Cover Design by Caroline Andrus

CONTENTS

"Just as ripples spread out when a single pebble is dropped into water, the actions of individuals can have far-reaching effects."

-DALAI LAMA

ACKNOWLEDGMENTS

As always, I'd like to thank my family for all of their love and support. Rich, Roo, Brittney, and Kaylee—you all rock—thanks for all your help! I owe another big thanks to Taj Holloway for being a big part of the conversation that got this book off the ground. Urban legends rule, Chica, and you're always welcome over for dinner! Another debt of gratitude goes out to my betas and my cherished advisors: Slick Rick, Jeanne Covert, Alexander Millard, Alexandra Burt, Barrie Davis, and Erin Winfrey. You guys are awesome! And last, but definitely not least, thank you to Mike Lynch. You are not only the best editor, but you are a true friend. I can never repay you for your kindness (and amazing wit!), but I'll keep trying. So much love your way, friend!

HELLO WORLD

Realistically, I know nothing has *really* changed. The ride back from Albany is no different than before. The car is still the same. But I'm different now. The route is still the same. The car is still the same. But I'm different now. On this Wednesday afternoon, I'm not only a high school senior or a military recruit. I'm officially sworn in. I'm officially an airman. Me. Meghan Marie Martin. I'm an airman. In a little over a month, I'll be eighteen years old, and in a little more than three months, I'll be heading to Lackland Air Force Base in San Antonio, where I'll start basic training and a new chapter of my life. Goodbye Middletown. Hello World.

"Penny for your thoughts?" Mom asks, startling me out of my reverie.

"Oh…" I look over and can't help but admire her profile. To me, my mom is the most beautiful woman in the world. She's a true bombshell. Blonde. Blue-eyed. Built. She's a little rough around the edges, and her reputation, unfortunately, precedes her, but she's my mom, and I love her.

"You have to quit worrying so much," she says as she reaches over and places her hand on my thigh.

I stare down at her hand for a moment and realize today marks yet another special occasion: my mother is sober. It's a rarity nowadays, and a rarer day yet when she's sober *and* motherly. Though, in her defense, Maggie May always tries to be a good mom. Most times she falls short on that, but I have to give credit where it's due. She tries.

On that note, I put my hand over hers and intertwine our fingers, my skin so much darker in comparison. When I was younger someone had told me we were like chocolate and vanilla. I don't remember who, but the saying has always stuck even though my mom isn't pure or sweet and I'm not rich or dark. I'm mulatto. I've been told that word is dated and offensive, but I've always liked it, and it's much better than the other things my sisters and I have been called. Mocha being another favorite. Oreo being one of my least.

"Your run times will get better the more you practice," Mom assures me with a squeeze of her hand.

"I know," I say, my future military physical fitness test being the least of my concerns at the moment. "I'll be ready by summer." Though I am worried about the heat. Texas in July, I'm told, is brutal. As a born and bred New Yorker, I'm not sure if I'll be able to handle it, especially under such stressful circumstances. *Great.* I hadn't been worried about it a second ago, but I am now.

"I know what will take your mind off it," Mom offers as she exits the freeway.

"It's not only that," I say as I try to figure out where she's going. "I'm just…" I glance over at her, the bags under her eyes noticeable even from this angle. In the past couple of months, since I started my recruitment journey, it's like she's aged ten years. Or maybe, now that I know I'm leaving, I'm starting to truly see her. I'm starting to realize how much I do for her, and I'm wondering if she's going to be okay when I leave.

"You're what?" she inquires as she weaves across two lanes of traffic to pull into the parking lot of a nail salon.

"I'm just worried about you and the girls," I finally admit, then I eye the salon suspiciously. "What are we doing here?"

"I'm treating you to a pedicure."

I roll my eyes. "Mom, I can do my nails at home for—"

"Yeah, yeah, I know," she says as she throws the gearshift into park, pulls the key out of the ignition, and then turns to face me. "But you're an airman now and your recruiter is worried about those ingrown toenails—"

"Mom—"

"No, ma'am," she says, wagging her finger in my face, "just because you're an airman and *this* close to being an adult doesn't give you the right to interrupt me. And don't try to talk me out of it either. I know we don't really have the money and I know we can do your nails at home, but here's my motherly advice to you, Peanut," my nickname for as long as I can remember, "always make sure you spoil yourself just a little bit. Otherwise, all that hard work with no play doesn't ever pay off. You understand?"

I nod even though I don't agree. The thing is, once my mom gets an idea in her head, it's nearly impossible to get her to change her mind, so I don't waste my breath. Instead, I try a different tactic. "I thought you said you had someplace you needed to be today."

Mom snorts. "It's way past noon, baby, so there's no chance of sleeping in today."

My brows furrow as I try to pick apart that particular mom-ism.

"Besides," she says, "this is more important. My baby is almost all grown up and gone."

When her eyes get all watery, I reach over and squeeze her hand. She's been on this emotional rollercoaster the past few weeks. I mean, I get it. I'm leaving, which is hard and scary for me too, but I can't express those feelings in front of her, because I'm her rock. If my dam breaks, hers will come crumbling down too, so I smile to lighten the mood.

"You're still stuck with me for a couple more months," I say as I throw open the passenger-side door and get out before the waterworks start. "You think they have an Air Force blue nail color?" I ask before I shut the door.

Mom gets out of the car and hurries after me. "I don't think blue will look good on you," she says, her voice back to normal. "Remember we tried it once when you were in elementary school." She pulls the door open, the strong smell of chemicals practically slapping us in the face. Thankfully, the potent odor is enough to keep Mom from coming apart at the seams over that particular Easter memory.

"Right," I offer as I hurry over to the sign-in sheet. "You getting your lip waxed today?" I ask without looking her way.

"No…" she says, but then she steps over to one of the mirrors. "Why? Do I need one?"

I shake my head. "I mean, I think it's okay…" I intentionally leave that sentence hanging, though.

"Maybe I should?" Mom says just as a young, petite Asian woman makes her way over to us.

"I'd like a pedicure, please," I tell the lady.

"Yes. Pedicure," the woman replies, her Vietnamese accent thick. "Go pick color," she orders while pointing toward the carousel of polishes.

I dutifully walk that way, but my attention remains focused on the conversation between my mother and the woman. They go back and forth about the price for a moment before they settle on a good amount. Then the lady signals my mother to follow her to the back for her lip wax. Relieved they're gone, I swipe a pretty, red polish off the shelf and then hurry to the counter.

I set the polish in front of the elderly Asian woman and smile. "Hi. I'd like to pay for my pedicure now please."

"You pay now?" she repeats, her English just as choppy.

"Yes, please," I say as I quickly grab my wallet from my back pocket and retrieve my debit card. I've been saving my meager Dollar Store paychecks so I have extra money to enroll my sisters in a summer day camp program that begins right before I leave. Mom isn't great at budgeting, and in the summer she always blows through cash trying to keep my sisters entertained, so the day camp will hopefully kill two birds with one stone: Mom won't run short on funds and my sisters won't kill each other out of boredom. If I had to bet though, I'd say my plan will partially work. The day camp will wear the girls out. My mother, unfortunately, will undoubtedly blow through her budget anyway, and so by virtue of her lack of restraint, I'm learning the art of saving. I won't let my little sisters suffer the way I once did.

"You need receipt?" the woman asks after swiping my card.

"No, thanks." I pocket my wallet and then follow her to the pedicure chair. I hadn't planned on anyone working on my feet, so I'm a little embarrassed when I toe my sneakers off and see all the holes in my socks. Thankfully, at this time of day, in the middle of the week, I'm the only one in the shop. I quickly snatch the socks off my feet and stuff them into my pocket, then I slide onto the chair. I've just gotten comfortable when Mom emerges from the back room, her upper lip a bright red.

"What color did you pick, Peanut?" she asks as she makes her way over.

I point at the bottle the woman had set on her pedicure cart.

Mom nods her approval. "I like it!" she says with a whistle. "Subtle but sexy."

I wasn't going for either, but I thankfully don't have to point that out because Mom is already on her way to the door.

"I'll be right back," she says as she fishes a pack of Marlboro Reds out of her purse.

I watch her disappear outside. She goes and leans against the hood of the car, lights up, and then grabs her cell phone out of her purse. I have no idea who she's calling. She used to talk to me all the time about her love life and her friends, but as I've gotten older—and I've started acting more like the adult —she's been more secretive around me and the girls, which is a good thing. We don't have different guys in and out of the apartment as much anymore, but that means Mom tends to disappear more and more often. I'm here now, so that's okay. I've always been able to handle the girls. But what about when I'm gone? Will they be okay? Will my mother make the right choices for their sakes?

As the woman begins my pedicure, I wonder about those questions and a million more. At the end of the day, I think joining the military is the best thing for me and for my sisters. I'll be the role model they've never had, and I'll be able to provide more for them because the military will eventually pay me more than the Dollar Store does. Not so much at first, when I'm lower ranked, but I plan to move up the chain as quickly as possible. Then one day, I'll be able to come back to Middletown with my head held high. And then I'll hopefully be able to get my mother and my little sisters out of this one-horse town.

1

JUST ANOTHER MONDAY

My recruiter looks at me with a smile, but I can tell she's a little annoyed. This isn't the first time she's come to meet me after school to work out and I've had to blow her off because my mother hasn't shown up to pick up my sisters at their school. She's also a little sad. I know that because after nearly a year of dragging my feet and finally swearing in, Staff Sergeant Hodge admitted the other day she was glad I had finally gone through with signing up for the service. "You're too young to be this old and responsible," she had once told me. In other words, she hates that I basically take care of my sisters and run our meager household while my mother falls farther and farther into a depression that's spiraling out of control.

As we make our way back to the bleachers, I glance over at her. "She's probably out grocery shopping and just lost track of time," I offer by way of the billionth excuse I've had to dish out for skipping yet another workout session.

"Probably so," she readily agrees, but I can see *that* annoyance in her eyes.

It's a look I'm familiar with because I've gotten it all my life. She's not mad at me—she's mad at my mom for being so irresponsible. She's mad at the system for not taking me and my sisters away when we'd probably be better off in some foster home—or three, since siblings aren't always kept together—especially ones like us: three different girls by three different dads. Sergeant Hodge isn't like other people we've met before though. She's a reasonable adult, and somewhere along the lines she learned you shouldn't punish kids for their parents' mistakes—she isn't the type to make us pay for their sins and shortcomings, which I appreciate. I've met the other type far more often. It's never a pleasant experience.

"What's your schedule like tomorrow?" she inquires as we make our way back to our gear. "Maybe we can try to squeeze in another run?"

"I'm working all week," I admit as I reach for my back-pack. I had begged for as many hours as the Dollar Store would allow because Mom's tips haven't been good—and she's been blowing through money like nobody's business.

Sergeant Hodge sighs. "You know, you'll be the first recruit who I'll actually be glad to see shipped off." She places her hand on my shoulder. "Compared to everything you do now, basic training is probably going to feel like a vacation to you, Meghan."

I meet her soulful brown eyes and sigh too. I'm sure that compared to my hectic life, basic training will be a breeze—even all the damn running I hate to do—but I don't know if I can go through with it, not when I'm so worried about Mom, Molly, and Misty.

"The best thing you can do for those girls is go," she adds like she can read my mind. "But right now, go on and get them from school. I'll be here tomorrow. Same bat time. Same bat channel?"

I nod, but just for good measure, I add, "Are you sure? You don't have to—"

"You're right. I don't have to come out here and do P.T.

with you, but I like helping all of my recruits prepare so they know what they're walking into." She pauses, her eyes boring into mine. "Plus, running isn't only good for your body; it's good for the mind too, so we'll do a quick thirty-minute workout tomorrow. That'll give you plenty of time to shower up and get to work on time, right?"

Yeah. But only if my mother can manage to pick up my little sisters from school. I don't say as much though. I don't have to. "I'll see you tomorrow," I say as I fish my car keys out of my bag and then sling it over my shoulder.

"Good night, Airman," Sergeant Hodge says.

"Night," I say and, as always, resist the urge to hug her. From the time I'd taken the ASVAB my junior year of high school until now, Sergeant Hodge has always felt like a mom to me. She isn't though, which I'm sorry for, and I'm trying my hardest to be strong, the way an airman is supposed to be, so I settle on a wave and then I hurry to my car. The piece of crap Hyundai is held together by duct tape and hope, but it managed to get me and the girls to school today, and I'm hoping it gets me to the elementary school, then home, and then to work tonight. The last thing I need is car trouble, especially with Mom once again being MIA.

Thankfully, the Hyundai starts and gets me to Carter Elementary just as one of the last cars in the parent pick-up line drives off. My two little sisters are sitting cross-legged with their backs against the red-bricked wall. Molly is braiding and then unbraiding her hair. Misty is reading. I pull up to the curb, turn off the car—since I'm running dangerously low on gas—and I get out. As I walk around the hood, Molly and Misty get up, but they know better than to head to the car, not with the way Mrs. Broom is looking at me.

"Miss Martin," Mrs. Broom says in her stern way. "Or should I say, Airman Martin. I see we interrupted your work-out. Again."

"I was just wrapping up," I lie. "And it's no problem. I'm sure Mom just lost track—"

"For the fifth time this month?" she adds, just to drive the nail home.

Has it been five times already? "Right. She's just been really busy helping Uncle Rusty—"

"No job, Airman Martin," she begins, her voice hitching up to that level that means she's about to go into lecture mode, "is more important than motherhood." Mrs. Broom, who for a woman well into her fifties is still remarkably fit, crosses her arms over her chest. "I've been telling her this since *you* were my student, Meghan, and whereas most mothers learn over time, your mother..." She leaves that sentence hanging and then looks between Molly and Misty. When she finally looks at me again, I see *that* look in her eyes. "Other people are beginning to notice."

That last part she adds by way of warning because as much as Mrs. Broom has always hated waiting on my mother, she wouldn't rat her out. Other teachers aren't as patient though, and neither are some of the parents—or Misty's dad. They're all watching us—everyone waiting for Mom to mess up just enough to snatch us away. To break our family apart.

"I'll make sure it doesn't happen again," I say, loathe to make promises I can't keep, though, at this rate, I may just ask Sergeant Hodge if we can work out here for the rest of the week. There isn't a track like at the high school, but I'm sure we can run around the fenced-in playground a bunch of times to get a couple of miles in before I have to head to work. And if Mom doesn't show up again, then I'll be here anyway. Just in case.

"I'll hold you to it," Mrs. Broom says, then she looks at the girls. "I'll see you two first thing in the morning, with your math homework," she emphasizes, though we all know that last part is for Molly's benefit. She isn't a homework kind of gal.

"Yes, ma'am," the girls say in unison.

If you didn't know them, you'd think they were twins. Fraternal, of course, because while they're both light-skinned mixed-raced girls with a mass of curly brown hair, Molly's eyes are a vibrant blue, like Mom's, whereas Misty's are a light brown, like her dad's. They aren't twins, of course, not in the fraternal sense anyway, but they are what people call "Irish twins," because they're only fourteen months apart. While Misty has always excelled in school though, Molly was held back a couple of years ago, so now she and Misty are both in the fifth grade together—and they're both in my former elementary school teacher's class.

Man, am I glad I'm finally getting out of this town.

Now I just have to make sure that when I'm gone my sisters follow in my footsteps and not in our mother's.

"Come on," I tell the girls as I hurry around the front of the car.

Molly and Misty slide onto the back seat, which is a small miracle. Usually they fight over who gets shotgun. Today though, and most times when there's trouble, they're wise enough to act right so nothing draws any more attention to us. The moment we drive away though, they pop off their seat-belts and lean closer to the middle console.

"Where is she?" Molly asks.

"Is she really at Uncle Rusty's?" Misty chimes in next.

I glance back at each of them for a quick second before I go back to watching the road. Our Uncle Rusty isn't really our uncle. He's Mom's boss, has been for about ten years now, but he's the closest thing to family I've ever known, and he's always taken care of us even though Mom has never been in line to win any bartender-of-the-year awards. In fact, I'm sure if it weren't for me and the girls, Rusty would have fired her a long time ago. He doesn't have any family left either though, so he always jokes that Mom is like the bratty little sister he never had or wanted, but we're worth all the trouble Maggie May throws his way.

"Put your seatbelts back on," I order, definitely not in the mood to deal with some stupid, nosy cop with nothing better to do than to bug a frantic teenager who's once again trying to work out the best way to deal with what life is throwing her way. "I don't know where she is and I don't have minutes on my phone to waste trying to track her down. When we get to the house, just run over to Mrs. Jackson's apartment and ask to use her phone." I glance in the rearview mirror and make eye contact with Molly. "You know what to say, right?"

Molly rolls her eyes. "Yeah, yeah," she replies, always annoyed I don't think she can maintain all the lies we tell in order to stay safe. "I'll leave a message pretending that she just ran to the store and I'm reminding her to grab extra snacks for our field trip tomorrow."

I nod. "Good girl." There is no field trip, of course, but we have to keep up the ruse even though, out of everyone, Mrs. Jackson knows that me and the girls are on our own the majority of the time.

For the rest of the car ride home, the girls tell me about their day, the two of them interrupting and contradicting each other several times before I pull into the driveway. Our apartment building used to be one nicely sized single-family home. At some point though, the owner had decided to divide it into four two-bedroom apartments. It isn't the nicest or cleanest place in town, and it isn't in the best neighborhood, but it's home, and the parking lot is big enough for each apartment to have two spots. I pull into mine now and notice Mom's car is still missing.

Where the hell is she?

For the past few weeks, she's been absent in the mornings,

so I've been stuck getting the girls ready and dropping them off at school, since I don't trust them to get themselves on the bus just yet, but Mom is almost always good about being there to pick them up. Lately, though, she's been really flaky—more so than usual, which worries me—greatly.

"I'm hungry," Misty announces as she scoots out of the car.

Molly gets out right behind her, chiming in on that sentiment.

I grab my backpack off the passenger seat and chase after them. "Well, there isn't anything to eat, so you guys can have a small bowl of cereal to hold you over until Mom gets back."

That idea is met with jeers, and both girls glance back at me and snarl.

"Hey, I lived off Toasty Oats for years and I'm fine," I say with an eye roll.

"But there's no sugar," Misty whines.

"You don't need sugar," I snap, always annoyed with how much they complain. Do they not realize how tight money is? Do they not realize we're doing the best we can? At least they have food! I remember when it was just me and Mom and we had to go days without really eating because, back then, she had too much pride to go on welfare. Now the girls survive on it. Sure, the food isn't great, but they always have milk, eggs, cereal, cheese, and bread, and when push comes to shove, you can do a lot with those ingredients.

"Mom will bring us dinner before she goes to work," Molly says, who—God love her—has never been book smart, but she's always been intuitive and very sensitive to my mood changes. She can sense my agitation, and we all know Mom is prone to disappearing and then lavishing us with tasty treats to make up for it, so she goes along with my logic, if for nothing more than to score brownie points with me. She slows down, giving me the chance to catch up to her, and then she looks up at me, searching for my approval.

I smile and nod. "Right. So for now, you girls can have some cereal while you do your homework. Mom will pop up before we know it, probably with a pizza—"

"Pizza!" Misty repeats, her voice echoing in the hallway. "I love pizza!"

"We know," I say as I watch her fish her copy of the apartment key from around her neck. She positions it just right, slides it into the knob, and unlocks the door. Just before she has the key completely out of the knob though, Molly shoves the door open, which pulls Misty's necklace taunt enough to warrant a gag. Molly laughs at Misty's distress and then she takes off into the apartment. This isn't the first time she's pulled that trick, so she knows she needs the head start. In response, Misty yanks the key out of the knob and charges after Molly, hellbent on killing her. I don't have time to play referee, so I figure the strongest will survive as I lock the front door and head for the bathroom. I get the water started, since even this time of year, it takes forever to warm up.

With the girls busy arguing, I'm free and clear to shower without interruption. I grab my Dollar Store polo and my work jeans from our bedroom—the girls' stuff on one side of the room with bunk beds and a small desk to share, while I'm on the other side with a loft-style bed-desk combo and an extra, mismatched dresser for my clothes. I drop my backpack onto my desk, pull off my sneakers and socks, and then I run across to the bathroom.

I've gotten my showers down to two minutes. Sergeant Hodge says most days I'll have plenty more time than that to clean up when I'm in basic training, but I've read otherwise online, and I've seen enough military movies to know better. Without washing my hair, I can get all the major spots scrubbed and rinsed in under two minutes. With the hair, since it's so thick and curly and requires immense amounts of conditioner, I'm still hanging at around ten minutes. The extra work and hassle of handling it has never bothered me before, so I'm loathed to even consider it, but I think right before I leave for basic training, I'm going to have to chop it off.

For today though, I skip washing it, since I know it's something I'm going to have to get used to, and I plan to just unravel it from the thick bun at the nape of my neck to replace it with the same style. It's how I'll have to wear it for the next few decades of my life since I plan to make the military my career. It's a dream that's been long in the making and one I hope my mother doesn't ruin, though at this point, I don't think there's any way the Air Force will let me out of my Delayed Entry Program status. I'm enlisted now. They're just letting me stay out long enough to graduate, so I doubt there are any loopholes to let me out of my contract, even if my mom can't take care of the girls.

I sigh, hoping I'm just overreacting. Mom is just trying to get as much fun and play out of her system while I'm still here. Once I'm gone, she'll have no choice but to finally get herself together…*right?* I step out of the shower and quickly towel off and get dressed. I have exactly nineteen minutes before I have to clock in to work, and I need to make sure the girls are settled before I go. I pull the bathroom door open and I'm just about to wipe the mirror off with my towel when I jerk to a stop. The words "I love you, M&M," are written in my mother's sloppy cursive and are enclosed within a lopsided heart. It's reminiscent of our signature goodbye, where Mom puts her hands in a heart shape over her heart and says, "I love you M&M." It's nice and universal since all our names start with the letter M. Initially, Mom hadn't planned that. She had named me in honor of my grandmothers, but when she realized she was Maggie May and I was Meghan Marie, we became the first M&Ms. Me the peanut version. Then, when the girls came along, Mom couldn't resist. She named them Molly Michelle and Misty Monroe, just to keep up the family tradition. By then, she had been divorced twice over, so she went back to her maiden name, Martin, which we all had because she hadn't been legally married to any of our dads at the time of our births. Of course, by then, we were M&Ms, so we sort of ignored that last M since it didn't go well. Who wants to be called M&M&M?

It's been a running joke in our family for as long as I can remember, but for some reason, as I stare at the steamy message, my stomach sinks at the sight of it even though I know it's probably been there for ages. That'll go to show how long it's been since anyone has cleaned the bathroom. Yet, despite telling myself that, I can't bring myself to erase the message.

"I love you too," I say as I hang my towel on my hook, then I turn to grab my deodorant from the medicine cabinet. After applying a healthy dose, since I know there's going to be plenty of inventory to stock tonight, I dab a little flowery perfume on my wrists—since the spritzer is broken, hence how I had gotten it for free from work—and then I apply some Vaseline to my lips, the contents just fine even though part of the bottle had gotten chipped and dented one long-ago night when the manager had accidentally crushed the case.

I turn to leave, planning to use the small mirror on my desk to fix my hair, but I stop short again when I see my mother's towel has fallen to the floor. I don't remember knocking it down, but it somehow fell even though I wasn't anywhere near it. As I reach to pick it up, glass shatters in the distance. From the sounds of it, I'd guess it was a dish. Of course, I don't have time to try to figure it out before the girls start going at each other. I sigh as I begrudgingly hang my mother's towel back on the hook so I can go and clean up another of her messes—not that I like to think of my sisters that way, but there are times when I resent having to take care of everything. There are times when I wish I could just be a fun-loving, lighthearted seventeen-year-old girl without a care in the world.

I never have been though, I remind myself, and I never will be.

With that resounding thought playing in my mind, I switch off the bathroom light and head toward the kitchen, my disapproving motherly face in place so I can hopefully scare the girls straight before I leave for work.

2

THE DOLLAR STORE

At work, I serendipitously run across a box of dishes on clearance because one of the bowls had broken at some point. What are the chances? I grab the box off the shelf and carry it to the break room. I'm usually never this lucky, though given how badly today has gone, it only seems fitting something finally worked in my favor. Even here at the Dollar Store, where life is usually quiet and predictable, we had several rude customers, and for about fifteen minutes, we had lost power because some drunk driver had crashed into a nearby utility pole. The darkness of the store wouldn't have been nearly so bad if we hadn't had about five families wandering around at the time, the kids literally going bonkers when the power failed. Not to mention that the manager went a little berserk too, worried about looting and people stealing stuff.

Even hours later, I still have the pulsing headache that sprang up from the minor blackout, so I start toward the first aid kit the manager keeps stashed in her desk. As I near the office though, the door chimes, letting me know someone has entered the store. *Dammit.*

"Welcome to the Dollar Store!" I shout out the mandated

message as I hurry to the manager's desk. I quickly rummage through the first aid kit to locate the opened Dollar Store brand of aspirin we always keep on hand. I shake two pills onto my palm, get the kit back into the desk, and hurry to the front counter.

To my horror, I see my two sisters standing by the register, both looking like the cats who ate the canaries. "What are you guys doing here?" I ask in a combination of dread and anger. I quickly glance at the clock. It's just past eight, but even in March it still gets dark way early.

Molly, always adamant about being the big sister and therefore the one who's designated to answer for the two of them steps forward and lets out a deep breath before beginning what I can tell she's practiced several times. "Mom still hasn't gotten home, and when the power went out…" She falters, so Misty takes over.

"We got scared," she admits, trying to sound proud of being able to admit that even though she knows I'm clearly upset with them for leaving the apartment.

"How many times have I told you girls to just wait out the storm!" I whisper-snap, then I look around to see if my manager is near. Thankfully, she's not. "That's why we keep the emergency kit in the closet with the flashlights and blankets," I add as I walk the rest of the way over to the register and grab the bottle of water I always keep stashed just beneath the counter. I swallow down the aspirins and then give the girls a proper stern look. "Do you know how dangerous it is for two young girls to be walking around at night?" I don't bother giving them time to answer that rhetorical question because I'm more interested in the reason they're here. "So Mom never called Mrs. Jackson back?"

The girls shake their heads.

Molly finds her voice again. "But her car is at Uncle Rusty's—"

"What?" I interject. "How do you know that...?" My eyes narrow as I study them and my brain switches gears so I can calculate what they've been up to. It's a talent I'm sure I'm going to need now that I'm a 1N0X1—the Air Force designation for an operations intelligence enlisted personnel, and one that I use now to deduce the girls' sudden appearance. As all the pieces begin to fall into place, I glare between them. "You walked to Uncle Rusty's in the dark?" I snarl out of clenched teeth—definitely more pissed now than concerned.

The girls sidestep closer to each other.

"Do you know how much trouble we could have gotten into if someone stopped you?" It's another rhetorical question, and one they'd better not try to answer.

The girls seem to shrink while I try to rein in my anger. I look around again, just to make sure we're still alone, then I turn toward the break room.

"Come on," I order without glancing back to see if they're following. Instead, I peek around corners to make sure my boss doesn't notice as we make our way to the back of the store, not that it would be the first time the girls have hung out here. They're frequent guests, but in each of those instances, I've given everyone ample warning. Tonight, I'm hoping my manager is cool about letting them stay until the store closes at nine since there's no way I'm going to let them walk back home at this hour. Granted, we only live a couple of miles away, but it's not the safest stretch, so there's that. Also, with Mom still being MIA, if some good Samaritan stopped to help them and got a little curious, that could land us in some very hot water with Child Protective Services. The last thing I need right now is some kind of custody issue before I leave.

The girls make it to the doorway of the break room just as I make it to the end of the counter. I point for them to go to the table, then I walk over to the Little Debbie end cap and grab two Honey Buns. After stopping for two bottles of water,

I march back into the break room. The girls' eyes, which are still ever sorrowful for disobeying orders and Martin family emergency protocols, still manage to light up when they spot the treats.

"To be clear," I say as I place the food and drinks on the table, "this isn't a reward for doing the wrong thing." I pull the manager's chair over, since the little table only has two seats, and then I look between the girls. "Listen, I know how scary it can be when the power goes out, but you know we can't let people find out you two are alone—"

"But we didn't say anything to anyone," Molly interjects. "And we were super quiet when we left the building so no one would notice."

"That's good," I tell her, "but what about all the people who saw you two outside?" I sit back in my chair and let them absorb that. "It isn't normal for two little girls—"

"I'm not little," Molly says and crosses her arms over her chest. "I'm eleven—"

"That's still not old enough for you two to be alone." I lean forward in my seat and give her one of my sternest glares. "You are the older sister, Molly, so you should know better. What if something happened to you? Misty wouldn't know what to do—"

"Sure I would," Misty chimes in. "I would call my dad."

When Molly and I both give her a killer case of rage over that stupid rebuttal, she slinks down in her seat. "He would take us all," she adds before looking down at her unopened Honey Bun.

A silence settles over us for a moment, probably because it's so hard for any of us to fully explain to Misty that while her dad has always been great with me and Molly, he isn't legally our father. And technically, he doesn't have to take us if he doesn't want to. And there's a big difference between taking Molly with him and Misty every other weekend to NYC compared to taking us all permanently. Also, he may not even have a choice on that matter because legally, he has no rights over us. It's something I know all about because I've looked into it a million times before. I think I can fend for myself at this point though, but that doesn't mean the thought hasn't occurred to me that the girls might be better off with Matt in a cramped little apartment in Manhattan rather than here in Middletown with Mom.

"Misty," I finally say, "there are laws we all have to follow, so we can't take the chance." This last bit I add because Mom has ingrained it into me. "And do you want to be the reason we're all separated?" I hate myself a little for saying it because I know the guilt that comes with it. We've all been on the receiving end of that line so often, but there's some truth to it. We're a family—a very broken and dysfunctional one, but we're all we've got. "I promise once I get to my permanent duty station, I'll find a nice apartment, and you guys can come and stay with me. We'll all be able to start over."

Misty still doesn't look at us, but she says, in barely a whisper, "You can't control where you go." She looks at me then. "I heard the teachers talking, Meghan, and they said you can go places we can't go. That you could go to war and die—"

"I am not going to war," I say vehemently, though it very well is a possibility, just one I'm hoping will come after I get a stateside assignment. Just long enough so I can move Mom and the girls far away from Middletown. Then they can get all settled someplace new and fresh.

"Knock, knock," my manager says from the doorway.

I jump onto my feet. "Ms. Latisha!" I start to roll her chair back to her desk. "I'm so sorry, my neighbor just dropped the girls off because she had to run out unexpectedly."

Ms. Latisha looks between me and the girls. "Mrs. Jackson was here, you say?"

I gulp. *Dammit.* That's the problem with small towns. Everyone knows everyone.

"Yes, ma'am," Misty says, her lower lip jutting out just a bit and her big brown eyes full of genuine honesty. She blinks, her long lashes seeming to take cue so the movement is accentuated to drive a dagger through anyone's heart.

She and Ms. Latisha standoff for a moment, the older black woman seeming to carefully contemplate her next move before she proceeds with caution. "Well, I hope everything is okay," she finally says, letting us take the win. For now. "You gals can stay in here while your sister finishes stocking these shelves."

"Of course!" I say as I shove her chair back in place and then hurry over to her. "And thanks for understanding! I'll just pay for their snacks first—"

"That's okay," Ms. Latisha interjects. "I'll get it this time, along with a couple of ice creams out of the freezer—"

"You don't have to do that," I say, hating it when people give us handouts, but my pride falls short because the girls squeal with delight and then take off, nearly knocking us over to get to the freezer. I watch them go then look at my boss. "Thank you."

Ms. Latisha gives me *that* look and then gently taps my shoulder a couple of times. "Just be sure to get those girls a decent dinner when you leave, okay?"

"I…" I stop myself from telling her they already ate because it's hard to *not* lie all the time at this point, but I know there's no use in keeping up the ruse with Ms. Latisha. Lying to people you see all the time is a nearly impossible feat I gave up years ago. It's just easier to stick to the truth—or as close as I can get anyway, so I settle on saying, "yes, ma'am," and then I duck out of the office before the conversation can get anymore awkward.

I hurry back to aisle seven and finish stocking the shaving

cream and deodorant. A couple of cans didn't make it through the shipping process well, so I stick those back into a box and then make a mental note to ask Ms. Latisha if I can take a few of them home with me...tomorrow though because I feel as though I've used up all her goodwill tonight. After breaking down all the other empty boxes and taking them out to the recycling dumpster, I make my way to the break room. The girls are huddled together, reading over one of the teen magazines, their pints of ice cream nearly empty; their Honey Buns gone.

"Did you say thank you for those?" I inquire as I reach for the wrappers. In response, they both absently nod and then start talking about some Disney channel celebrity I've never heard of. I don't have time to watch television, and while we don't have cable, Mrs. Jackson usually lets them swing by for a couple of hours in the evening to "keep her company." Of course, I personally know that after working all day at Walmart, Mrs. Jackson likes to be alone—Mr. Jackson having passed away a couple of years earlier—but she's always looked out for me and the girls, which I appreciate.

I tuck the box of leaking, oozing bottles of shaving cream and broken deodorants under the manager's desk and then turn to look at my sisters. "Did you guys finish your math homework?"

They nod, once again still too enthralled by whatever celebrity gossip they're reading to pay me much mind. Glad that they're quiet and occupied, I head back out to the store and help tidy up and cash out the drawers for the evening. At exactly nine o'clock, Ms. Latisha ushers us to the door.

"You girls go on and go," she says, giving me one final push to let me know she means business. "Go on now," she says in that older black woman way of hers, "get them girls to bed and you do the same, Ms. Meghan."

"Will do," I assure her, so exhausted I plan to take her up

on that offer. "Thanks again for everything." The girls chime in with their thanks and then goodbyes.

Ms. Latisha waves and then closes the door, locks it, and shuts off the front lights. I take that as my cue to start ahead; the girls follow along like ducklings. They once again slide into the backseat, probably because they're still glaringly aware they've messed up big time and have mostly gotten away with it, so they don't want to push their luck.

I say a little prayer before I put the key in the ignition and then breathe a sigh of relief when the car starts. I'm *so* ready for bed, but even though every part of my body wants nothing but sleep, I don't go straight home. Instead, I take a right when I get to the Dollar Store's exit and head toward Uncle Rusty's. There's no way I'll be able to wait up for her tonight, so I'm going to her first, and she damn well better have a good excuse as to why she ditched us all day without so much as a word.

3

WELCOME TO RUSTY'S

My mother's car is parked in her usual spot at Rusty's Bar & Grill. The carport is adjacent to the back door and is officially for staff use only, but I pull into one of the empty spots by my mother's piece of crap Chevy Malibu anyway, because, by proxy, I count as staff.

"Wait here," I tell the girls, and then before they even have a chance to answer, I get out and slam the door way too hard. I look back to see if they're okay, but Ms. Latisha had bought them that magazine so they're still too engrossed by it to notice my tantrum.

I take a few steps ahead but I stop short when I notice Rusty's car is parked on the other side of the Malibu. *Where's my moped?* Well, technically, it isn't *my* moped. Yet. Rusty had found a BMS Legend a few weeks ago and was working on fixing it up little by little. He had been driving it to work the past couple of days, trying to get the last of the kinks out—or so he claimed. Secretly, I think he had gotten it for me in the first place, but it was one of the few times my mother's dysfunctional motherly instincts had kicked in, so he was trying to butter her up about it. Show her it was safe. Of course, the keyword in all this is dysfunctional, since on things she should be worried about, like abandoning her children for the day to do god knows what, she's totally oblivious! Me learning how to ride a moped though, well that's too dangerous.

I swear that woman is a walking contradiction.

On that sour note, I stomp my way to the back door of Rusty's and yank it open. For a second, I'm assailed by the delicious smells of bar food, so my hunger overrides my anger. I peek inside, the kitchen vacant, which on a Monday night during the off-football season isn't entirely unusual. I walk over to the condiment table and scarf down two pickles and have just reached for a slice of cheese when Uncle Rusty walks in through the swinging door.

"Meghan!" he says, looking as though he's seen a ghost. "Jesus, kid. You scared me."

Uncle Rusty is a big guy—like over six feet tall, and he's broad like a linebacker, so I never thought he'd be one to scare easily. I mean, he has done some serious jail time. Though I guess when I think of it that way, he probably would get jumpy if people snuck up on him. Plus, the music is blaring from the jukebox, *and* I had just come in through the back door unannounced, so his reaction might not be entirely unexpected. Still, there's something about it that strikes me as odd.

"Hey," I say lamely, my hand still hovering over the cheese. "Sorry. I didn't mean to scare you. I was just looking to borrow Mom for a couple of minutes..."

A strange expression clouds his big, bearded face. "Borrow your mom?" he echoes.

I drop my hand to my side and then look around. "Yeah. My mom," I say, not sure why this conversation feels so weird. It isn't as though this is the first time I've just popped in before. "Is she busy or something?" I ask, shifting my attention to the order window that isn't too far away. It has a pretty decent view of the bar. There are a couple of regulars sitting at a high-top, but the place looks pretty deserted, so they can't be that busy.

"What I mean is," he says as he walks toward the grill, "your mom never showed up for work today."

My gaze snaps back to his. "What do you mean she never showed up? Her car is out back."

"I know," he confirms as he reaches for his cell phone. "She left it here last night because she took off with a friend. She said she'd just get a ride to work tonight." He swipes at his screen, types something in, and then he finally meets my bewildered gaze. "I texted her a couple of times but I hadn't heard anything. Then the power went out and the cops showed up, so I lost track of time..." Uncle Rusty looks me over. "Have *you* not heard from her?"

My heart skips a few beats and my mouth suddenly goes dry. Mom's disappeared before. But this time, I'm getting a really bad feeling about it. I shake my head sullenly, a million thoughts swirling through my mind, making my skull feel like it weighs a thousand pounds.

"Well, let's not panic," he says sort of clumsily—the way adults do when they realize they've said something they aren't supposed to. "You know better than anyone that Maggie May has a tendency to lose track of time."

I nod, but I can't help but evade his eyes. "I know..." Because I do know better than anyone how flaky and unreliable she can be. And this seriously isn't the first time she's been gone for this long. One time, when I was fourteen and the girls were eight and seven, she had run off to Foxwoods Resort Casino with some guy, and somewhere along the way, she had gotten arrested for a DWI. We were home by ourselves for two days before Uncle Rusty found her and posted her bail so she could get back to Middletown.

And then there was "her accident" about a year ago. The one where she had careened off the road by Monhagen Lake and had been pinned inside her car for almost three days before someone finally spotted what was left of the Honda Civic. She had nearly died of dehydration then, and if it hadn't been such a mild winter, she could have frozen to death, but Mom always jokes and says she has nine lives. Nothing or no one can hold Maggie May Martin down, she always teases— not even death.

"You said she left with someone?" I finally have the sense to ask, my brain once again switching back into investigative mode.

Uncle Rusty nods. "Yeah. Some dude from Newburgh..." He seems to ponder that for a moment. "Will, I think... yeah...big black guy with dreads. I've seen him around a few times the past couple of weeks."

That sounds exactly like the kind of guy my mother would wander off with, and Newburgh isn't that far away, but it's far enough that if she got stranded, she wouldn't be able to make it back so easily. "When did they leave?" I ask, my operations intelligence hat completely on now because if she is stuck again, I don't want to leave her stranded without at least trying to help. When she had her accident last year, I had gotten so mad I hadn't even bothered to look for her, and she could have died because of that. It was a mistake I wasn't going to make again. So I'm pissed that she's off on one of her "Mad Maggie May" adventures, but at least this time around, I'll keep an eye out, just in case.

"Hmm..." Uncle Rusty says, once again seeming contemplative in his response. "It was pretty dead last night..." He walks over to the grill and starts cleaning it. "I think that guy —Will and his crew—showed up around eleven or so." He heads to the refrigerator, pulls out three burger patties from the freezer, and heads back over to the grill. "They mentioned something about stopping by here on their way back from somewhere." He drops the patties onto the grill, the sizzling sounds and smells making my stomach do a couple of flips. "I just caught bits and pieces of the conversation though, 'cause your mom waited on them."

I consider that for a moment. "So she left with him and his friends?"

"No." He flips the burgers. "His friends left around one. Him and your mom left closer to two." He shrugs. "Like I said, it was dead, so I let her go a couple of minutes early and I closed up shop."

I sigh since that definitely sounds like something my mom would do. The problem, of course, is that without any other information, it would be impossible to find her. "Can I use your phone?" I ask him.

"Of course," he motions toward it and then goes about dropping a batch of fries into the deep fryer. "Can you keep an eye on these for a second while I check on the customers?"

When I nod, he disappears through the swinging door. As I move to stand in front of the grill, I shift the cell phone between my shoulder and ear. When I lift the spatula off the counter, my mom's voicemail picks up. The familiar robotic recording begins to play.

"Hey," I say after the beep, "it's me…" I sigh, trying to contain my temper. It helps, marginally, but I can't hold my sarcasm at bay. "Thanks for the heads up about getting the girls today…and for ditching out on dinner…" I flip the burgers. "Anyway, I've taken care of everything." *As usual.* "It's like 9:30 on Monday night. I just came by Rusty's and he said you never showed up for work, so whenever you're done doing whatever it is you're doing, give him or Mrs. Jackson a call so we know when you'll be back." I shift and grab the phone, ready to hang up, but before I hit the end button, I add, "We love you. Bye."

I hang up, more pissed now than I was a second ago. I place Uncle Rusty's phone on the counter, then I go about flipping the burgers. Afterward, I top them with cheese.

"Put those in to-go containers," Uncle Rusty says as he walks back through the swinging door. He steps over to the deep fryer and shakes up the fries in the boiling vat. "Any luck?" he asks.

"Nope," I say, just as curtly as I feel. I walk over and grab three to-go containers and three buns. I toss the bread onto the grill to brown them and then go about setting up the containers—in a very meticulous manner—just because I'm that annoyed.

"Were you guys hit by that power outage earlier?" he asks conversationally.

"Yeah." I move the middle container to the left a tad, just so it's in line with the other two boxes.

"That was one of mine," Uncle Rusty says as he lifts the fry basket to hang.

I look over at him. "Excuse me?"

"The drunk guy…he was here when I opened today at four and he started hammering back beers like nobody's business." He dumps the fries onto a stainless-steel tray he keeps on the other side of the counter and then he seasons them with his special sauce—which is just an equal distribution of salt, pepper, and that Spanish seasoning called Adobo. "I actually had to cut him off, and I was relieved when he finally left, but then the power went out and the damn police showed up."

Uncle Rusty visibly shudders. As a convicted felon, he hates the cops. Unfortunately, when you own a bar, which in Uncle Rusty's case had happened through a series of very fortunate events, you very often have to deal with law enforcement. That's one of the reasons he keeps Mom around. She has a way of handling the cops even though she's been in a boatload of trouble herself. I snort at that particular thought though, since now that I'm older I understand why she "handles" the cops so well. According to the town's gossip mill, it's because she's "been" with most of them. I don't think that's true…mostly.

"Those buns are going to burn," Uncle Rusty warns, his sharp tone snapping me out of my reverie.

I quickly get the bottom buns into the containers, top them with burgers, and then place each of the tops on the other half of the Styrofoam lids. "Sorry," I say, looking back at him sheepishly.

"Nothing the girls wouldn't have eaten anyway," he adds lightly as he reaches for the tongs and dumps a boatload of fries into each box. "Can you grab a couple of tomatoes and lettuce for me?"

"Yeah…of course," I finally say, still a little in shock that I didn't realize he was cooking for us. Talk about needing to sharpen my investigative skills. "Thanks."

"Don't…" he sighs and then shakes his head. "I figured with Mags being gone, you gals haven't had a decent dinner."

I shake my head. "No…if I would have known she was gone I would have made something before I went to work."

He just nods his head as he dresses the burgers. "So listen, since your mom isn't home, I want you to take my cell phone tonight—"

"Uncle Rusty, I couldn't—"

"It's fine, Meghan. I have the phone here at the bar, so it's no hassle on my end. Besides, we don't know if the power was restored back at your place, so I don't want you and the girls freezing to death overnight if it's still off." He closes up the lids, stacks the boxes one on top of the other, and then hands them to me.

I take them, my hunger entirely too fierce to refuse the free, delicious-smelling food. "Thanks…" When he places his cell phone on top of the boxes, I stare down at it. "I promise I'll take good care of it," I assure him.

"I know you will, kiddo." He grabs the top of my head with his palm and wiggles my skull around a bit in that weird way of his. "Now get out of here and get those girls fed and in bed." He releases me and then drops his hand to my back and guides me to the door. "Call me if anything happens, and I'll text in the morning to check on you guys, okay?"

"Okay," I say, and then, for good measure, I drop my chin onto the phone to hold it in place.

"Come on," he says with a chuckle. He helps me out and then walks with me to the car. When he pulls the driver's side door open for me, he's enthusiastically greeted by the girls.

"Uncle Rusty!" they shout as they scramble out of the backseat to hug him.

In usual form, Uncle Rusty lifts and then bear hugs Molly, then Misty. He makes small talk with them while I get into the car, then he orders them back inside, waits until they have their seatbelts on, and then closes the door. He taps on the window two times and then takes a couple of backward steps. We all wave as I drive by him and head toward the exit. I get us home in record time and before I know it, we're all sitting at the table, stuffing our faces with burgers and fries.

With the girls fed and tired after a long day of school and then walking around town, I manage to get them tucked into bed with the lights out by ten o'clock. I quickly change into my pajamas too, but I know I won't be able to sleep, so I pull our bedroom door closed and make my way down the short hallway to the living room. It's a small space, just big enough for the mismatched sofa, loveseat, broken end table, stained coffee table, and lopsided entertainment unit. We have a television at the moment—the girls getting old enough now that they haven't broken this one yet, but there's no cable or internet, just an old DVD player.

I switch on the lamp, a tiny, misshapen, broken one I had gotten from the Dollar Store. The light it cast is pitiful, but as I reach for Uncle Rusty's cell phone, I know it'll be good enough to see the screen—and hopefully bright enough to alert my mother to my presence when she walks in the door. I pull a blanket over my legs and get comfy. Uncle Rusty has a smartphone, which I'm immensely envious of—we've never been able to afford one for me, and the one Mom has is paid for by one of her mystery friends, so it's off limits, even to me. I know how to use them though, mostly, so I turn the phone on and swipe through the screens.

Uncle Rusty doesn't have a lot of apps, but he's never bothered to organize them, so there are several screens, some with just one or two random apps on it. I ignore the majority of them and focus my attention on the phone icon. There are no missed calls or voicemails. I check the text message app next. The icon doesn't show a new text has arrived. I hit the button anyway. There are plenty of messages listed, but the one I'm interested in is right at the top, the ID name listed as Magpie —Uncle Rusty's nickname for my mother. I tap on it and stare at the first of only three messages.

"Hey, where you at?" Uncle Rusty had texted at 4:32.

There had been no response.

At 8:00 p.m., he sent another message. "Guess you're not coming in today???"

No response. No sign to show she had even read the message.

Then, at 9:15, he texted again. "Meg's here looking for you."

Still nothing though.

I tap the screen to pull up the keyboard. Then I type, "Hey, Mom. It's me. Uncle Rusty lent me his phone for the night. Call me when you get this." I hit the send button. For some reason, as I stare at the green message bubbles, an image of mom's steamed bathroom message suddenly springs to mind. I roll my eyes at the memory of it, but then, without thinking, I type, "We love you," and hit send again.

Maybe that way she won't think I'm so mad I'm not worried.

And maybe then she'll actually take the time to call me back.

4

THE PING

I toss and turn for an hour before I finally give up on the notion of sleep. The sofa isn't the most uncomfortable thing I've slept on before—at one point, Mom and I had been homeless and stayed at a women's shelter for a few months. When we were there, the first few days, I had slept in a sleeping bag on the floor. Then I got upgraded to a cot, which wasn't much better, but I had learned a valuable life lesson: if you're tired enough, you can sleep anywhere. Unfortunately for me at the moment, my body is exhausted but my brain is still firing on all cylinders.

I throw back the covers and walk to my mother's bedroom. Her door is always closed because she's a slob, and she also likes to believe she can smoke in her bedroom with the window open, as though that somehow negates the fact we can all still smell it and that there's a strict no-smoking policy in the building. Nothing or no one can stop Maggie May from doing what she wants though, so I take a deep breath before I push the door open.

I'm smacked in the face with what Misty's dad likes to call a generous helping of patchouli and ass. It's a quote from one of his favorite movies, but it doesn't nearly seem to do the smell of Mom's room justice. To be fair, I have no idea what patchouli and ass smells like. I do, however, know what a bar smells like in the morning when all the people are gone and all that's left behind are cigarette butts, empty bottles, and broken dreams. It's an acrid kind of odor, and stale, and that's what Mom's room always reminds me of—an old, empty bar, where, at some point, good times had been had, but now it's just an empty, dirty place in need of a good scrubbing.

I flip on the light switch and look around. The room is in its usual state of chaos. Clothes are thrown into piles all over the floor. Shoes are strewn about. The bed is unmade. The window is wide open. I roll my eyes as I make my way over to it. I look outside into the small fenced-in backyard. Thankfully, it hadn't rained, and more importantly, nobody had climbed in to rape or murder us. Granted, we live on the second floor and the fire escape doesn't run back to this room, but leaving the window open was a risky move. And now that I think about it, we're really lucky nothing had happened, since the window must have been open all day and then all last night too.

As my brain switches back over to calculation mode, I realize now that when I had peeked into the room this morning, all I had really paid attention to was the fact that Mom wasn't in it. After that, I had pulled the door closed behind me, and then I had stormed off to the living room window to look outside at the parking lot. Her car wasn't in her spot, which had sent me into an enraged frenzy that involved me silently cursing her out while I hurried to get the girls ready for school. We had left without me even thinking about the window, so the apartment had been unsecure all day, and then I had left the girls here with it wide open. As I slide the lock back into place, I make a mental note to add that to the already long list of things I have to do before leaving the house.

I roll my eyes again. *Thanks, Mom.*

When I make my way back to the door, I remember why I had come in here in the first place. For clues. For some iota of information as to where she is and who she's with. I shift so I have a good view of the entire room, then I sweep my gaze across the tiny ten-by-ten space. Mom had taken the smaller bedroom so the three of us had the master to share—not that it's much bigger than this one, which barely has enough space for Mom's queen-sized bed, single end table, and bureau.

Despite the tight spacing though, her furniture matches, and it's actually quite nice, but that's only because it was a hand-me-down from Mrs. Jackson. It had been the bedroom set she and her late husband shared, and she couldn't bear the thought of sleeping on it with him gone, so she had bought an entirely new set the week after the funeral and had surprised Mom with the offer. It was a welcomed gesture because Mom's room had always been a hodgepodge of garage sale and thrift-shopped goods.

I begin my inspection with the bureau; the long, sleek-looking cherry wood six-drawer chest probably the best place to start. It has an attached mirror that Mom has taped pictures to, so there's only a small portion to use for its intended purpose. I walk over and look at my reflection. There are bags under my eyes, and my pajamas, even for my tiny five-foot-tall, petite frame, are too small. I've had them for years now, which is something I pride myself on. One day I won't always be poor, but even then, in that better-off future, I'll still take care of my things, and I'll still try to get the most use out of everything before I toss it. Otherwise, Mom always says, I'm just being wasteful, and the world doesn't need another wasteful person.

I sigh again as I run my finger over a picture of the four of us at Lake George the summer before. Mom, as always, looks gorgeous in her bikini top and denim shorts. I lean over and study her closely, a mixture of anger and sadness washing over me as I do. How can someone be so wise and so dumb all at the same time? I lean closer to get a better look at the other pictures. There are several others from our many trips to Lake George—Uncle Rusty's in a couple of them because either me or my sisters had taken the pictures. He owns a timeshare up there, so for as long as Mom has worked for him, we've spent the Fourth of July there. It's become a tradition we all look forward to, along with all the random day-trips we can manage, depending on how busy it is at the bar.

A smile creeps onto my exhausted face as I glance over all the photos of the girls. Several are of them being goofballs at the lake, while others are just random times of them playing dress up in the house, or playing out front. There are, of course, the proofs from their school pictures. We can't ever afford to buy them, but Mom meticulously cuts each one off the order sheet and tapes them to the mirror. She has all of mine from high school, which sort of annoys and embarrasses me. I guess it's just a cutesy mom thing to do, so I try not to harbor any ill will toward her in that regard, but as I closely examine myself, I wonder what those pictures look like in a yearbook. And I wonder if they're the only ones of me in there, or had I made the cut in some other way, perhaps by accidentally photo-bombing some cheerleader, or as a spectator at one of the football games.

That, of course, would be the only way I could have made it into the yearbook beyond just the standard annual picture since I had never participated in any school activities. Mom hates all the other moms, and she always needed me to watch after the girls, and there has always been that pesky money problem too. School activities and sports aren't free. The only way I even got to go to the football games the past couple of years is because my best friend always gets free tickets and the girls are old enough to leave alone for a few hours—not legally, of course. New York doesn't have an actual set age limit for when it's okay to leave a kid home alone, but Mom has gotten into enough trouble with Child Protective Services that we're trying to wait until, at the absolute earliest, they're in middle school, which hopefully will be later this year. Just as long as Molly can pass all her end-of-year tests.

I sigh again. *That girl.*

I make a mental note to check on her grades tomorrow and then I continue poring over the pictures, my attention now focused on the ones I don't recognize.

I shift to the other side of the mirror and immediately set my sights on a picture at the very top. It's of Mom and a handsome guy—he's tall, dark, and built—just the way she likes them. They have their arms around each other and they're standing cheek to cheek in front of the Christmas tree at Rockefeller Center. Mom is bundled up in her heavy winter coat and that stupid hat with the ball on top of it. From the looks of it, the picture had to be taken recently, definitely this past Christmas, but I don't remember her mentioning a trip down to NYC. As far as I knew, she rarely went down there anymore. Usually now, to avoid having to deal with Misty's dad, she puts the girls on the 3:45 Short Line bus to Port Authority every other Friday. It's an arrangement that's been working well, especially because that gives me and Mom plenty of time to work without having to worry about them.

I study the picture a little more closely. Maybe this guy had driven them down to drop the girls off one weekend and then he and Mom went sightseeing? I mean, it's definitely a possibility, but I'm sure the girls would have mentioned that to me, and I would have remembered meeting him, or at least hearing about him…whoever he is.

I search the rest of the pictures. I can easily place most of them—like those taken at the bar with Mom's regular customers, but there are others I can't place, like two others of Mom with the mystery Rockefeller guy. I take those off the mirror, and then I grab three other pictures of Mom with three other black men. That's a total of four unfamiliar men. Could one of them be the guy she left the bar with last night? What did Uncle Rusty say his name was? Will? I flip through the six pictures again, slowly this time, and I force my weary mind to focus, but I don't recognize them. In total, there are four black men; two with dreads and two with short hair. Surely, one of them has to be Will—maybe the Rockefeller guy, since he's in three of the pictures. Mom spending that much time with him has to mean something, right?

I turn toward the door, intent on taking pictures of the pictures so I can send them to Uncle Rusty, but just before I reach for the light switch, I catch sight of the bed. The sheets are rumpled into a ball at the foot of the mattress and the comforter is hanging halfway off, draped across part of the floor. Jeez. How had I ended up being so neat and meticulous with a mother like her? I walk over, set the pictures on the nightstand, and then begin to make the bed since I know it'll be easier for her to get in without a hassle when she finally gets back...from wherever she is...

On that sour note, I finish making the bed, then I reach over to switch on the lamp, just in case she stumbles back in tonight, and then I reach for the pictures. As my fingertips brush against them though, I stop short. Mom's phone charger is haphazardly thrown across the dusty Cherrywood surface the way it always is. For a moment, I'm not sure why that bothers me so much, but as I lift the pictures back up, it suddenly dawns on me. Mom never goes anywhere without her charger. Well, anywhere but work, since Uncle Rusty keeps a bunch of chargers there, in the bar and in the kitchen area.

And she always keeps one in her car...but she hadn't taken her car...

That woman is never far from a charger because she has an older model phone and the battery pretty much dies if it isn't plugged in. Would she have left without one? I mean, I'm pretty sure she probably grabbed one from work, or maybe from her car, though without being able to see the car or ask her, it's impossible to tell. I can call Uncle Rusty about that last question though, so I hurry to the living room.

I flip on the overhead light and then I line up the pictures in two even rows on the coffee table. I grab Uncle Rusty's phone off the couch and swipe at the screen. Thankfully, there's no passcode, so I scroll through the home screens, looking for the camera app, but when I stumble upon the "find my phone" app, I once again stop short. Now why hadn't I thought of that sooner? I tap on the icon and watch as a map appears. The phone is logged into Uncle Rusty's account, so the little blinking phone icon zooms in just above our apartment building. That isn't helpful information, but I'm not looking for Uncle Rusty. I'm looking for Mom. I sign out of Uncle Rusty's account and then I try to jog my memory for my mom's information.

She almost always uses her full name with no spaces as her User ID, so I type that in and then try her usual password: meghanmollymisty@2334. Our first names and the first part of our home address. That isn't the password for the account though—or so the message tells me, so I try again: martinmartinmartin@5938. Our last names with the last four of her social. Probably not the best or safest idea, but when it comes to Mom's bad memory, especially when in combination with her excessive alcohol use, it's better to border on basic. Otherwise, she'll lock herself out of accounts.

Thankfully, that password seems to do the trick. A map appears over Middletown, the blinking phone icon searching around for a painstaking moment before it finally hones in on Mom's phone. As the indicator blinks over the address, I zoom in on the screen. That's it. I found her phone! I found Mom! She's at Rusty's.

She must have gotten there right after we left and then probably got busy with trying to catch up with everything at work. *Figures she'd forget to take a second to call or text to let me know.* I spitefully hit the "play sound" action button, which I'm hoping, on her end, isn't easy to switch off, and then I call the bar's landline since it's one of the few numbers I have memorized.

"Rusty's Bar and Grill," Uncle Rusty shouts into the phone, the music blaring in the background, making all the noises crackling over the line all the more excruciating.

"Hey," I whisper-shout, not wanting to wake the girls. "It's Meghan."

"Meg!" he shouts, and then he starts moving. I can tell by the way his beard scratches against the ancient phone receiver. "Hey," he repeats, this time the music not as loud. "Everything okay? Mom make it home?"

I shake my head, confused, especially because now I can hear the faint pinging coming from her cell phone. "No. I thought she was with you?" I strain to hear. "That's her phone, right?"

"What…?" he starts, clearly not tracking at first, but then he suddenly must have an epiphany, because he finishes with, "Is that her phone?"

"Yes," I snap. "Yes, it's her phone. Isn't she there with you?"

"No…hang on…" he says, the rustling sounds of him moving around while he searches grating on my last nerve. "I hear it…"

So do I, and I'm miles away! "Is she not there?" I ask, needing some clarification. I mean, why would her phone be there without her?

"No," he says, the pinging loud enough now that he must be right on top of the damn thing. "Aha! Here it is." There's some heavy breathing into the receiver. "It's here. I've got it." The obnoxious pinging finally ceases.

Where was it?" I eagerly inquire, anxious *and* pissed off now too.

"In the pantry…in her purse…"

"Her purse?" I shake my head, not seeming to understand even though it's all so simple. "So she left without her phone or her purse?" I shake my head one more time, hard. "But… she wouldn't do that…she wouldn't…" I mean, she's pulled some harebrained stuff before, but she's never left the bar with some guy without taking her phone and purse.

"Maybe it's about time we call the cops," Uncle Rusty says, saying what my brain refuses to admit.

I drop onto the couch, my body suddenly numb. "Yeah," I somehow manage to say. "Yeah…"

"Listen, Meg, it's dead here. There are just a few regulars, so let me kick them out, and then I'll be right over, okay?"

I nod, but then realize he can't see me, so I say, "Yeah. Okay."

"Hang tight," he says. "I'll be there as soon as I can."

"Yeah…okay…" Those seem to be the only words I can say, so I just hang up, and then I force myself to pull it together. You're an airman. You're a future hero. You can't freak out. Besides, I tell myself as I pull up the keypad to dial 911, my mom is Maggie May Martin, nothing or no one can hold her down, and she's always okay, so there's no need to panic. Or at least I tell myself so.

5

THE OLD FLAME

By the time the police show up, my mom has been missing for nearly twenty-four hours. Of course, the police aren't really worried, which is why it took them over an hour to get here. On a bright note, that had given Uncle Rusty enough time to get the bar closed so he could come over and try to calm me down. "She's fine," he kept saying while I had him on the phone. "She does this all the time," he reminded me.

I know she does—believe me—out of everyone on the planet I know she's done this before. I know she's prone to disappearing. I know she's irresponsible. And I know she's a bad mom. That thought makes my stomach sink because even though I know it's true, I hate admitting it. I have a bad mom. No one wants to admit that. No one wants a bad parent. Unfortunately, I got stuck with two. I guess, on the grand scale of things, Mom is way better than Dad. She had kept us when she could have tossed us into dumpsters or put us up for adoption. We've always—for the most part—had a roof over our heads. We have food.

I know all these things. I realize all these things. I'm grateful for all of these things, but that doesn't change the obvious. She's a bad mom. I know that doesn't make her a bad person. She's actually really funny. And she means well…she's just…I don't know. She's damaged in her own right. But she tries. Even on her bad days. Even when she clearly resents us. Even when she slips into long, painful bouts of depression or fits of rage. Even on the days I wish the worst things for her, she tries. And she's my mom, and I love her.

"Congrats, by the way," Officer Dunbar says as he takes a seat on the couch and flips open his notepad. "Airman Martin," he says with a chuckle, in that cheesy dad sort of way. "That has a nice ring to it, kid. We're all proud of you down at the station."

I'm not sure why I blush, but I do. "Thanks, Jesse—" The inadvertent, disrespectful slip of his first name actually causes me to jerk into a stiffer posture. I coyly meet his amused gaze. "I mean Officer Dunbar."

"It's fine, Meghan," he says, seemingly unfazed by my blunder.

Though, in my defense, it's hard to call him by his official title when most of my prominent memories are of him sneaking out of my mother's bedroom in his Mickey Mouse boxers.

"So, when do you ship off?" he asks like this is some kind of social call and not a genuine emergency.

"July eighteenth," I offer, that date forever emblazoned in my mind now.

"Ah. So you at least get to celebrate the Fourth with us before you go," he says absentmindedly as he scribbles something into his notepad.

"Yeah…" For a moment, my mind wanders to our upcoming holiday at Uncle Rusty's place, but I try not to focus on that at the moment. Instead, I try to steer the conversation back to the reason Jesse is here in the first place. "So about my mom…"

"*Oof,*" he says and then he actually *tsks.* "Texas in July." He looks at me and grimaces. "I was stationed at Fort Hood for three years, and I can tell you that Texas summers are cruel." He shakes his head. "Brutal. So be sure to stay hydrated, Meg. Okay?"

I nod. "Yeah…I didn't know you were prior service."

"Oh, yeah. Eight years as an M.P." He chuckles. "Or, I guess in your world, that would be S.F."

I'm still trying to learn all the lingo, and each branch of service has different terms for the same things, which makes it even more difficult to grasp.

"Security Forces," he clarifies with a wink. "What's your AFSC? Which, by the way, in the Army is called an MOS."

Jeez! Why does it all have to be so different and complicated? "I'm an 1N0X1. Operations Intelligence," I add, just in case that's called something different in Army-speak.

"Sweet! You get to spy on the bad guys."

"Yeah…" I say, sort of enthusiastically. I love talking to veterans and getting the lowdown on what I'm about to experience, but tonight isn't the time or place for that. Tonight, I have to force myself to stay on task. "Speaking of which…I've been doing a little investigating and I think Mom may be in trouble."

Jesse taps his pen against the notepad, almost as if that'll help him switch gears back to the reason he's here. "Right. Okay," he says, seemingly back in full police mode. "Let's start from when you first realized she was missing." He looks at me for a moment but then looks at Uncle Rusty.

I skip a beat, not sure if I'm the one who should be doing the talking. When another moment of awkward silence passes though, I clear my throat. "Well…I suppose I *realized* she was missing this afternoon. I mean, she wasn't here when I woke up this morning—or, you know, yesterday morning." Since it's technically Tuesday now. "But I hadn't been concerned about her then…" I bite my lip, but I don't bother to backpedal. They know Mom sometimes gets stuck sleeping *things* off first thing in the morning. "Anyway," I say, trying to keep on track, "Sergeant Hodge met me after school for PT, and we had just started our warm up when Mrs. Broom called to say Mom hadn't shown up to pick up the girls."

"Okay," he says as if prompting me to continue.

I look at Uncle Rusty. He gives a slight nod of his head, so I recount the afternoon and evening—mostly. I, of course, leave out the part about the girls walking miles and miles in the dark. Instead, I tweak the truth and tell him they had called the Dollar Store from Mrs. Jackson's phone to let me know Mom still hadn't made it home.

"But she was due to work tonight?" Jesse asks Uncle Rusty. In response, Uncle Rusty nods. Then Jesse looks back at me. "So, as of right now, it hasn't even been a full twenty-four hours since she's been missing?"

It's a little after one in the morning, so technically, no, it hasn't been twenty-four hours. I reluctantly shake my head. "No…not yet…but she left her car! And her purse and her phone!" I bite my lower lip to keep from shouting out more, but I can't seem to help it. Something is wrong. I can feel it, and I need to make Jesse understand the urgency. "I know she can be a flake, but she's been getting better at keeping in touch…" Even I can tell how lame that sounds though. I've never done a good job of covering up for her crappy parenting skills, but I give it one more try. "And you know she hasn't disappeared like this in a while."

Jesse sighs and drops back into his seat. He gets that look on his face. The one where adults are trying to think of a nice way to say something mean.

"Oh, and I found some pictures," I quickly add. I fumble the photos out of my back pocket, place them on the coffee table, and then spread them out so Jesse has a clear view of each. "I'm not sure who everybody is, but Uncle Rusty said this is the guy she left with last night." I point at the picture in question; the one of Mom and Will standing in front of a park.

Jesse leans back over and closely examines each photo. After another long moment of scrutinizing, he points to one of the other pictures—the one of Mom and an older, light-skinned black man. "This is her P.O., so no worries about any foul play there."

I know that P.O. means Probation Officer. For as long as I can remember, Mom has been on probation for something. This latest round of state-mandated supervision was because she had written a couple of hot checks—on top of the fact that she was still on probation for her DWI. I roll my eyes since I had sat in the parking lot of that building often enough, but I had never actually met her probation officer before. At least now I know what he looks like.

"Okay," I say as I pull that picture off the coffee table and set it aside. That at least gets one person off my who-the-heck-are-you checklist.

"I think I recognize this guy…" Jesse says as he points to another photo.

According to Uncle Rusty, the guy in that picture used to stop by the bar often, but he hasn't been around much lately and Uncle Rusty can't remember his name now.

"I'm pretty sure I've arrested him before…" Jesse says as he lifts the photo to examine it more closely.

"I wouldn't doubt it," Uncle Rusty says. "I can't think of his name at the moment, but he comes by every couple of months. Drinks a lot. Drops a lot of cash."

Jesse nods. "Hmm. Yeah. It's starting to ring a bell." He looks up at Uncle Rusty, who in turn holds his steady gaze.

I get the feeling there's some unspoken stuff going on between them, but I can't decipher any of it.

"But he isn't the guy she left with," I remind Jesse, tapping on the picture of her and Will. "This is the guy." Then I point to the three photos of Mom and the mysterious Rockefeller man. "Do you happen to recognize him though?"

Jesse switches out the picture of the one mystery guy for these three. "No…" He flips to the second one. "From the look of him though, I doubt he's from around here."

My brows crease as I consider that. "Why?"

He shrugs. "Hard to say. It's more just a gut feeling since I don't recognize him, and he's dressed pretty nicely. Maybe a business guy from New York?"

When you live upstate, New York means the city, which would make sense since the pictures were all taken there. I take the photos from Jesse and reexamine them. The man *does* look nice; his clothes are expensive, and there's something regal about the way he's standing.

Jesse lifts the picture of Will and Mom and holds it toward Uncle Rusty. "Do you have any information on this guy?" he asks.

Uncle Rusty shrugs. "I'm pretty sure his name is Will, or at least that's what I remember hearing. And I know he's from Newburgh. I can go back to the bar and go through the receipts, but I'm pretty sure he paid cash. You know most those guys do."

Jesse nods as he sets the picture back down on the coffee table.

"What guys?" I inquire, feeling disrespectful by asking but needing to understand all the unspoken undercurrent that's going on between them.

To Uncle Rusty, Jesse says, "If you can do some digging and let me know if you find anything, then I can run the information through the system and see if we can track them down." Then he looks at me. "You eighteen yet?"

I shake my head. "No…not yet…" At first, I have no idea

where he's going with his line of questioning, but then I get it. Legally, the girls and I should have adult supervision. "But I will be on Saturday," I add, even more grateful I'll finally be old enough to officially handle everything.

"Well," Jesse says on a sigh, "seventeen is a really gray area, especially this close to your birthday, and I think you'll be fine minding the girls until she gets back, right?"

"Oh, yes," I quickly assure him, not wanting Child Protective Services involved if we can avoid it. "You know I'll take great care of them."

"And I'll be here," Uncle Rusty adds. "You know, not here," he motions around the apartment, "but I'll make sure Meg has all the help she needs and that the girls are taken care of."

"Good. So we have the bases covered for now and hopefully Maggie May will pop up before we know it." He stands and slips his notepad back into his breast pocket.

"But…" I get onto my feet and look up at him with pleading eyes. "What if she's in trouble?"

Jesse puts his hand on my shoulder. "Meg…" he stammers a bit and then drops his arm to his side. "Listen, you know me and your mom dated for a little while, right?"

I nod.

"Look, there are times when she just goes into these manic —" He cringes at his word choice. "I mean…she's bipolar, you know…"

For some reason, my body always tenses up when I hear that word. I cross my arms over my chest. "She's been really good at taking her meds," I say in her defense even though I'm not entirely sure of that. I make a mental note to count out her pills when they leave.

"I'm sure she is," he says, "but sometimes she has these episodes and she's just got to get things out of her system." He places his hand back on my shoulder again. "I'm sure when you wake up in the morning, she'll be passed out in bed."

Usually, I would agree with him. Usually, I would just be pissed and annoyed by her irresponsible behavior. Today is different though. I can't explain it, but it feels off, and my anxiousness over the entire situation causes tears to sting my eyes. I swallow over the lump that lodges in the back of my throat and I fight to keep the tears from spilling onto my cheeks. "Yeah, I know," I say, trying hard to sound casual. "It's just..." I look between him and Uncle Rusty.

"I'll drive by all the major points heading toward Newburgh," he says, undoubtedly in reference to her last disappearing act out by the lake. "And I'll make some calls and make sure no one with her description was admitted to a hospital, okay?" He pats my shoulder a couple of times before he takes a few backward steps. "I'll call if I find anything, but I'm sure we have nothing to worry about."

I nod, trying to seem confident, but I'm glad when Uncle Rusty steps over and slings his arm around my shoulders. "And we'll call when she shows up," he says.

"Sounds good," Jesse calls over his shoulder as he makes his way to the door. "Get some sleep, Meghan," he adds as he pulls the door open. "I'll call you in the morning to check in."

When he glances back at me, I nod again. "Yeah. Okay. I have Mom's phone."

"Okay. Night, guys."

"Night," Uncle Rusty says and then makes his way over to the door. When Jesse disappears down the hallway, Uncle Rusty closes and locks it. "If you don't mind, I'll crash on the couch."

"Ah...yeah. Sure." I smile a little, relieved that he volunteers to stay. "I'll go get you some bedding."

Uncle Rusty walks over to his jacket, which he had slung over the couch when he first arrived, and he retrieves the small, rectangular camouflage case he keeps his meter, test stripes, insulin, and needles. A buddy had made it for him decades before because Uncle Rusty has suffered with Type 1 diabetes all his life, which for a long time was pretty stable. Now that's he's getting older and putting on the pounds though, he has his good days, but more often than not, he has bad ones. Bar food and booze aren't a good combination for anyone, especially old men with bad pancreases.

When he disappears into the kitchen, I head into the hallway and pull open the linen closet door. We have a ton of mismatched sheets and pillowcases. Some from sets gone-past; others that were randomly picked up along the way. I gather a decent bunch, along with a blanket, and then I set them on the couch. It isn't the first time Uncle Rusty has crashed at our place, but I always feel bad because he's a big guy and our couch is sort of small in comparison. I don't say as much though, because I know he'll tell me it's fine; he's slept on much worse.

I have too.

After saying my goodnights, I make my way back to my room. Usually, I close the door because Molly is a light sleeper, so the noise and lights will rouse her and eventually get us all up, but tonight I leave the door wide open, hoping to hear when Mom finally makes it home.

6

THE FIRST TEXT

For barely having slept or for only really taking the time to do anything more than brush my teeth, I still somehow manage to make it to school early. That probably wouldn't have been the case if Uncle Rusty hadn't stayed over and volunteered to make sure the girls got off to the bus on time. I'm grateful, but I'm still annoyed that any of us have to go through all the trouble because my mother isn't here.

Which brings me back to the most pressing issue at hand. Where the hell is she?

I pull her cell phone out of my back pocket and check everything. There are no text messages or voicemails, but there are lots and lots of emails. I skip going through those for the moment because in the back of my mind I somehow know there's probably stuff in there I don't want to see. Instead, I focus my attention on her text messages. Again. I know I'm treading on dangerous territory, but I think it's the best place to start my investigation. I tap on the icon and have just glanced at the list when my best friend hurries into the classroom.

"Hey," Phil says as he drops his backpack onto the desk next to mine. "Any news?"

I forgot I had texted him the night before to let him know what was going on. He looks at me expectantly, clearly waiting for a response, so I finally shake my head and then watch as he unloads his books.

Phil and I have been best friends since kindergarten. I always say that it's by virtue of our last names; me being a Martin and him being a Martinez, but Phil always likes to correct me on that point. He says I'm his best friend because he's just a cool guy. I agree. He is, by far, the coolest person I know, but the truth of the matter is that I don't think he would be friends with me if he hadn't stood next to me all his life. Granted, *he* used to get bullied a lot when we were kids because he has a very mild case of fetal alcohol syndrome—which is easy enough to notice if you're familiar with the physical characteristics that come along with such a condition—but now, in high school, Phil is legendary, so he doesn't need me to stand up for him. In fact, it's usually the other way around now because he's a pretty famous gamer, of the ELeague variety. They call him King of the Creed —for the one first-person shooter game he plays called *Commando's Creed*. Personally, when I get a chance to play, I'm a *Desolation Peak* kind of girl, but I'll cheer Phil on while he plays anything, and I'm not alone on that. He has fans because he's made it to the playoffs three times. He never lets that get to his head though, which makes me love him even more.

When he's gotten everything he needs for our math class set up on his desk, he plops into his seat and looks me over. "She does this all the time, Meg."

I roll my eyes since I'm very quickly tiring of hearing that phrase. "I know," I say, trying hard not to sound snippy with him. "But I couldn't get to sleep after I texted you, and then I got this idea to ping her phone…" I look down at the screen and stare at the list of text messages. "She left her purse and everything at the bar, Phil." I hold up the phone as if that alone could convey my worry. "I'm just…I don't know…" I finally meet his concerned gaze and shrug. "Something just doesn't feel right this time…"

The thing about Phil is that for a guy, he's pretty intuitive and sensitive. Mom says it's because of his condition. I agree with her, but not because I think there's something genetically wrong with him that makes him more empathetic. I just think he knows what it's like to be treated badly, and so he goes out of his way to be kind and attentive to everyone. He does so even more with me, I think, because for so long, I defended him. I was his bodyguard when no one was willing to stand up for him, and so now, in return, he takes care of me while I learn how to parent my mom and sisters.

"What's different?" he asks, not harshly, but with enough gusto that I know what he's trying to do.

I just shrug and surprise us both by not taking the bait.

His small, dark eyes soften. "She's fine, Meg." He reaches over and gives my shoulder a squeeze. "I mean, what are the chances of her being stuck in a ditch again?"

I know he's trying to make light of the situation, but I can't help but cringe at that. The guilt of it is seriously weighing me down.

"Meg. She's fine," he offers again, this time gently, and then when the teacher walks into the classroom, he releases my shoulder and takes a seat. "She'll probably stagger in this morning and then get mad at you for taking her phone."

I snort at that since I can picture it. And because I'm hoping he's right.

When the teacher begins to take roll, I sit back and scroll through my mom's messages. There are a ton, some dating back to years earlier. The older ones are with some of my mother's "friends," though I use that word loosely since Mom's friends are usually just Uncle Rusty's regular customers. I guess, for Mom, that counts as friendship. There are newer text messages with people I don't recognize, and some of them are just phone numbers, since she hadn't bothered to enter their contact information.

I figure the best way to dive into my investigation is to start with the most recent messages. It's one of the phone numbers without contact information, but the area code is the same as ours, and it has to be between Mom and this Will guy because the last message she received from him was on Sunday night. He had written, "We're heading your way." When I tap on it, I see the text message string is lengthy, though it mostly consists of one-word responses or very short phrases like, "Yeah, I'm here," or, "See you then." I read through them quickly, but when the teacher clears her throat, signaling she's ready to begin, I turn off the phone. For now.

Phil thinks it's nuts that I'm still determined to get straight As even though I'm going into the military. He always jokes and says that if he could join, which he can't because of his disability, he would sail out of high school with the bare minimum. Under different circumstances, I may have done just that, but I plan to make the Air Force my career, so that means I'll have to go to college. Sergeant Hodge says they'll promote me for a while without a degree, but if I want to make senior enlisted rank, I'll need to go to college, and with them picking up the tab for my tuition, there's no way I'm going to turn down the opportunity. So I pay attention in math class and then I hurry across campus to get to English. It's my least favorite subject, so my mind wanders a lot, and I only manage to resist the temptation to check the phone because I sit in the front of the classroom.

Forty-five minutes feels like an eternity when you're going over Shakespeare, so I busy myself with jotting down notes of everything I know so far. I even attempt to make a timeline to see if that helps. I start with Sunday morning, because I remember I had peeked in on Mom right before I had left for work at around 7:40 a.m. She had been lying face down; the covers pushed to the floor because she had passed out in her work clothes. It definitely wasn't an unusual sight for a Sunday morning, so I pulled her door closed and left.

Had her window been open then? I strain to remember, not sure why I get hung up on that detail for a moment, but then I finally relent. There's no way to know for sure, so I get back to work on the timeline and focus on Sunday evening. Rusty's is always painfully slow right after football season ends, so Mom was able to slip away to bring us some burgers and fries. She hadn't been in the best mood; I remember, because she and Matt had gotten into an argument when he called to let her know the girls were on their way. I'm not sure what the fight was over, though. If I had to guess, I'd say it was about money. It's always about money with them now, since enough time has passed that neither is interested in the other's private lives unless it's affecting the girls. Thankfully, Mom has at least learned the art of keeping men out of our lives—mostly in part because of my nagging.

I sigh as I shake that thought off because, for the first time, I realize how much that plan has backfired. I used to beg her to keep her love life separate from her family life. Now I wish I knew more about what she did when she wasn't with us. Who was she with? Where did she go? What did she do? I sigh as I go back to studying my very pathetic-looking timeline. I place a tick mark in the middle of the line and write "7:00 p.m.," because that was just around the time she had left to go back to Rusty's—give or take a few minutes. Once she had gone, I had gotten the girls ready for bed and we all sat in the living room, the girls watching a movie while I caught up on homework.

A little after nine, we went to bed. On Monday morning, I

had poked my head into my mother's room and realized she wasn't there. In response to her absence, I had slammed the door shut and stomped to the living room window to find her parking spot empty. Fuming, I had gotten the girls ready and driven them to school, but I figured she'd pick the girls up after school. That's the way it's always happened, so it hadn't occurred to me she wouldn't be there in the afternoon. I mean, it hadn't crossed my mind to worry—to assume I may never see her again.

"Meghan?"

I startle when Mr. Terrell places his hand on my shoulder.

"Everything okay?" he inquires as the class chuckles at my reaction.

"Yeah…" I slam my notebook closed as I look up at him. "Sorry. Can you repeat the question?"

Mr. Terrell looks me over for a moment, clearly concerned. He's one of the nice adults, but I'm sure the gossip mill has gone buck-wild over my mother's latest disappearance.

He starts walking back to the front of the classroom. "I asked you to name a distinguishing characteristic of one of the witches?"

"Oh…" I jog my memory and thankfully come up with something right off the top of my head. "They had beards?"

"Correct," he says, and then, for the remainder of the class, he goes into his own lengthy soliloquy about the witches. He's pretty passionate about it, and I try to pay attention, but my mind keeps wandering over all the details I had just compiled. Nothing sticks out as unusual though. Nothing screams foul play. Yet, in my gut, I know something's wrong. Call it a daughter's intuition.

When the bell rings, I shoot out of the chair and beat everyone out of the room. When I'm in the safety of the hallway, amidst a sea of other people all in a rush, I pull my mother's phone from my back pocket and go back to the first text messages from Will. I read through them again, this time paying closer attention to the actual conversation, though he isn't the most talkative person, at least via text anyway. Since the entire string of messages is only really of them setting up times to meet, I suppose there isn't much to say.

As I near my science classroom, I scroll down to a picture of my mother. It was taken a couple of months ago, in front of a building with huge Greek columns. I don't recognize it, but I do recognize the smile that's plastered on her face. She's definitely drunk, or very close to it. I zoom in on the picture, hoping to pick up on some kind of clue as to where she is, but there aren't any signs posted or any other landmarks.

"Any luck?" Phil says as he falls into step with me.

I look over at him curiously. "What are you doing here?" He should be clear on the other side of the school.

"I can be a little late to psychology and not worry about it." He bumps his arm against mine. "Any word from her yet?" he inquires as he helps me dodge a group of jocks.

I shake my head. "Nothing." I show him the picture of Mom in front of the Greek-columned building. "You recognize this place?"

Phil takes the phone from me and carefully examines the photo. Most kids with fetal alcohol syndrome have some cognitive impairments. Fortunately, Phil can hold his own intellectually, though he swears his condition is responsible for his poor memory. "It looks…" He uses his fingers to zoom in. "Hmm…it's ringing a bell like I should know it, but I can't think of it—" The bell rings. He hands me the phone and starts backing away. "You should text Rusty. See if he's heard anything."

"Good idea," I say as he accidentally bumps into someone. "We still on for lunch?" I ask when he's done apologizing.

"Yeah." He nods. "Meet at my car?"

I nod in return. He gives me a thumbs-up. I watch as he

swivels around and hurries down the hallway, then I do my own about-face and head into my classroom. I slip into my seat, which is thankfully in the middle of the classroom, and I send Uncle Rusty a text message.

After double-checking to make sure the volume is muted, I set the phone face-up on the desk and get my books out. As I flip my spiral notebook to a blank page, the teacher starts his lecture. I begin to take notes earnestly since science is one of my favorite subjects, so I get so immersed in the discussion it takes me a moment to notice that Uncle Rusty had replied.

"Not yet," he had texted.

I stare at the words until the screen goes dark. Then, when he texts again, I stare at the new message for a long moment.

"She'll turn up, kiddo."

After another moment of staring at the message, I roll my eyes. *Yeah, yeah,* I think with a sigh. That's what everyone keeps saying. I just really, really, really hope they're all right.

7

THE LUNCH HUNCH

My social studies teacher tends to drone on. On any other day, I wouldn't mind, but on days when Phil and I have lunch plans, I hate it. My class is on the other side of the building from the student parking lot and with spring in full bloom, all the juniors and seniors are heading out to grab lunch now, so it takes forever to make it to the parking lot. It takes even longer to get off campus, and then the drive-through at McDonald's is always a nightmare. I mean, at the end of the day, is a Big Mac really worth all the hassle?

Hell. Yeah.

When the bell finally rings, I bolt out of my seat and weave through the hallway traffic like a pro. Before long, I'm outside. Phil's car is in my sights and, oddly enough, he's leaning against the hood of his Mustang and he's signaling me —kind of like a madman.

"What?" I ask, my voice hitched up so the single word carries across the lot to him. Unfortunately, the higher tone also makes it sound as though I'm annoyed when I'm just genuinely curious.

He cups his hands around his mouth to amplify his voice. "Check your phone!" he shouts.

My phone? He knows I don't have any minutes on it. But when I catch a glimpse of his exasperated expression, I suddenly understand. "You mean check *my mom's* phone?" I say as I make it over to him and pull open the passenger side door.

In response, he just rolls his eyes and stomps his way over to the driver's side door. I pull the phone out of my back pocket before I get into my seat and buckle up.

"I remember where I saw that house," he says after starting the car and revving the engine a couple of times.

"Oh?" I ask calmly as I make my way to the message that says exactly the same thing. "Care to share?"

Phil tosses a sidelong glance my way. "Newburgh. It's one of those historical sites that Gramps dragged us to a couple of years ago."

"Oh," is all I can think to say to that. "Why would Mom be there?" I backtrack to her messages with Will and pull up the picture to study it again.

"It's the Dutch Reformed Church, built back in the 1800s." He tosses another glance my way. "I read up on it in class while I was waiting for you to reply."

"Well, excuse me for not being used to having a working phone all the time."

"Grams has offered you our fourth line for years—"

I cut him off at the pass. "You guys can't afford that," I say before he even thinks of continuing with that line of thought. Phil was raised by his grandparents because his mother, a diehard alcoholic, lost her rights to him when he was just a baby.

"It isn't that much extra," he adds, but then quickly changes the subject because it's an argument we've had for years and one he's always lost. "Anyway, it's an old church in

Newburgh. I don't think it's used for worship services anymore." He glances my way again, really quickly. "Not that I think your mom was there for church…"

I try not to take offense to that. I mean, it's no secret Mom isn't in line to win a mother-of-the-year award, and we all know she isn't the most religious person in the world. At times, when she's coming off one of her manic episodes, she can be remarkably deep and spiritual, but she's never been an active churchgoer, even on her best days.

"You said this guy Will lives up there?" Phil continues with his speculations. "Maybe he lives nearby or something?"

That would definitely be a better explanation for her being at a church. "Are there lots of houses down that way?" I ask as I use his phone to go online for a map of the area.

"I think so…" He pulls into the drive-through at McDonald's then peers over to look at the phone. "Like I said, it was a couple of years ago, so I don't remember all the details, and Gramps dragged us all over that day." He shrugs. "Who knew Newburgh had so many colonial sites?"

"Hmm," is all I say to that since it isn't really a question. Plus, I've been on enough Martinez family daytrips to know how Phil's day had gone. Gramps had undoubtedly gotten them up bright and early. They drove the hour to their destination, and then he proceeded to take them to every historical marker he had placed on one of those huge, old-fashioned maps he always orders months beforehand from the town's visitor's center. He can be pretty thorough and aggressive when it comes to the schedule he creates.

"That's it," Phil says as I go in for a street view of the church. He reaches over the center console and zooms in on the map. "See, this is right downtown, just a block or two off the water." He does some more moving around of the screen, and then he settles on taking the phone out of my hand.

"Looks like it's surrounded by houses. And I'm betting most of these have been turned into apartments."

Like mine. Those old Victorian houses are big enough that it only makes sense to split them up to make more rent. As the thought of home resonates, I remember I had shoved the pictures from Mom's dresser into my backpack this morning. I fish the six photos out of my bag and flip to the one of Mom and Will standing in front of a park. I study it for a long moment. Mom and Will are standing in front of a tree. I have no idea what kind, but it's huge, so the leaves and branches obscure nearly everything around it. I can tell it's a park because to the left of the tree there's a metal bench; to the right, a soccer net. Behind them is definitely a sports field of some type. I'm betting it's a multipurpose one that can be used for baseball or soccer. I can also make out a couple of buildings to the left too, with green tin roofs, but I don't see anything that resembles the church.

Maybe this is the view across the street?

As I take the phone out of Phil's hand, he leans closer so our heads are touching. "What is it?"

I hold the picture of Mom and Will next to the screen. "I just…" I move the phone closer to my face. "I'm trying to figure out if these were taken at the same place."

Just as Phil tries to lean closer to examine the pictures, someone honks their horn. We both startle and then giggle as Phil puts the car in drive and pulls up to the payment window. It's my turn to treat, so I hand over my debit card and wait until we've picked up our food and are parked in our usual spot before I hold the photo and phone side by side again.

Phil dips into the bag and uses a handful of fries as pointers. "Definitely not the same place," he observes before stuffing his face.

I ignore the crunching by my ear and study the pictures again. Phil seems positive these are two different locations, but

I'm not so sure where his confidence is coming from. I mean, it's really hard to tell, especially with the way the tree is blocking the view of nearly everything in the park and, in the church picture, Mom is center stage, so you can't see anything around the church except a couple of the pillars and the front doors.

Phil hands me my Big Mac and fries. Given the time factor and my hunger, I opt for researching later. Besides, I've started timing myself while I eat too because one of the old veterans who comes into the Dollar Store all the time tells me that during basic training, they have an "eat it now, taste it later" policy. He was in the army, but for stuff like that, I'm pretty sure it's military-wide. After getting the pictures and the phone safely tucked onto the dashboard, I open the cardboard box, drop my fries into the top, and then prep myself. There's an art to eating your food quickly while still trying to enjoy it. I think I've nearly gotten it mastered. I wait until the clock changes to the next minute and then dive in.

I'm really going to miss my weekly Big Mac treat while I'm in basic.

"You're going to get heartburn doing that," Phil warns as he stuffs more fries into his mouth.

I only grunt because I won't do anything to mess up my system. Bite. Chew five times. Swallow. Eat a handful of fries. Repeat until done. Then chug the soda. In basic training, there won't be any Coke, but another old veteran who comes by Rusty's told Mom I'll have something else called "water drills." It's their way of making sure we stay hydrated. The thought of that kind of turns my stomach though since I've never been a water drinker. It's all you have when you're poor, and most times, from the tap, it's gross.

"So Rusty is sure she left the bar with this guy?" Phil asks in between bites of his Double Quarter Pounder.

For a smaller guy—or smaller than average guy, I should

say, since at five feet six, he's still way taller than me, he can put away some food.

I nod as I continue with my eating ritual.

"Have you tried calling him?"

That gets my attention. I look over at him. Chew. Chew. Chew. Chew. Chew. Swallow. Mouthful of fries. In between more chewing, I shake my head.

"You mind then?" he asks as he shoves the rest of his burger into his mouth, wipes his hands on a napkin, and then reaches for my mom's phone.

I watch as he unlocks the phone, pulls up the text, and then navigates through the steps to call the number. He taps the little icon and then holds the phone out in front of him and puts it on speakerphone. For some reason, my heart sinks as the phone rings, and even though I'm only one bite away from being done with my food, I don't stuff the last bit of burger into my mouth after I swallow down the last of my fries.

The phone rings again and again, and just when I'm sure the voicemail is going to pick up, the last ring cuts off and an automated female voice tells us the mailbox for the phone was never set up so we're unable to leave a message. Three short obnoxious sounds play before the call ends. I pop the last bite of Big Mac into my mouth and force myself to chew and swallow since my stomach is now in knots.

"Hmm..." Phil says as he navigates to the photos and then somehow manages to pull up the locations of where the pictures were taken. He scrolls through the options and makes it to the one of Mom and Will at the park. "It was taken in Newburgh," he says as he holds the phone toward me for a better view. "On Robinson Avenue."

I shudder, since it's a little creepy and invasive that the phone keeps track of where you take the pictures, though, at the moment, I'm glad for it. "Robinson Avenue..." I grab the phone with one hand and my drink with the other. I thumb through the pictures while I start on my soda. It's not so easy with the carbonation, so I just sip as I scroll through more and more images. Mom has tons of photos. They're mostly of us, but I find the six that I have hard copies of, which turns out to be unhelpful. The ones of her and the Rockefeller guy were all taken in NYC. The one with her probation officer was taken in Middletown. The one with her mystery guy, who Jesse claimed to have arrested, was taken in Newburgh, on Lawrence Avenue.

"She sure does spend a lot of time up there," Phil observes.

"Yeah…" She hadn't in years, but now it seems as though she was back to hanging out here again. It's my dad's home-town, and while I've been there plenty of times according to everyone, he had died when I was six, so I only have a few memories of him or the town.

"Are you working out after school?" Phil asks as he moves the gearshift into reverse so we can try to beat the traffic back to campus.

"Yeah." I start gathering the trash. "Sergeant Hodge is meeting me at the girls' school…" I glance his way, but then just as quickly look away, for some reason feeling ashamed now. Embarrassed that my mother is still gone.

"She'll turn up," he says, sounding as sure as everyone else does when they utter those words, though, at this point, I'm not sure where they're getting their confidence. It's been a day and a half since she's disappeared and it seems like there are more questions than answers, and this time around, something feels off—and there's some evidence to prove that. She left without her car; her purse; her phone; her charger. Those are things she rarely separates herself from on a normal day, so it's weird that she would choose to leave all of them behind when she was going out. Not unless she ran out thinking she'd be right back. Not unless something bad had happened. I once again shudder at that thought.

"When we get back to the school, we can pull up a map of the city on my laptop and see if we can figure out her movements. Maybe there's some kind of connection we'll be able to make out with a bigger view," Phil says.

"Good idea." And one that I should have thought of sooner. This entire experience is beginning to worry me—not only for my mom's sake but because I should be able to figure this out. I *am* going into the intelligence field, but at this point, I'm not sure if that's a good idea. I don't seem to be any good at it.

As that somber thought replays in my mind, I shove the last of the trash into the bag and quickly finish my soda. I drop the empty cup in next and then pack everything else into a tight ball that I set on the footwell. Then I grab my mother's phone. The battery is nearly dead, so I plug it into Phil's charger, ever grateful that he has the same model, and I go back to her pictures. These are the keys to finding her. Somewhere in here, there's a clue as to where she went and who she's with. Right now, all roads are leading to Newburgh, so I need to get up there and figure out the rest, because Mom's life may depend on it.

8

PETE'S HOT DOGS

The problem with cutting everything close to the wire is that if one thing goes wrong, then your entire plan goes to hell in a handbasket. Hence the case with us making it back to school on time. There was an accident—a minor fender-bender, really, but the drama that ensued afterward held everyone up. It all started when Triston McFadden tapped the bumper of Flo Henderson's Volkswagen Beetle right by the entrance of the student parking lot. According to the gossip mill, everyone swore that Flo had gotten out of her car and given Triston the slap of the century. They claim it happened all so quickly that no one had time to get their phones out fast enough.

With a bunch of social media guru-wannabes hanging around that seemed hard to believe, but with no one being able to confirm or deny that, the slap of the century hashtag had spread through the school before we had even inched close enough to see anything for ourselves. It took about ten minutes, but Flo was, indeed, out of her car. So was Triston. There were about ten other people milling around the vehicles too, along with a police cruiser parked long ways so he could take pictures from all angles.

By the time Phil pulled into a parking spot, we were already late by five minutes. Phil threw the gearshift into park, shut off the engine, and reached for his backpack behind my seat in one fell swoop. I wasn't nearly as gung-ho to get inside. The problem, of course, is that my last two periods of the day are B.S. electives—psychology and astronomy. And while I actually enjoy astronomy, psychology tends to get on my nerves. I think it's because the more I read into it, the more I realize how messed up my mom is, and how, between her and my dad, the cards are kind of stacked against me.

"Let's go," Phil says as he gets out of the car and slams the driver's door so hard I flinch.

I sling my bag over my shoulder, grab Mom's phone, and hurry after him. He's moving fast to make it to class, but I start to fall behind because my attention is back on the phone. In the ensuing madness of the fender-bender, while we waited for the traffic to clear up enough to get moving again, we had placed all three points on a map: The park on Robinson, the church near Grand, and the mystery guy on Lawrence. The three points all fell within a three-mile radius, so it would have been easy enough to walk to each, though why anyone would choose to do that is the biggest mystery of all.

"Come on, Meg!" Phil shouts as he holds the door open for me.

I look at him, then at the door, and then back at him. Then, without consciously thinking about it, I take a backward step. "I'll catch up," I say as I take another step back. "I forgot my book in my car."

Phil looks at me curiously. Probably because he knows I'm not the type to forget a book.

"And I think I have to…" I shrug, "you know…use the bathroom before I get to class, anyway."

His eyes squint even more, to the point that he probably can't see a thing. "I told you eating that fast wasn't any good for you," he finally says, but there's still suspicion in his eyes. "I'll see you next period then?"

"Of course," I spout out, but my faltering voice probably doesn't help convince him.

He looks me over, then looks toward the parking lot, then looks back at me. "Meg…"

I grunt and jut my hip out, like a pouting toddler. "It'll be easier to get a sense of where she went if I just go up there and check these places out—"

"Are you insane?" he says as he releases the door and makes his way back to me. "That's like looking for a needle in a haystack, *and*," he emphasizes as he takes the phone from me and then adjusts it so we can both see the screen clearly, "do you have any idea how many houses are in this area?" He looks at me, his eyes searching mine. "We can't just go door to door—"

"Why not?" I snatch the phone out of his hand, shove it in my pocket, and then cross my arms over my chest. "If I leave now, then I can make it back in time to get the girls and then get to work."

"Meg. Listen to yourself. You're talking about ditching school to go on some wild-goose chase—"

"She's missing!" I snap so loudly I'm sure the people in the nearby classrooms hear me. I huff out a breath and then continue in a steadier, lower tone. "Why doesn't anyone but me seem to care that she's gone? I mean, you guys just keep making light of it, but she's not here. She hasn't turned up, and I'm the only one who even cares enough to be worried!"

"We're all worried, Meg," he assures me with a hand to my shoulder. "Of course we're worried, but we don't want to add to your anxiety by saying that, okay?"

I look up at him, tears welling in my eyes after hearing his admission.

"And she's done this before," he emphasizes in that soft,

gentle way of his, "so yes, we're all worried, but we're trying not to be for your sake because she's going to turn up."

I snatch my shoulder out from under his grip. "Stop saying that!"

He sighs but then nods. "Okay. Fair enough. I won't say it again. But that doesn't mean you should drive up to Newburgh to search for her yourself. I'm sure Jesse can call someone up there to check it out."

"Jesse is just like you and everyone else! He doesn't care that she's missing."

"That's not true, Meg, and you know it. He cares. And I'm sure he'll have a buddy he can call."

I shrug and then spin on my heels. "Fine. I'll call him as I'm driving up there."

Phil falls into step with me. "That's not what I meant and you know it. Also, there's no way your piece of crap car can make that trip."

"Then lend me yours," I say as I shoot him a sidelong glance.

He actually trips a little bit at that suggestion. "Ah. No."

I snort, though I don't blame him. The Mustang was his eighteenth birthday present. It's a base model, with only the barest of upgrades, but he loves that car more than anything—except for maybe his grandparents and his girlfriend.

"I'll take you," he says as he clicks the remote to unlock his car.

I stop short and shake my head. "Oh, no. I'm not dragging you into this and getting you in trouble."

He turns to look at me. "Then what, Meg? Because your car won't be able to handle that trip and you won't let go of this ridiculous idea to do reconnaissance, so what do you suggest?"

"I…" I look between him and the school. Being put on the

spot sucks. "If you lend me the car, I'll say I stole it if something happens."

Phil rolls his eyes. "No one will believe that."

"Fine," I retort. "Then what do you suggest?"

For a moment, he stares at me, deadpan, then he walks over and tosses his backpack into the trunk. Without even bothering to look my way, he gets into the driver's seat. I stand there for a moment, not wanting to get him in trouble, but I'm desperate to find Mom, so I know I can't skip this opportunity. I walk over and slide into the passenger seat. Without a word, Phil starts up the car and gets us going. I don't move until we're on I-84, Newburgh bound. After getting my backpack comfortably settled between my feet, I pull Mom's phone out of my back pocket and hook it up to the charger. I study the map for a long moment before I finally dare a glance at Phil.

"The dates don't add up," I offer by way of the lamest apology ever.

"What do you mean?" he asks, his voice back to normal, as though nothing just happened.

Grateful for the reprieve, I switch back to the photos. The three taken with the Rockefeller guy were in the winter. December for the Christmas tree one; December again for the one of them posed cheek to cheek, and January for the last one of them standing by the Columbus Circle monument.

"I mean I think it's weird she has these three pictures of Rockefeller guy from months ago on her dresser right next to these other guys." I scroll to the one of her and the guy who Jesse said he arrested. "They took this one last July." Then I scroll to the one of her and Will in front of the tree. "And this one was taken last month."

"Maybe they somehow all know each other?" Phil suggests. "I mean, Jesse did say that he's arrested that one, right?" He glances over at me. I nod. He goes back to looking at the road.

"So…and I know you don't want to hear this, but what if these guys are involved with drugs?"

I sigh. I knew it wouldn't be too much longer until that word started making an appearance. Mom drinks. Mom does drugs. Both are habits that she's tried to break many, many times. Each time, she's failed miserably.

"So what, because they're black, they're drug dealers?"

"You know that's not what I mean." He looks over at me again, long enough to roll his eyes, and then he goes back to staring straight ahead. "If you want help, Meg, you're going to have to quit being so defensive."

"Yeah." I cross my arms over my chest. "Well, if I remember correctly, ten years ago, you liked how defensive I was."

"I did, and I still do, but I'm not the enemy here."

Silence descends upon us. After a few minutes go by, I unfurl my arms and place my hands on my lap. I look down at them and sigh. "That thought has crossed my mind," I finally admit, not daring to look at him. "I'm still not sure how Rockefeller fits in, but it would make sense that these two guys know each other, especially the way Uncle Rusty describes them…"

He nods. "And the addresses aren't that far apart, so I think it's as good a guess as any," Phil adds, thankfully still not sounding upset or cross for all my tantrums. "I'm not sure how the church ties in yet, so I think we should start by finding the park and then checking out Lawrence Avenue. See what pops out at us."

"Sounds good," I agree, glad he has a plan because I hadn't really thought this far ahead. Now that I have the wherewithal though, I make sure to use my time wisely and go back to studying the text messages between Mom and Will. As I start at the top and work my way down, I'm actually glad there aren't any real messages to decipher or read through, as the series of "I'm here" and "On my way" are easy to scroll past. The problem, of course, is that without any meat in the content, I'm short of material to use for ideas. As I get to the bottom of the messages, which Mom had exchanged with Will about six weeks earlier, I finally find something useful. "They met at Pete's!" I say, sounding a lot more triumphant than I intended.

"Who's Pete?" Phil asks.

"I have no idea…" As I scroll through the messages again, I sigh. "He only mentions him once."

"So Will tells your mom to meet at Pete's?"

"Yeah." I stew on that. "Maybe Pete's the mystery guy who lives on Lawrence Avenue?"

He nods. "Could be…yeah…"

He doesn't seem to know what to say beyond that. Neither do I, so as we make our way to the park, I go over the messages again, making sure I don't miss anything.

"All right," Phil announces as he makes a righthand turn. "Here we are. Robinson Avenue."

I look up at a normal-looking street. There are some businesses and houses scattered around for a couple of blocks, and then I see the sign for Delano-Hitch Park. My heart begins to race. My palms begin to sweat. I lean forward in my seat and lower the window as we drive past what looks like a water park in the distance, and then a couple of buildings with green tin roofs. *Those are them!* Those are the ones in the picture!

Phil seems to sense my eagerness because he slows down. My stomach lurches as we continue along, an empty field before us, and then a tree. *The* tree. And the metal bench.

"That's it, right?" Phil asks as he continues ahead at a snail's pace. "There's a car behind us," he adds, by way to explain why he isn't stopping, and of course, there aren't any parking spaces on this side of the street. "I'll swing around and find a spot on the other side," he assures me.

Naturally, the next intersection is for a one-way street, and with the car right on Phil's butt, he doesn't dare try to pull a U-turn right in the middle of the road, so instead, he continues ahead. I stare out at the park, hoping to gain some kind of clue as to why my mother was here. What's so special about this place?

"Um…" Phil says as we near the next intersection.

His tone piques my curiosity so I turn to look at him. "Um?" I echo, hoping that prompts him to finish his thought.

"Look," he says, motioning ahead with his chin.

I look up at the red light and then at the street sign. "South Williams?" I say though I'm not sure why that would be important.

"No," he says, shaking his head. "Not there." He points a little to his left, at eye level. "I think we just found Pete."

I follow his line of sight and see the sign on the curb. It looks like a dancing hot dog standing beside a vending cart. It reads "Pete's. Established 1932."

"Meet at Pete's…" I say, sounding as stunned as I feel.

Phil pulls into the parking lot so we're facing the small, one-story restaurant that's nestled into the neighborhood. "I wonder how long it'll take you to down a dog?" he says with a chuckle.

I pop my seatbelt off and fish my wallet out of my backpack. "Guess there's only one way to find out."

9

THE RELUCTANT NEIGHBORS

Without a doubt, Pete's hot dogs are the best I've ever had. I lick the last of the ketchup and mustard off my fingers and then I stare down at my time. Fifty-seven seconds. I'm sure that isn't a world's record or anything, but it was quick enough to get them down and still enjoy them, so I'm still claiming it as a double victory.

"You're going to make yourself sick one of these days," Phil says as he takes a bite of his first dog; the second still sitting on the table.

I sit back in my seat and smile. "That's the point. To figure out my limits now."

"Well, I guess we've learned that you should go with less ketchup and mustard next time." He motions toward my chest.

I look down and see a large red-and-yellow wad of messiness had made its way onto my shirt. "Dammit," I say as I reach for a napkin.

"Don't. That'll just set it in," Phil says around a mouthful of hot dog.

Just before my fingers reach the napkin dispenser, I let my

hand drop back onto the table and sigh. He's right—or rather his Grammy Anne is since she's the one who always tells us stuff like that.

"Just swipe off as much as you can with your finger and then use some cold water to get out the rest," he adds before he takes another bite of his hot dog.

"That would require me to take my top off," I say as I stand. "Do you have an extra one in the car?"

He shakes his head.

I sigh again, but then I make my way to the bathroom, hoping it's at least a private one so I can stand in my bra as I work out as much of the stain as I can. Poor people don't have the luxury of just throwing stuff away, so either way, I'll have to strip down. I know I'll have to get used to that—you can't get through basic training without getting naked in front of a bunch of strangers, but the longer I can hold off on that particular experience, the better. Thankfully, I'm in luck. It's a private bathroom, so I lock the door and very gingerly pull my shirt off. The stain landed in a nearly perfect oval right in the middle of my chest region, so I turn on the tap while I try to figure out the best way to maneuver the material under the faucet without getting the rest of it completely soaked.

After three folding attempts, I get the fabric to a place where I can stick it under the water without too much collateral damage. With two unsteady hands, as if I'm about to perform life-saving surgery, I move the shirt toward the water but jerk myself to a halt when I finally notice the steam. What the hell? I reach for the handle but I once again stop short when I see a huge letter "C" painted on the edge in an elegant font. That definitely means cold, so what's with the steam?

My hand is hovering just above the sink, the warmth of the water engulfing my hand just enough to cause a sheen of moisture to form on my down-turned palm. I quickly turn the faucet off, if not for anything other than to quit wasting water.

Then I just stand there, uncertain of what to do for a moment. Has the world gone mad? Is it backward day? I shake my head at that thought, since it's ridiculous, and as a future investigator, I need to stop coming up with cockeyed theories. Right. Focus. The most plausible explanation would be that some kids switched them out as a prank. I reach for the other handle and turn it on, this time with a slower drip, and then I give it a second. When I'm sure the residual heat from the previous session doesn't bleed over into this watering, I gingerly swipe my index finger under the stream. Yup. That's hot too. I've never been to a restaurant where there wasn't an option for cold water. I mean, no hot water makes sense. I've seen it happen before when an owner doesn't want to get sued because someone gets burned, or because something is wrong with the plumbing or hot-water heater. But no cold water at all? That's just bizarre.

As more steam begins to rise, I turn off the hot-water tap and I've just started to reach for the cold-water knob again when I finally notice the mirror above the sink. The running water had steamed it up pretty well, blurring my reflection. Instead of turning on the faucet, as I had intended, I reach out to clear the fog, but just before I place my hand on the mirror, I stop. I'm not exactly sure why I do, or why I leave my hand there, rigid like a statue, but for a moment, it feels as though I have no control over my arm.

Chills begin to creep up my legs, like weird, invisible tendrils of ivy, so I look down, frightened it might be more than just my imagination—like a spider, or a rat, or a couple of those nasty water-bugs. Nothing's on me though, and those cold sensations continue to climb up my legs, up into my stomach, and all the way to the top of my head, freezing me in its wake. My teeth chatter from the sudden drop in temperature and I begin to shiver.

The tremors make their way to my fingertips, sparking

life back into my dead, frozen arm. In response to the tingling, I jerk my hand away from the mirror, both relieved and a little terrified by the odd experience, but the moment my hand is out of the way, I don't have time to appreciate the return of my dexterity. I can't, because I'm too mind-blown by the fact that there's a message written there now. A message surrounded by a lopsided heart. A message that's written in my mother's sloppy cursive that reads, "I love you, M&M."

I drop the t-shirt to use my one hand to hold myself steady against the sink while with the other hand, I reach for the message. My fingertips hover just above the heart, my mind racing to come up with a plausible explanation. Think, Meghan. How could this be here? I lean closer to the mirror to examine the words. *It can't be,* I think to myself as I lean back so quickly I lose my footing and stumble backward a couple of feet.

"Mom?" I whisper, my breathing is coming in spurts now, so it sounds just as ragged and overwhelmed as I feel. I stumble back to the sink and reach for the message once again. I don't touch the mirror, not wanting to smear the words, so I hover my hand about an inch away, and then I trace them with my pointer finger, trying to confirm the obvious. That's my mom's handwriting. I've forged it enough times to know with utmost certainty. "Mom?" I say again, an awful feeling settling in the pit of my stomach as I admit to myself what this must mean.

"Meg?" Phil says through the door, startling me so badly I literally jump and crack my knee against the sink. Then he knocks a few times. "Are you okay in there?"

I look at the door and then back at the mirror. The message is gone. The steam evaporated. "Dammit!" I say as I lean over the sink and start breathing onto it. "Come on," I say in between pants.

"Meg?" Phil says, this time trying the knob. "Hey. Are you okay in there?"

When I'm close to hyperventilating, the solution to my problem suddenly becomes obvious. I turn the hot water back on and then I whip around to open the door. "Come here," I order as I grab onto Phil's arm and pull him toward the sink.

"Meg!" He yanks his arm out of my hand and turns around. "You're naked!"

"What?" I quip, but then I look down at myself. Right. I'm standing in my bra. I scramble to grab my t-shirt, but then I realize the glob of ketchup and mustard is still sitting there. I swipe it off with my index finger, rinse the sodden digit off under the steaming water, pull my t-shirt back on, and then I turn back to the mirror. "I'm dressed," I tell him as I reach back to slap his arm. "Come here. Look at this!"

The water is hot, steam billowing out of the sink, but it isn't fogging the mirror the way it had before. I wave my hands near the faucet, in an upward motion, hoping to speed up the condensation process. "There was a message…" I say, so he has some idea of what to look for, but I don't want to give specifics, so he can confirm it for me.

"There's a what?" he asks, though he's clearly confused and concerned over what he's just walked into. Despite that, he still leans closer to the mirror.

"Just look," I promise him as I point to the region of the mirror where the message had appeared. "It'll come back."

"What will?"

"The message!" I snap.

"Meg—"

"Is everything okay?" an employee asks from the doorway.

Phil and I whip around. I shake my head as I stare at the older lady. "No, ma'am…it's just that…"

"Yes?" she inquires as she searches the small room, undoubtedly checking for damage.

"She was trying to get a stain out," Phil chimes in, pointing at my shirt. "And she made it worse because she used hot water instead of cold."

I nudge him in the ribs with my elbow. "That's all that's coming out," I say in my defense, which is beside the point. I turn back around and look at the mirror. There's only steam. "There was a message," I say, more to myself since I'm so disappointed by the emptiness I can hardly breathe.

"If you wrote or tagged up that mirror," the lady says as she makes her way over, "you'll have to pay to get it fixed." She squeezes in between me and Phil to take a look for herself.

I step aside to give her more room, but my eyes never leave the mirror.

The lady turns off the water. "I don't see anything," she says.

"No…" I confirm sadly. "I'm sorry…I thought I saw…" I look between her and Phil. They both search my eyes—the lady with suspicion. Phil with concern. "It's just that my mom is missing and…" When the look in the lady's eyes changes from wariness to confusion, I sigh. "I just haven't been getting a lot of sleep," I finally admit, which is true. Maybe all the worrying is messing with my head.

"Well…" the lady says, wringing her hands together now, clearly unsure of how to proceed. "I hope she turns up soon then." She takes a couple of backward steps. "When you're done in here, just shut off the light and pull the door closed behind you."

"Of course," Phil says for me. "Yes. And we'll be right out." Phil grabs my hand. "Sorry for the confusion…and thanks for lunch. It was delicious."

The woman nods and then disappears back into the restaurant. We stand there for a moment, hand in hand, but then Phil finally shifts to stand right in front of me.

"Are you okay?" He brushes a lock of hair out of my face and looks me over closely. "What happened?"

"I..." At first, I'm hesitant to say anything, fearful to admit the truth for a couple of reasons, but then the words spew out of me like lava.

When I'm finished, Phil just stands there.

I can't maintain his bewildered gaze, so I look back at the mirror. "I swear it was there, Phil. I swear it on the girls' lives."

"I believe you," he says. I dare to look back at him. His expression is still woeful though. "I think our minds are capable of doing all sorts of things to help cope—"

"I didn't imagine it, Phil, and I didn't hallucinate it," I snap. "I saw it. It was right here!" I circle the empty space.

"Meghan. How is that possible?" he asks, always testing my theories, even when they're so close to the heart.

"I don't know," I admit, "but it was there."

He sighs. I do too.

"Come on. Let's get out of here before they call the cops." He offers me a hand. I take it.

We walk out of the bathroom, being sure to turn off the light and to close the door behind us, as instructed, and then we head toward the exit.

"Bye," the lady says, still looking at us warily. "I hope your Mom gets home soon."

That stops me in my tracks. I look at the lady. She's definitely still suspicious of us—probably thinks I'm doing drugs or something, but there's something sincere in her eyes. I pull my hand out of Phil's so I can grab Mom's phone out of my pocket. "Thanks," I say as I lean against the counter and turn on the phone. "You wouldn't happen to recognize her, maybe?" I quickly navigate my way to the photo of her and Will and then turn the screen so she can see it. "She's about five foot five. A hundred and ten pounds or so. Blonde. Big blue eyes. She has a couple of tattoos on each wrist," I add, trying to think up all the things that may have stood out. "M&M on one and M&M on the other."

The woman reaches for the phone. "May I?" she inquires, gesturing for me to hand it over. I do. Then I watch her face as she examines the picture. "Hmm," she says, a spark of recognition illuminating her face. "I can't say for sure about your mom…" she zooms in on the picture. "But I know this guy." She looks up at me, her eyes wide, and then she scans the dining room.

I get a sinking feeling in my gut as I watch her. "We think his name is Will," I whisper, because it somehow seems appropriate given her reaction.

She nods. "Yes. Will.i.am—"

"Like the rapper?" Phil interjects, his voice so loud in comparison that the lady and I cringe.

She nods and then quickly scans the dining room again as if someone could have miraculously materialized.

I lean closer and then do my own search of the area, suddenly feeling exposed. "Does he live around here?" Phil asks, his voice just as hushed. "Her mom has been missing for a couple of days and he was the last person she was with."

The lady makes the sign of the cross and then hands the phone back to me. "I'm sorry to hear that," she says, sounding even more sincere now. "He's not a good person." She looks at me. "He lives nearby. When you find your mama, you should tell her he's not worth her time." She pats my hand. "But if anyone asks, don't say I mentioned it."

That's a surefire sign Mr. Will.i.am is probably on the wrong side of the law. Most normal, law-abiding citizens like this lady probably hates that he's her neighbor, but snitches get stitches, so as much as she would like to see him gone permanently, she's not looking to take the credit for it.

"Would you mind if we left our car in your lot while we

walk to the park?" Phil asks. "I can leave you the keys or something, so you know we'll come back."

"Oh, no," she says with a don't-worry-about-it hand gesture. "You guys go ahead. The car will be fine for a little bit while you explore." She points toward the window. "That park bench is just around the corner, so there's that. I'm not sure exactly where that fella lives, but it can't be too far because he always walks over here, even when the weather is bad."

"Okay, thanks," Phil says. "We appreciate your help."

"Yes," I add, feeling the need to also thank her for her kindness. She could very well have thrown us out, but instead, she's been the biggest help so far. "Thank you."

"Don't mention it," she says, seeming bashful now. "I just hope she turns up soon."

"Me too," I say as I follow Phil outside.

"You want my hoodie?" he asks as we head toward the corner.

I glance down at the stain and sigh. For a March afternoon, it's actually nice out. Probably somewhere in the mid-sixties, which is a welcomed rarity. The stain is obnoxious though, and so while it's pleasant enough that I don't need it, I agree to take it anyway. I slip it over my head just as we make it to the intersection, right by the Pete's Hot Dog sign.

"Twenty bucks says that's his place," Phil says as he points down the block, toward a police cruiser and an ambulance, their lights flashing but their sirens off.

Before I jump to agree with him, I take a moment to examine the scene. The police cruiser and ambulance are parked about halfway up the block, a little past the bench and tree from Mom's picture. There's an officer standing on the sidewalk, in front of one of the houses, and a short distance from him, closer to us, are a group of people. Probably neighbors.

"Come on," I say as I head for the crosswalk.

"I take it you aren't up for a little wager then?" he asks, though his tone is intentionally light, probably because he knows that none of this is a joking matter.

"It could just be that some elderly person fell and couldn't get up," I say, just as casually. Secretly though, I'm hoping he's wrong because I don't want that to be Will's house. My luck has held out enough to have gotten me here—to the right place at the right time, but I don't think it's going to extend to Will's house.

10

THE RIGHT PLACE

There's a group of old people standing just ahead of us. The two elderly couples are clearly interested in what's happening at the house a few doors down, but it's impossible to tell if they're neighbors or if they just happened by and then stopped to rubberneck. Phil, who's a lot cooler under pressure than I ever realized—though, given that he's always playing those role-playing games, I guess that would make sense.

"Is everything okay?" Phil asks as he leans a bit closer, like he's trying to get a peek inside the house.

"We don't think so…" the guy finally shifts to turn toward us, his brow furrowing as he studies us. "You two aren't from around here," he observes, which gets everyone's attention. The two older ladies turn to look at us, and the other older gentlemen glances at Phil for a moment before his steel-gray eyes bore into mine.

"No," Phil says. "We're from Middletown. Her mother has been missing for a couple of days…" He looks at me, winces, and then looks back at the group. "Well, just a day really, but it's under some unusual circumstances…"

Now everyone is looking at him.

I pull Mom's phone out of my pocket and show them the picture. "This is my mom. Her name is Maggie May. This guy's name is Will." I look over at Phil for moral support. He nods as if in agreement, so I turn back to look at the group and continue. "The lady at Pete's Hot Dogs thinks he lives around here…"

The old people lean closer to the phone.

"Yeah," the older lady with the bad blue-black hair-dye job says. "We recognize him. You say this is your mama?"

As her beady dark eyes settle on me, I gulp. I've met her type before. She's the kind of older white lady who can't wrap her brain around the fact that I'm Maggie May's daughter— me, the mocha-skinned, brown-eyed, frizzy-haired girl who's standing before her. I can't tell if her disbelief is stemming from the fact that she's just appalled by the notion of a white woman bearing a black man's child or if she just doesn't see the obvious family resemblance. Regardless of the reason, I've learned that whatever the cause of her obvious disdain, it's always best to try and steer the conversation in another direction.

"He was the last person she was seen with," I finally say, shifting the phone closer so that each of them can get a good look. "We think this picture was taken around here somewhere."

"That's right over there," the man with the gray eyes says. He points across the street, toward the tree and metal bench that's a little farther up the road, then he shifts to point back at the house with the ambulance. "And *that's* Will's house—"

"He's a drug dealer," the other older lady cuts in. She has a deep Brooklyn accent. "And we're hoping it's him and not his grandmother—"

"Rose!" The lady with the blue-black hair slaps the women's hand. "That's an awful thing to say! Especially to children."

The women launch into a bickering match that's too fast-paced and sharped-tongued for me to make any sense of. For my part, I do at least catch the other lady's name: Katherine; and I come to the very safe conclusion that she and Rose quibble like this often, so I watch the exchange as if it's a tennis match, and I'm actually a little saddened when they begin to settle down, seeming to have come to an impasse of some sort. When they turn and set their sights on me again, I instinctively take a backward step, since I'm not sure if I'm about to bear the brunt of their anger.

"Not that I would wish anything badly on anyone," Rose says, emphasizing her words for Katherine's sake, "but that boy has been nothing but trouble since he's moved in with his grandmother."

"Yes," the man with the gray eyes agrees—this one undoubtedly Rose's husband.

Katherine and the other bald man—probably her husband, nod their agreement.

"Drugs," Rose repeats in the same loud whisper. "He's had all sorts of people in and out of here the past year, and we've had to call the police on him more than once."

The group of old people nod collectively.

"Damn shame for Dolores," Katherine says. "Up until Will came along, she was always a good neighbor."

That sentiment draws more nods and murmurs of agreement from the men.

"So my mom," I say as I wake up the phone to make her picture visible again and try to get the conversation back on track. "Have you seen her around lately?"

"It's hard to say with all the folks in and out of here," Rose says, "but if I were you, I'd tell your mama to find better company."

Yeah. That seems to be the going consensus.

"Any idea why the ambulance and cops are here then?" Phil asks, thankfully diverting the attention off me.

"We didn't call them," Rose offers. "And it came as a bit of a surprise, since it's been pleasantly quiet the past few days."

"Oh?" I say, my brain finally switching into investigative mode. "For about how long?"

"What do you mean?" Rose asks.

"I mean how long has it been nice and quiet? Just for today?"

"Oh. No. All weekend, actually. See, Dolores likes to go visit her daughter in Port Jervis, so Will drives her over there every few weeks." The lady leans closer to me. "Those are usually bad days for us, mind you, because he'll misbehave all the more while his grandmother is away."

The men nod and murmur.

"Most times we have to call the police by day's end of Dolores going off like that," Katherine adds. "Thankfully, this weekend was the first exception."

That piques my curiosity. "So he was finally quiet this time around?" I ask, hoping to keep the conversation moving in the right direction.

"No. Well, yes," Rose answers for the group. "What I mean is they both left on Saturday morning, but neither one of them came back." She shrugs. "We just assumed he had stayed over with Dolores. Maybe they had a wedding or something?"

"So, the last time you saw them was on Saturday morning?" I ask, just to confirm I'm getting the story straight.

"That's right," Rose says; the group nodding in unison with her. "It's been the nicest, quietest weekend we're had all year."

I look over at Phil, my one brow raised quizzically. "I guess that makes sense…" I shift through all the details I have stored in my memory. "Uncle Rusty did say Will and his friends had just come in from out of town, so maybe they had a wedding or some family event in Port Jervis?" I shrug and then look at the elderly couples as if they're going to miraculously provide me with the right answer.

"I guess that could explain everything," Phil says, "*in theory*, but then why would the police and paramedics be here now?"

Before I can even begin to ponder a plausible explanation for that, two officers begin their ascent down the long driveway. They're very engrossed in their conversation, which, for some reason, causes my stomach to sink. Would they be so enraptured if nothing was going on in the house? I doubt it. Unfortunately, with where we're standing and how the house is situated, there's no way for us to get a good look inside. As I take a step forward, hoping to peek into one of the windows, the women gasp. That draws my attention back to the top of the driveway.

My jaw drops as I stare at the white-shrouded gurney and the two paramedics.

Rose begins to recite the rosary. Katherine makes the sign of the cross over and over again.

"Do you suppose it's Delores?" Rose whispers, still loud enough for all of us to hear.

"I don't know," the other lady starts, but just then we hear it, a sob like a wounded animal; a sound that sends chills running down my spine. I look over just as Delores hurries after the paramedics, or at least that's who I'm assuming the hysterical older black lady is.

"Delores!" Rose calls out, confirming that fact for me. She takes a few steps toward the driveway. "What's happened?"

"Oh, honey," Katherine calls as she follows after her friend. "Are you okay?"

In response, Delores just sobs again, and now she seems confused as to how to proceed. Does she keep following the gurney, or does she go to her neighbors, who, at least for their parts, do seem genuinely distressed? In the end, the old lady follows after the paramedics, her sobs gut-wrenching to endure as the four of us—me, Phil, and the two old men, just stand there watching.

"Ladies," one of the officers interjects, halting the women in their progress, and then he walks toward them, almost as if he's going to push them back toward us, but then he seems to think twice about that. "Do you know this woman?" he asks no one in particular, but then he looks between them expectantly.

"Yes. My name is Rose Wienerwald. I live right there," she says, and then points at the house we're standing in front of. "Delores and I have been neighbors for over twenty years—"

"And I'm Katherine," she interjects as if this suddenly became a morbid type of competition, pointing in the other direction of Delores's house, a little farther down the block. "I'm also her neighbor."

The cop seems to pick up on the odd tension too because he smiles and then places a hand on each of their elbows as if he's about to guide them somewhere. "That's good to hear," he says in a firm but oddly soothing way, "because Mrs. Armstrong has just had the very unfortunate experience of discovering a family member—"

"Was it Will?" Rose asks.

"Her grandson?" Katherine tosses in as if to clarify.

The officer nods. "Yes. Unfortunately, she found him, which can be a highly traumatic event for anyone, especially a close family member."

"Of course," Rose says, and then nods and places her hand over her mouth.

"Yes, of course," Katherine agrees.

"We'll be taking her grandson down to the coroner's office now, so I was wondering if you ladies wouldn't mind helping

Mrs. Armstrong back up to her house. Perhaps help her clean up some and call some of her family members?"

"Of course!" Rose chimes in, this time as though her life depends on those words.

"We'll bring her over to my place," Katherine declares. "Since surely going back in there would be too difficult at the moment."

"My place is much closer," Rose quips.

"Perhaps you ladies can take shifts," the officer recommends, his tone gentle but firm. "After all, these will be very difficult days for Mrs. Armstrong and I'm sure she'll need all the help she can get."

"Of course!" Rose says, suddenly so demurely I practically don't recognize her.

"Yes. Of course," Katherine agrees.

On any other day, I would have found these two women to be deliciously delightful—in that soap opera sort of way. Today though, their pettiness is driving me to the very edge of my patience.

"This is my card," he says as he releases their arms and reaches into his back pocket. He retrieves his wallet, pulls out two cards, and hands one to each.

Well played, I think to myself as I take mental notes on how to handle overwhelming witnesses and neighbors.

"She'll undoubtedly have many questions when she finally calms down." The officer pulls two more cards out of his wallet and hands another to each woman. "Here are a few extras to hand out to her or family members." He looks between them pointedly. "She'll want to plan for a memorial of some sort, since we'll need to hold onto her grandson's remains for a little while, for tests and such. You understand?"

"Yes," Rose says firmly.

"For how long?" Katherine inquires.

"I can't give a definitive answer to that question, but have

Mrs. Armstrong contact the medical examiner's office in the morning. She'll be the only one they'll speak with, of course," he adds, "or any immediate family members if she has someone else who can call to check on the status."

"Her daughter will surely come right away," Rose offers.

Katherine nods. "Will she be able to call them?"

"Sure." The officer takes a backward step. "If you ladies can help guide her back inside now, we'll be getting on our way."

With me being so involved in their conversation, I hadn't even noticed the paramedics had gotten Will's body down to the ambulance. The two women follow the cop over and practically have to pry poor Delores off the siderail. I tear up a little as I watch. Not because I should—that guy could be the reason my mom is missing after all, but because watching his grandmother so heartbroken even though it sounds like he was an awful person is both sad and touching to watch. I guess everyone—no matter how bad—has someone sitting on the sidelines loving them. Probably secretly rooting for them to turn a new leaf.

I know that feeling too well.

I sigh as I lean against Phil to watch as the two older women finally convince Delores to walk away from the stretcher. They both place an arm around her and while I can't tell just from watching, the women veer toward Rose's house— a point of contention I'm sure she'll brag about to Katherine for years to come since, at the moment, they both look genuine as they help their neighbor toward the house.

As the women near, the two men finally snap to attention and hurry ahead to get the screen and front doors open, respectively, and Phil nudges me back a bit, as if to give the ladies a wide enough berth to get past without having to side-step anyone. I instinctively take several backward steps but then surprise even myself as I barrel toward them.

Delores doesn't even notice, but Rose and Katherine do

because they pull her to a gentle halt and then stare at me expectedly.

"Yes?" Rose inquires.

"I'm sorry," I blurt out. I step even closer and take Delores's hand. "I'm very sorry for your loss, Mrs. Armstrong," I say softly, "and I hate to bother you at such an awful time, but my mother is missing—"

Rose huffs. "This is not an appropriate time, young lady—"

"It is," I insist, once again surprising myself with my brazenness. I look back at Mrs. Armstrong, her eyes swollen from crying, snot dripping out of her nose and over her upper lip. For a fraction of a second, I reconsider, but then I decide it would be a wasted moment if I remained quiet. "Was your grandson alone?" I dare ask, my voice hitching at the end though.

Delores studies me closely for a moment but then finally nods. "Yes, child." She sniffles. "He was alone…just sitting there on the couch…" A few tears slip onto her cheeks. "At least he looked at peace…" she whispers and then looks skyward. "He looked at peace."

My brows furrow at that and as I look over the old woman's face, I think I understand. She must have found him when she got back. Apparently on the couch. *At peace.* So there mustn't have been any obvious signs of forced entry, so it couldn't have been some violent gang-related killing. At least I don't think so. Not if he looked "at peace."

"Come now," Rose says as she pats Delores's hand gently. "Let's get you inside."

"We'll call your daughter for you," Katherine adds, me and Phil all but forgotten as the women head inside.

Phil and I stand there watching and don't start moving until the old men go inside and close the door.

"You okay?" Phil asks as we near the intersection.

I shake my head.

"At least we found the right place," he offers as we wait for the light to change. "It was just at the wrong time."

I finally look at him and then shake my head again. "No. It was the right place and the right time because now at least we know…" Tears blur my vision and I have to hold my breath to keep from bursting into tears.

"I bet Jesse can call up here and get some information about Will," Phil says softly. "Maybe talk to that cop and see if they know anything about your mom."

My mom. Those two words suddenly feel as though they've sprouted hands and are choking the life out of me. I fight back tears for a moment longer, but as I catch sight of the Pete's Hot Dogs sign and the memory of her heart-shaped message resurfaces in my mind, I lose it. Thankfully, Phil is here to help me pick up the pieces.

11

THE SECOND TEXT

I can't bring myself to go to school on Wednesday. I get up. I go through the motions, but just as I'm about to leave, I can't muster the strength to lift my keys off the hook, and the idea of opening the door seems like an impossible feat—like time travel, or people living happily ever after. I stand there for a moment longer, until Uncle Rusty steps beside me and places his hand on my shoulder.

"Meghan," he says, but then he sighs.

I look up at him, daring him to tell me I'm overreacting; that she's going to turn up any minute, but I think Phil and I have finally convinced him to let go of that ridiculous notion. Mom is missing. That's the simple truth of it. She left the bar in the wee hours of Monday morning with a guy named William Henry Armstrong; a two-bit drug dealer from Newburgh, and now she's gone and Will is very, very dead.

Uncle Rusty drops his arm to his side and I head over to the couch. I'm still so exhausted from yesterday the emotional toll drags me onto the cushion. I rub my temples, the memory of the lengthy discussion Phil and I had with Uncle Rusty and

Jesse in this exact spot coming back to me as I sink farther into my seat.

"Maybe you should stay home today," Uncle Rusty suggests. He makes his way over and then leans against the arm of the loveseat. "After we get the girls to school, we can head over to Shirley's and see if she wouldn't mind helping us whip up some missing-person posters that we can hang around town."

The fact that he's acknowledging what I've known from the start has the opposite effect on me. Instead of feeling relieved, I'm terrified. Saddened. Angry. My mom is missing. Those four words have resonated so many times inside my head the past few days that I'm sure they've left a permanent groove in my brain—like one of those fault-line cracks after an earthquake. I lean forward and drop my head into my hands. Aside from the throbbing in my temples, my sinuses are swollen from the constant tears I can't stop shedding. My entire body hurts, like in that way mom describes when she's about to fall into one of her major depressions.

It is hereditary, I remind myself. All of her crazy is.

"I don't think the girls should miss school though," he says as he glances over his shoulder, toward our bedroom.

"No," I agree, my voice sounding muffled because I'm still rubbing my temples. "They shouldn't." I sit back in my seat and sigh. "And neither should I." I force myself onto my feet. "The last thing we need right now is for CPS to stick their noses into our business."

"But I'm here," Uncle Rusty reminds me.

"Yeah, I know." I look deep into his soft brown eyes. "And I appreciate that more than you know, and I'm sure it'll help if they do come poking around, but you know how they get with all that legal guardian crap."

He nods. "Yeah. I know." He peeks over his shoulder then looks back at me. In barely a whisper, he says, "I overheard

Misty telling Molly last night she was going to find a way to call her dad—"

"What?" I shout, which causes Uncle Rusty to flinch.

"Ssh!" He puts his finger to his mouth and then motions for me to keep it down. "Without trying to be so obvious, while we were doing the dinner dishes together, I reminded her that it wouldn't be a good idea to call him."

I roll my eyes. "Definitely not." I mull over the thought of him coming up here with Mom missing. Can he take her? Will he try to take Molly too then? Would he offer to take me? Is that all even possible? What about school? What about work? I've already missed every night this week.

"The truth of it is," Uncle Rusty starts in that tone I'm starting to recognize—in a way that means he's about to dish out some harsh realities, "is that when I walked Jesse out last night, we talked about that because, at some point, he's going to have to notify him—"

"He can't—"

"Meghan," Uncle Rusty says firmly, "he has a right to know."

I violently shake my head and those damn tears that are always hanging around start sliding down my cheeks again. "He'll take her—"

"And is that really a bad thing?" he counters, his tone back to gentle. He leans forward, grabs a tissue off the coffee table, and hands it to me. "We all know Mags is infamous for disappearing, but," and he holds up a hand so I don't interrupt, "it's been a few days now and Matt has a right to know."

He's said that already, but I still don't agree. I mean, it isn't that Matt is a bad guy. I honestly love him and wish all the time that he and my mom had gotten married. I think my life would have turned out so differently if he had stuck around— in a good way—so the thought of calling him isn't because I don't agree that he should know Mom is missing, it's just that I don't want him to separate us. The girls are all I have left if Mom doesn't come home.

"Listen, if we hadn't learned about what happened to Will last night, I would be on your side all the way, kiddo, but that's kind of like a game-changer..."

I consider that for a moment but then shake my head. "Why? She wasn't there, and when Jesse called his buddy in Newburgh, they said it hadn't looked like he'd had company."

Uncle Rusty nods and then shrugs. He sighs next and then runs his hands over his face. "I know," he finally says. "It's just that..." He looks at me. "Why don't we give it today, see if she turns up, but if not, I think it's time we call Matt—"

"But Uncle Rusty—"

"No buts anymore, Meg. If Mags isn't back by the time you girls get out of school then we'll call him together, see if he'd be willing to come up here for a few days..."

My shoulders sag in defeat but I nod because I know it's inevitable. The only thing I can hope for is that Mom suddenly turns up and that Matt will volunteer to take Molly too because as much as I don't want to be separated from them, I especially don't want them to be separated from each other.

Uncle Rusty gives me a hug. I lean into him and allow myself the moment of comfort, but then I step away from him. "I'll go and wake them up before I leave."

He tucks one of my frizzy curls behind my ear and nods. "Yeah. Sounds good. You want some toast or something else for breakfast?"

I shake my head, since the thought of food just makes me feel worse.

"You have to eat, Meg," he says, sounding more fatherly than I've ever heard him before. "You have to take care of yourself before you can take care of anyone else. After watching your mom all these years, I really, really hope you've learned that lesson."

I've learned tons actually, but sometimes knowing what's right doesn't help you deal with what's happening. Life is so awful sometimes. Cruel, really, and I don't think our frail little bodies were designed to withstand all the heartache that comes with so much worry and fear day after day. It's exhausting.

"I'll make you some toast," Uncle Rusty says as he turns and heads for the kitchen. "Be sure to stop long enough to wash your face before you go," he adds.

Instinctively, I touch my cheek and realize the advice isn't because I'm dirty, per se. I'm just snotty and probably puffy and swollen from crying again. I make my way to the bathroom, turn on the water, and lean over the sink. *Come on, Mom,* I think as I scoop a handful of cool water into my hand and splash my face. *Get home already,* I plead.

After soaping and rinsing my face off, I blindly turn off the water and then reach for the hand towel. I press it against my eyes, hoping the pressure will help with the swelling, then I stand tall and look at my reflection. The snot is gone, but even if I didn't cry again today, it would probably take a week for my face to go back to normal. I sigh as I reach over to hang the towel and then freeze in place when I spot Mom's "I love you, M&M," message. My heart races as I look at the faucet. The water is off, and I know that when it was on it had been cold. Definitely not hot enough to warrant steam.

"Mom?" I whisper, searching the room through the reflection of the mirror.

A shadow in the darkened portion of the hallway causes the hairs on the back of my neck to stand on end, and then a frigid phantom breeze blows, causing my entire body to shake.

"Mom?" I breathe out, both petrified and elated by the paranormal experience.

I hear the rusty creak of a door a second before I see my

mom's bedroom door open slowly. A ray of light seeps into the hallway and evaporates the shadow. With its absence, the chill in my bones subsides, and when I look back at the mirror, Mom's message is gone. I reach for the glass, to where the message always appears, but I stop short of touching it, fearful that by doing so, I'll somehow smudge or wipe it away.

"Mom?" I whisper again, this time looking around the room. I turn around and check every inch of the small space, then I let my gaze drift to her partially open bedroom door. Had it just been the wind? I mean it couldn't have been, but the rational part of my brain insists on asking and then pondering that question. *There are no such things as ghosts*, I remind myself. But if there were, then seeing my mother would be a very, very bad sign, because that would mean she's dead.

"Please don't be dead," I say softly, over the lump that's forming in the back of my throat, threatening to release more tears. "Please," I repeat, hoping that somehow helps the universe know how opposed I am to that notion.

Slowly, I make my way across the hallway and step in front of my mother's bedroom door. I peek in through the thin crack for a second and then I push it completely open. My gaze immediately drifts to the calendar that's lying in the middle of the floor. It hadn't been there the last time I'd ventured into the room. Normally, the little calendar, which had been an extra, smaller version of a cat-themed calendar Misty had gotten at a book fair, was thumb-tacked to the wall by the mirror. I look in that direction and focus on the pinhole for a moment, then I let my gaze drift to the thumb-tack that's lying on its side on the dresser, as though it had fallen. Finally, I calculate the distance between the calendar and the dresser. *If* the calendar had just randomly fallen, then it could have landed where it is. It's a very real possibility and it's not like stuff like this doesn't happen all the time. My family is notorious for over-using pinholes, so it could have just fallen.

I don't think it did though.

I step into the room and pick up the calendar, noticing that it had fallen face down, onto the month of July. On the eighteenth, in Misty's very jittery but nearly flawless script is a sad face and the words "Basic Training." For some reason, that makes me smile even though it should make me even sadder. I sigh as I adjust the calendar around and then flip to March. The second Wednesday of the month is circled, and in my Mom's handwriting, the initials MEPS are sloppily placed and underlined.

The acronym stands for Military Entrance Processing Station. She must have put it there to remind herself that it was the day I was swearing in. I think about that day, about standing with my hand raised, taking an oath to serve my country, and then later, at how Mom and I had gotten our nails done and then went to McDonald's afterward. It was two weeks ago today. Funny how that suddenly feels like it was a lifetime ago.

"Hey," Uncle Rusty says from the doorway, spooking me. "Your toast is ready."

I turn to face him.

"Everything okay?" he asks, his attention on the calendar in my hands.

"Yeah…" I say, since I still have no idea how to tell him about the messages. Instead, I look back at the calendar. "I was just…" I sigh and realize I don't have the strength to try to come up with an explanation.

"Go eat up," Uncle Rusty says, seeming to sense I need the reprieve. "I'll wake the girls."

"Right." I nod. "Yeah. Okay."

"Try to have a good day," he says. "I'll call if I hear anything."

I nod, and then I make my way to the door, but my attention is still on the calendar. There's nothing else annotated in March, but for some reason, I get the sense I was lead to the nearly blank calendar for a reason. *But why*, I wonder as I make my way to the kitchen. And more importantly, will the ghostly shadow return to give me another clue?

———

Mom's cell phone goes off just as I pull into my parking spot at school. I still haven't entirely gotten used to having a working phone all the time, so I have to fish it out of the bottom of my backpack. On the home screen, there's a notification, but it only shows it's from a number that isn't saved to her contacts. I make my way to her messages but I stop short of tapping on it because I suddenly realize it has a 917 area code. That's a New York City area code. I tap on the message and my curiosity and confusion only deepen.

The message reads, "You sleeping inn today?"

I just stare at it, not sure how to respond. Even my body seems to freeze in time.

Someone knocks on the window, startling me so badly I fumble and drop the phone.

"Sorry!" Phil shouts through the glass, then he pulls the door open. "Sorry," he repeats, but this time he can't hide the grin. "Damn, if I didn't know how pissed you are right now for spooking you, I would be laughing so hard." He cackles but chokes on it, but then he bursts out laughing.

"Not funny," I snap as I reach for the phone.

"It was though," he says through more obnoxious snorts. "You literally jumped out of your skin."

The phone is blank when I lift it, but after I tap the screen, it comes back to life and the cryptic message stares back at me.

I'm still very confused by it...I mean, who asks a sleeping person if they're sleeping in?

"Oh," Phil says, suddenly somber.

I look up at him. His expression is positively sour.

"Jeez, Meg...I'm sorry. Is it your mom?" He puts his hand over his heart. "Did you hear something?"

"No." I quickly pull the keys from the ignition, grab my stuff, and then get out of the car. "We still haven't heard anything, but I just got a message." I slam the door shut and lock it.

"From Jesse?" he inquires as we fall in step.

I shake my head. "No. But Uncle Rusty did tell me this morning that he's planning on calling Matt if Mom doesn't show up today."

"But..." Phil sighs. "But if he calls and tells him your mom is missing then won't he come up here and take the girls?"

I just look over at him, because he knows that's exactly what's going to happen.

"Not for nothing," he says, "but me and Grams were talking about it yesterday and maybe it won't be such a bad thing if Matt comes up, Meg—"

"What?" I snap, incredulous. "Phil!"

He looks away. "Meg, I know you don't want to be separated from the girls."

"Yeah," I say, my arms going out to my side to emphasize that. "Duh."

He looks back at me, his eyes narrowed now. "Look. You know he'll take both of them." He holds up a hand before I can interrupt. "We all know he will. No one wants to separate you guys, and no one *especially* wants to separate the girls."

"I..." I stop walking and put a hand on my hip. "We can't know that for sure, Phil," I finally say, since there's no arguing that point. Until we actually call Matt and see what he says, it's all a moot point.

"And you can stay with us," Phil says softly. "Grams and Pop are totally cool with letting you have the guest room until you leave for basic—"

"I…!" My chest puffs out, preparing to read him the riot act. My hands flutter around, getting ready to emphasize my outrage, but nothing comes out, and in that moment, I feel more exhausted than I ever have in my entire life. For the first time ever, I've got no fight in me. I exhale loudly and almost fold into myself.

Phil places his arm around my shoulders. "Meghan…"

But we just stand there, because sometimes there aren't any words for the horrific moment you find yourself in. Sometimes, silence is the best response.

12

THE RENDEZVOUS

Mom's cell phone chirps halfway through first period, letting me know that a new message has arrived. Thankfully, someone's phone accidentally going off during first period isn't too unusual, so no one but Phil looks my way. I quickly turn off the ringer and then make my way to the message. It's from the 917 number—the one with the cryptic "sleeping inn" message. With a shaky finger, I tap on it and then blankly stare at the single question mark that had just arrived. That's it. There's no other text; no other explanation as to who it could be or why they're texting such weird messages.

I tilt the screen so Phil can see it, then I put the phone on my desk and stare down at it. "You sleeping inn today?" the first message reads, which for some reason keeps nagging at me, not only because it's cryptic, but also because it reminds me of something I can't place.

The phone vibrates again and a notification pops up showing that Phil just sent a message. I tap on it.

"Reply to it!" he texts.

I look over at him and shrug, not out of disinterest but because I've been considering that option the entire class period. I just need to find the perfect thing to say so I'll get a response I understand.

The phone vibrates again.

"Say something vague," Phil suggests. "Like yeah or no."

I consider that, since it's a better option than just letting this window of opportunity pass me by. I make my way back to the mystery messages and stare at them again. "You sleeping inn today?" I read and then I go back to racking my brain, trying to decode the message. No matter how hard I try though, I can't quite access the information I need.

Maybe a good response from the mystery writer will help jog my memory?

I pull up the keyboard and type, "Yeah. You?" I reread those two words for a full minute before I shift the screen so Phil can see it. He leans closer and then after a second, he nods. I hit the send button before I chicken out, then I set the phone on the desk and stare down at it. A minute ticks by. Then two. By the time the bell rings, my eyes feel bloodshot and weary. I gather my books and slip the phone into my back pocket.

"Let me know when he texts back," Phil says as we file out of the classroom.

"How do you know it's a guy?" I ask as I scoot around a couple who are walking entirely too slowly.

Phil catches up to me but he doesn't bother dignifying my question with a response. We both know it's a guy. Mom doesn't have female friends.

"McDonald's?" he asks as we near the hallway where we have to go our separate ways.

I stop short and look at him curiously. Wednesday's are usually his day to hang out with his girlfriend. "Rebecca still sick?" I inquire.

"Yeah," he says with a shrug. "They think it's the flu."

"Really? I thought flu season was over?"

He shrugs. "Me too, but it's something. She's been running a fever for a couple of days and she can't hold anything down."

I raise a brow and give him a cryptic smile. "You sure that's it?" I ask coyly.

Phil rolls his eyes. "You know we're extra protected."

Yeah. I know. Phil isn't about having a baby anytime soon, so he always uses protection, and Rebecca had gotten one of those birth control rods shoved into her arm, so I'm sure she's just sick. I just like messing with him. "So, Big Mac?"

"Quarter Pounder," he says as he bumps his arm against mine and then starts to veer off toward his hallway. "Stay positive, Meg. And text me the second you hear anything, okay?"

I give him a thumbs up and then hurry out of the way of a group of guys walking my way, as though they own the school. I catch sight of Phil a second before he turns down his hallway. I give a wave and then make my way to English, my mind a million miles away.

You sleeping inn today?

Those four words play on a loop in my brain as I take my seat and pull out my books. I grab the calendar too, since I have no intention of actually following along with the lecture today. I can't do Shakespeare on a good day, so trying today would be downright torturous. Instead, I go through the calendar, page by page, trying to discern a clue, but the only dates marked off are ones that I already know. My MEPS date, my basic training date, my birthday, the girls' birthdays. And because Misty had done most of the annotating, Mom's, Matt's, and Uncle Rusty's birthdays are also circled. It's all stuff I know, which frustrates me in a way I've never been frustrated before. *Why can't I catch a break?*

As if on cue, the phone vibrates. I shift to pull it out of my back pocket, and then I stare at yet another cryptic message.

"227."

I sigh as I drop the phone on the desk. *What the heck is*

that supposed to mean? Is that a time? Is something supposed to happen at 2:27? Oh…maybe that's when he's sleeping in to? I look at the clock over the whiteboard. It's a quarter to nine, so that's hours away, which makes me wonder why he would be up now, texting to tell Mom he isn't waking up until this afternoon? That makes no sense.

Another problem is that I have no idea how to respond to that to get more information. Should I text 228, or maybe 226? Is there a pattern I'm missing? Is it even a time?

I drop back against my seat, close my eyes, and rub my temples. What kind of investigator am I going to make if I can't figure anything out? A bad one. *A very, very bad one,* I tell myself. *No.* I won't accept that. There has to be something I'm missing; something obvious that will help me find her. I sit up and reach for my notebook. After flipping to the right page, I review the timeline I had created a couple of days ago. I go over it carefully, making sure I didn't miss anything, then I continue where I left off. I place a tick mark at 9:00 p.m. on Sunday, to indicate when we had gone to bed. Then I place another at 2:00 a.m. on Monday morning, to identify the last time Uncle Rusty had seen her. Next, I create another column for Tuesday and I notate the approximate time when Will's grandmother had found his body. Could Mom have come home in between any of those times? I consider that for a moment longer, but after another second of mulling it over, I let it go for now because if she had come back somewhere in the middle of the night, she had left before we had woken up.

I go back to the timeline after we had left for school. Could she have come home during the day on Monday? I mean, Will's neighbor had said the house had been quiet all weekend and on Monday, so maybe they had stayed at our house? I shake my head at that, since I would have noticed if a strange guy had been in our apartment. So maybe they left the bar and went back to Port Jervis? I tap my pencil against the page as I let that sink in—the idea intriguing enough for me to give it some serious consideration. Maybe that's it—maybe I've just been looking in the wrong place the entire time?

I go to reach for the phone to text Jesse, but the bell rings. I stick the phone in my back pocket, pack my books into my bag, and then stand.

"Meg," Mr. Terrell calls. "Can I talk to you for a second?"

My stomach sinks since it's never good to have to stay after class. I dodge a couple of students and make my way over to his desk. "Yes, sir?"

He drops into his seat and looks up at me. "Any word on your mom?" he inquires, his voice low so the students scurrying out of the room can't overhear.

I shake my head.

He sighs and runs his fingers through his shortly cropped hair. "I'm sorry, Meghan…" He drops his hands to his lap, as though he doesn't know what to do with them. "Listen, about the test on Friday…" He clears his throat and then starts messing with his tie. "I can tell you're distracted—with reason, of course," he adds quickly, "so if it takes some of the load off your shoulders, we can reschedule for you to retake it when we get back from break."

My mouth drops open for a couple of reasons, the first being that his kindness and concern always touches my heart. He's a good guy and I'm glad he's my teacher. The second reason is because I had totally forgotten that next week is Spring Break. Our school district always takes it last, so it always coincides with my birthday. The fact that I've forgotten about both shouldn't surprise or bother me, but it does. In fact, the realization of it suddenly makes me very angry at my mother. I'm going to be eighteen on Saturday. This is my senior year—my last Spring Break as a high schooler, yet here I am, so worried about her that I've once again been deprived of enjoying my life—of being a kid.

"Thanks, Mr. Terrell," I say, my voice level and sincere because I've spent years learning how to pretend everything's okay even when it isn't. "I appreciate it." That part I mean sincerely. I'm really not in a good head-space to deal with Shakespeare. "Maybe the Monday after we get back?" I suggest.

"Yeah. That's fine." He stands. "And try to get some rest, Meghan. You look exhausted."

"I…" I run my hand over my hair. I had slicked it back this morning but it was already starting to frizz.

"I don't mean…" Mr. Terrell starts, "you know…" He clears his throat again, clearly unversed in speaking to distraught teenaged girls even though he's a high school teacher. In his defense, he doesn't even look like he's in his thirties yet, and I'm pretty sure he doesn't have kids.

"I know what you mean," I reassure him. "Let's just hope everything finally works out so I can get some rest."

"Right. Yes. Of course," he says, now shifting his weight between his feet.

"Well, thanks again," I say, backing away, since this already awkward moment has somehow morphed into a downright cringe-worthy experience. "I should go…" I point behind me. "You know, or I'll be late."

"Great. Yeah." He does that I'm-practicing-to-be-a-corny-dad wave. "See you tomorrow."

I quickly whip around and hurry out of the room, and I don't slow down until I make it all the way to my next classroom. I stop just outside the door to take a deep breath. *Wow.* My body had just run the gamut on a ton of different emotions so quickly I actually feel nauseous. I lean against a locker and then yelp when Mom's phone vibrates in my back pocket.

"You okay?" Kaylin asks as she walks past me. She stops

just shy of the door and looks at me with genuine concern. "Meghan?"

I nod. "Yeah…I'm okay," I finally manage, though I realize I don't sound convincing. I extract the cell phone from my back pocket and hold it up for her to see, hoping to save face. "I just spooked myself," I add, lamely.

She eyes the phone for a second but then looks back at me. Kaylin has always been polite to me—her mother is one of the moms who hates my mother, and she talks badly about her all the time. Thankfully, that apple hadn't fallen anywhere near the tree, because Kaylin has never been rude, and like a lot of people, she seems to genuinely pity me. "That happens to me all the time," she says about the phone, trying to sound chill but coming nowhere near it. "If you or your sisters need anything…" She bites her lower lip and then looks around, almost as if to gauge if anyone can overhear. "I mean, I hope they find your mom soon—" Her eyes meet mine for the briefest second, and in that moment, I swear I can see her soul. It's good and kind and sad. She looks down at her feet then. "So like I said, if you and your sisters need anything, call me okay?"

"Yeah. Okay," I say with a nod. "Thanks," I offer, and I mean it. For my entire life, I've seen nothing but darkness, cruelty, contempt, and judgment from the people in this town, so I'm amazed that in my family's lowest moment—at that precise time when we're so open to being kicked while we're down—we've seen nothing but kindness and compassion.

"You coming in?" she asks, braving a look my way.

"Yeah. In a sec…" I hold up the phone to remind both of us that I got a text. Kaylin nods and disappears into the classroom. I go to the message. It reads, "Yes or no?"

What? I place a hand to my suddenly flushed forehead and I read it again. *Yes or no to what?* My heart races as I reread the message over and over again, and my stomach churns, the buttered toast threatening to erupt. I hurry to the bathroom and slam open one of the metal stall doors. I stand there, my breathing erratic, my thoughts frenzying. I'm going to puke. I lean forward and squeeze my eyes shut.

Breathe through it, Peanut, Mom always used to tell me when I was sick. *It'll pass,* she used to promise, and most times it did. Today it does too, but while I don't throw up, I still feel sick. I turn to go and rinse my face, but I stop cold when I see the message.

"Yes." The steamy word is surrounded by a heart.

My knees buckle, so it takes me a moment to make it over to the sink. "Mom?" I whisper, looking around. There's no response, but the heart-shaped message persists despite there being no steam or rational explanation for its existence. I go to reach for the single word but in all of the running, I still have the phone clutched in my hand. I stare at the dark screen and then look at the mirror. "You want me to say yes to this message?" I ask.

There isn't a verbal or written response, but the temperature around me suddenly drops. I shiver and half expect to see the shadow again. I search the reflection behind me, taking a second to look at each stall carefully. Nothing pops out at me. The lighting doesn't change. But for a brief second, I see Mom. It happens so quickly I feel as though I imagined it, but I somehow know it was real enough; a glimpse of her from not too long ago. It was of the day we were driving back from MEPS. Two weeks ago on Wednesday. *Yes.* I remember now. We had just pulled into the parking lot of the nail salon when she said, "It's way past noon, baby, so there's no chance of me sleeping in today."

Sleeping in. It hadn't made sense then but now I get it. Mom hadn't meant sleeping in, as in getting a few more hours of rest, and the mystery person who was texting hadn't made a typo with his misspelled "inn." It's all so clear now. They meant the Sleep Inn. The hotel.

I quickly pull up the messages and stare at the number. 227 is undoubtedly a room number, the one for this week anyway, since I suddenly get the sinking feeling this is where Mom has been disappearing to on Wednesdays.

I look at the message on the mirror, then I look at the text messages. Without really even realizing it, I type "yes" and then hit the send key. With my decision made, I put the phone in my back pocket, rinse my face off, and stand tall. There are so many things I want to say to my mother right now—and there are so many questions I want to ask because I get the feeling she's listening, but I can't bring myself to say anything because I fear her responses—or lack thereof. There's something hopeful about the quiet between us; maybe because there's no surefire acknowledgement of what I've been dreading to hear, so instead of asking any questions, I simply say, "I love you, M&M."

My declaration is met with silence, which I appreciate more than anything at that moment. I stare at the heart-shaped message on the mirror for a moment longer then I hurry out of the bathroom, hotel-bound.

———

The Sleep Inn hotel is located on a not-so-busy street near a car dealership. I pull into the parking lot and stare at the building for a long moment. I have no idea what to do now, so I just go through the motions of putting the car into gear and pulling the keys out of the ignition. My hands shake as I palm the keys and reach for the door handle. *Get out of the car, Meghan,* I order myself, and my body thankfully obeys. After stuffing mom's phone into my back pocket, I lock the car and then march straight to the hotel entrance. As I near the sliding double doors, I slow my pace. *Do I stop at the front desk?* I've seen movies with people using hotels as a rendezvous place before, but off the top of my head, I can't remember how they handle this part of the script.

I'll have to improvise.

I step into the hotel and keep moving, my eyes shifting around the lobby quickly so I can locate the elevators.

"Hello," a man calls from the front desk.

The elevators are a few feet away, so I keep moving, hoping he isn't talking to me.

"Can I help you ma'am?" he asks next.

That was definitely directed toward me. "I'm fine," I call over my shoulder. "Just heading to my room."

At that exact moment, the elevator nearest me opens. I hurry over and get on. As the doors slide closed, my heart practically pounds out of my chest. My hand is shaking so badly I almost can't press the button, but I somehow manage it and then lean against the cold steel walls as the elevator ascends. The second floor gets there too soon though, so I nearly chicken out. *Go,* I tell myself, and I do, as if my feet are a disembodied part of my body. They carry me to room 227 and I stand before the door. My one hand is still clutching my keys like a vice, but my other one seems to have a mind of its own. It rises up, balls into a fist, and knocks. With its heinous job complete, my arm snaps back to my side, locked against me as I stand at attention, and then I wait for someone to answer, my body shaking and my breathing ragged.

13

THE BAD NEWS

I hear someone grab the doorknob and then, in slow motion, I watch as the handle on my side of the door moves. My knees almost give out at the same time that bile rises in my throat. I suddenly feel very, very faint. As the door swings open, my heart pumps waves of blood that *whoosh* past my ears, deafening me so badly I can't hear anything, but I'm able to watch on, mouth agape, as Rockefeller comes into view.

He seems just as shocked as I feel.

"Meghan?" he asks as he steps out to look up and down the hall.

"I…" I croak out. "You know me?"

He searches the hallway again, almost as if he's expecting a camera crew to jump out of the shadows to tell him he's on some hidden camera television show. He finally looks at me, clearly still shocked. "Meghan…what are you…?" He pulls the door completely open. "Where's your mom?"

Rockefeller is thankfully still dressed in expensive-looking slacks, a long-sleeved button-down shirt, and a very nice tie. I peer around him, into the room, and see he's kicked off his shoes, but aside from the desk chair being pulled out and a bunch of files scattered about, the room looks as though he's just checked in.

"Is your mom okay?" he asks, snapping me out of my inspection.

I look back up at him since he's tall—just the way Mom likes them, and he's as handsome as he seems in the pictures; cuter actually, since the pictures don't do his light brown eyes and dimples justice.

"Meghan?" he says, this time with a sense of urgency. "Is your mom okay?"

I stay rooted in my spot even though I somehow know I'll be safe with him. "She's missing," I finally offer.

"Missing?" he repeats, almost as if it's a foreign word to him.

I nod. "Yes. Since Sunday—well Monday morning, actually. Early," I add, my frayed nerves finally getting the best of me. "The last time anyone saw her was around closing time."

Rockefeller motions me to come inside. "Can you come inside please?" he asks, though it doesn't sound like a question.

I stagger into the room.

He waits until I drop onto the corner of the bed, then he leans against the wall and crosses his buff arms in front of his chest. "You don't look so good," he says, his tone more concerned than judgmental.

"But you know what I look like?" I inquire, trying to stay focused on the logical, tangible stuff. "So my mom has talked about me?"

"Of course," he scoffs, as though he's offended that I asked. "All the time," he adds, much more softly. "She's very proud of you, Meghan."

Tears blur my vision and I have to swallow over a huge lump that suddenly lodges in my throat.

Rockefeller sighs as he makes his way over. He stops long enough to grab the desk chair, and then he rolls it over to me.

He takes a seat right across from me. "Why don't you start from the beginning," he says.

"What's your name?" I counter, suddenly unwilling to bring him up to speed unless I finally have a name to put with his face. "And how do you know my mom?"

He sits back in his seat, crosses his foot so his ankle is resting on his knee, and then he places his hands on his lap.

It's something I recognize as a business-type power move.

"I'm John. Your mom and I met a couple of years ago, after her accident."

That gets my attention. "When she wrecked the Honda?"

He nods. "Yes. I was one of the claims adjusters she met while she was trying to settle everything afterward." He fidgets with his tie. "We reconnected about a year ago, just randomly one night when I ended up at Rusty's."

Of course. Rusty's. That's how it always happens.

"So you're John? Just some insurance guy?" I say as I look around the room. Funny. He doesn't look like a John. That name seems so plain for him. "So is this where you normally do business then? In a hotel in Middletown and occasionally down at Rockefeller Center?"

John is a light-skinned black man, so his sudden, scorching cheeks are easy to notice.

"No. Never." He loosens the knot of his tie. "I…look, given that you're here, I'm sure you can…" He runs his hands over his face, his confidence gone. "I'm married," he blurts out, "so this thing we have is…"

I start blushing now too even though I know my mother has messed with married men before.

"It didn't start out like that," he admits, still stumbling over his words. "I was surprised when I bumped into her at the bar, but then we got to talking about how life was going after the accident, and she was so down on her luck, you know, so at first I just wanted to help…"

My blush deepens, but now from embarrassment *and* shame. I hate when people categorize us as down on our luck.

"Over time it's just sort of morphed into this." He motions around the room. "But that was never my original intention, Meghan, and it doesn't diminish the fact that I genuinely care about you guys."

"*Us?*" I blurt out. "Have you met the girls?"

"No." He shakes his head. "Your mother has been very adamant about shielding you girls from her..." he seems to search for the right word, "*social* life."

I let that last statement settle in for a moment before I say, "Which is actually what's working against us now. She's been missing since Monday morning and we have no idea where to look for her."

His brows furrow. "But you've managed to find me, which is good, so maybe if you catch me up, I can help some. Though I will say that the last time we spoke was Friday since it's hard for me to keep in touch over the weekends."

Yeah. I'm sure his wife wouldn't much care for the interruptions. Of course, I let that go, since it isn't going to help anyone. Instead, I tell him everything I know, including all the emotional upheavals I've lived through, but I don't mention the supernatural stuff because I can't bring myself to tell anyone about that yet. I don't want people to think I'm coming unhinged. When I'm done recounting the last week in great detail, John sits back in his seat and rubs his chin, as if in deep thought. After what feels like an eternity, he finally looks at me.

"Did Molly hurt her ankle last week?"

I'm so confused and taken aback by his strange question that I can only shake my head. But then I think back to the week before, just to make sure I'm not lying. In my head, I play a quick recap of the days' events. Everything had been normal—or normal for us, anyway. In fact, now that I think about it and know how much everything has changed in such a short span of time, the more I realize that the mundaneness of that week had been blissful. In my heart, I know life will never be that simple again. My already difficult, abnormal life is over. I had always thought it would only get better. I had never imagined it could get worse. So drastically worse.

"Are you sure?" he asks as he leans forward and places his elbows on his knees. "Did any of you have to go to urgent care?"

I shake my head again, this time more firmly. "No. Last week was normal. No one got hurt or sick."

He sighs. "So she was using again?"

My heart skips a beat and a sheen of sweat erupts on my forehead. It's an automated response when I'm put on the spot, especially where lying for my mom comes into play.

"Meghan…" He looks at me so intensely, I squirm. "I know this is all hard on you, but if what you're saying is true— if your mother is missing, then you need to be honest with everyone. Including yourself."

My bottom lip begins to quiver, but I tip my chin up and cross my arms over my chest. "She's been a little stressed lately—"

"She's blown through your rent money two months in a row," he interjects. I'm not sure how he manages to sound so firm and so gentle at the same time, but when he puts a hand on my knee, my composure nearly fails. "So no one went to urgent care or needed prescriptions filled?" he inquires again, his eyes boring into mine.

I shake my head, this time because I know I'll start crying if I try to say anything.

He drops back in his seat and looks up at the ceiling. "If you guys are sure she wasn't with that Will.i.am guy then maybe you should start checking her spots."

A tear slips out of my left eye as I repeat those two words.

Her spots. Meaning places she likes to go when she shoots up. Even with all the facts sitting before me, I don't want to admit she had relapsed *that* badly. I was hoping it was just some weed. Maybe coke. The thought of her messing around with heroin or meth again practically destroys me, and the idea of her being dead somewhere in the woods, a needle jammed in her arm, almost pushes my fragile mind over the edge.

I jolt off the bed and start pacing, needing to walk off my frazzled nerves. "You're wrong," I finally declare as I wipe tears off my face. I had started crying at some point and hadn't even realized it. "She's just…she's stuck in a ditch somewhere." I turn to face him and square off my shoulders. "You of all people should know that! She wasn't off stoned somewhere the last time and she isn't this time. I can feel it. She wouldn't start using again. Not this close to me leaving."

He stands and heads toward the desk. "I hope I'm wrong too, but I've been seeing the signs for a few weeks now, Meghan, and now there's this…" After grabbing the tissue box, he pulls out a few out and hands them to me. "I want to believe that she's okay, but I think we both know that even if it isn't about the drugs, we need to start being proactive *right now* because she's been missing for over forty-eight hours." He pauses, almost as if for effect. "She once told me that there's a place she used to always go to off Lake Avenue."

The street name instantly rings a bell, because it's by Fancher-Davidge Park. I wipe my tears and then blow my nose. It's one of the places she used to go. I know because as part of her therapy, one of her many substance-abuse counselors had told her it was best to share everything with her loved ones. It was supposed to help with her recovery, which obviously hadn't worked.

"And she's mentioned going back to the crash site a lot," he adds. "She says it helps put life in perspective when she's having hard days." He reaches for my hand. "Have you started checking anywhere yet?"

"No—"

My mom's phone rings, cutting me off. I fumble it out of my pocket and stare at the screen. It's Uncle Rusty. I debate answering it, since a part of me wonders if he's only reaching out because someone told him I left school. If he is, I can't imagine him being too upset—he's stepped in as a paternal figure for years now, but he's never acted like a dad like that before. I'm hoping today isn't the day that changes. I answer the call.

"Hey," I say, for some reason looking at John for guidance. "Everything okay?"

"Where are you?" he snaps.

I gulp and more sweat erupts on my forehead. "I...I got a lead that I had to check out," I admit.

"Where are you, Meghan?" he repeats, his tone leaving no room for argument.

I blurt out the story, the word vomit probably difficult to keep up with it, though Uncle Rusty must follow along just fine because he doesn't interrupt me. When I'm finally done recapping, silence permeates the line for a long moment. I don't dare speak again, so I just wait. Thankfully, Uncle Rusty finds his voice.

"Normally I would have a bunch of questions for him and for you," he says that last part with a definite hint of paternal disappointment, "but this isn't the time or place for it because I'm currently standing outside of your school. I came because I wanted to tell you in person that someone called Matt and told him. He's with the girls now, at their school—"

"No!" I shout, my heart racing so quickly a sharp pain shoots down my left arm. I hurry to the door, desperate to get to my sisters' school before Matt can do anything rash. "Who told him? What is he going to do?" I ask as I reach for the door and actually yelp when John clamps onto my wrist to stop me. I spin around and face him. "What are you doing?" I ask as I yank my hand away from him.

He quickly holds his hands up and backs away from me. "I just wanted to give you the cash before you left."

Dumbfounded, I shake my head. "Excuse me?"

"For your rent," he adds quickly. "I've been helping out for a bit now and I have it with me, along with some extra because…well, you know…she said she needed to pay the urgent care bill and get Molly's prescriptions."

"I…" I don't know what to say.

"Listen, Meghan, I know this is all so much for you to take in, but this isn't the time to turn down anyone's help, especially with this." He runs over to the desk and reaches into his laptop bag. He pulls out a white envelope. With his back still turned to me, he grabs his wallet from his back pocket, pulls a bunch of bills out of the fold, and then stuffs those in the envelope too. "I know you probably don't know where to go, but give this to Rusty and tell him to get it to your landlord." He turns, hurries back over to me, and extends the envelope so it's just within my grasp. "That'll cover you guys until the end of June, and I'll keep the phone on, so you can keep using it."

"John…I can't…"

He grabs my free hand, places the envelope in it, presses my fingers closed over the crisp, white edge, and then gives me a reassuring squeeze. "I'm not taking no for an answer." He drops his hands to the side. "Be sure to tell your mom to call me when she gets back." A glint of something flashes in his eyes—like a shadow of doubt—but he seems to force it aside with a fake smile. "I'm sure she's fine," he lies.

I don't know why, but I hug him. He wraps both arms around me and squeezes me tight. Then before breaking away, he kisses the top of my head. "It's going to be okay," he says softly. "You still have my number, right?"

I nod.

"Good. Keep me posted, okay? And call if you need anything."

I nod again, tears welling in my eyes so badly I once again don't dare speak, so after a slight nod of my head, I turn and leave. I rush down the hallway and make it as far as the stairwell before the tears begin to fall.

"You okay, kid?" Uncle Rusty asks, which startles me because I had somehow forgotten I still had the phone pressed to my ear.

"No," I say, unable to contain my emotions anymore. "Can you meet me at the school?"

"Of course. I'm already on my way."

14

FRIENDS IN LOW PLACES

As I stare out my kitchen window, I realize there's an art to negotiation that I haven't quite mastered. I'm sure, given enough time, I'll learn how to get what I want out of a deal, but as of today, I'm still a little rusty, so I've had to settle on a few things. Thankfully, though, I'm not out too big. Yes, Matt is here to stay until Mom gets back home, but he's agreed to stay here in Middletown with us until the end of the week, just so the girls and I don't miss school. Unfortunately, he has to be back at work Saturday afternoon, and since no one but me thinks the girls will be okay at his apartment while he's at work, I have to go down to Manhattan over the weekend, and potentially all of Spring Break, if Mom hasn't shown up by then. It's a situation I don't even want to think about for so many reasons; the most obvious being we have no idea when she'll return, if ever.

My stomach ties up in knots every time I think about it, so I instead focus my attention on another dilemma. Money. John had given me enough to cover the rent until June, but Uncle Rusty and Matt don't think it's wise to pay it all at once. I know the reason is because they don't want me to pay it and we end up having to move. That train of thought causes those knots to start forming in my gut again, so I begrudgingly remind myself I agreed to take part of it to pay April's rent. The rest, Matt will hold onto just in case we need anything major. Of course, none of this would be that big of a concern if I could keep working, but with my time now slotted for babysitting in the city, I'm going to be short a substantial amount of hours from work. Granted, when I called the Dollar Store a little while ago to let them know what was going on, my manager, Ms. Latisha, had been graceful enough to let me work tonight, tomorrow, and, Friday night to help out. I appreciate it. I really do. But fifteen hours of pay isn't going to amount to much, not when we have a ton of bills that need to be paid come the first of the month.

"You know," Matt says from across our small table, "I've never known you to ignore a Big Mac before."

I glance down at the sesame seed bun before I look back at him. He's right. I've never turned down a Big Mac before, but in my defense, I hadn't planned on eating my favorite food today. Matt had run out while I was on the phone with Ms. Latisha and brought McDonald's back to the house, no doubt in order to butter me up. "I guess I'm just not hungry…" I grab a fry out of the carton before I sit back and force myself to chew.

"I'm not the enemy here, Meghan," he says softly, and for what feels like the hundredth time.

"I know." I swallow the last of the fry and then sit up straight. "And I'm sorry I didn't call. I just figured…you know…" I lift the Big Mac out of the carton, if only to avoid having to look at him.

"Water under the bridge," he says. "I'm here now and I want to help look for her. Maybe after this we can swing by the station and talk to that officer?"

With a mouthful of Mac, all I can muster is a nod. We eat

the rest of our food in silence and then, as we clean up, I tell him about everything that's happened since Mom disappeared —minus the supernatural stuff. He listens intently and then agrees to stop to check all "her spots" on our way to the police station. His supportiveness shocks me, and it admittedly gnaws at my consciousness. Maybe I should have called him sooner since it's nice to have someone who seems just as concerned and willing to go out to search for her.

Before we head out to leave, I make a pitstop at the bathroom. As I go about my business, my mind is so acutely focused on where we need to stop I don't notice the water turning on until it's on maximum pressure, the hot water coming out in spurts. I quickly finish taking care of business before I hurry over to the sink, my heart pounding painfully against my chest.

"Mom?" I whisper as I search the reflection in the mirror for any sign of her.

Steam begins to form, so I lean forward, waiting for the inevitable message.

A fingertip impression appears, the sight of it causing my heart to race into overdrive. I grab onto the sides of the sink for support, since the sudden rush of blood makes me dizzy. I blink several times to clear my focus, and then I watch on, always in awe, as my mother's cursive handwriting appears out of thin air.

It says, "Go with him."

I read those three words several times before I turn to search the bathroom, hoping to catch a glimpse of her once again. "Go with who? Matt?" I'm so tired of the riddles. "Mom...can you...where are you?" I ask, pleading. "Just give me a straight answer and I'll go to you! Please." That last part comes out as a sob.

Icy tendrils begin to wrap themselves around my arm, almost as if someone is grabbing onto my forearm and tugging on it. I turn to face the mirror and gasp when I look upon my mother's beautiful, radiant face. She smiles lovingly and then disappears, the word "Bowery" replacing her image. I reach out to touch it, for some reason hoping I can feel her, but it's just a mirror, and with the hot water losing steam, the message begins to fade.

I stand there for a moment longer, watching as the word vanishes, then I use the tepid water to rinse my face. I wash my hands next, methodically for some reason, and then I dry my still-trembling hands with the towel. *Go with him,* I think as I replace the towel—she had to mean Matt, or so I can only assume since I can never get a straight answer from her. Her next message though had pretty much affirmed that. Matt works at the Bowery Hotel. He's one of the executive chefs at the adjoining restaurant. But why would she want me to go down there? And what does that mean for her?

All this time, I've been telling myself she's stuck somewhere and that this thing she's doing is just some cool mother-daughter psychic connection—that she's alive somewhere and she's trying to give me hints to find her. If she's in Manhattan though, would she be able to communicate with me? I mean, it's all supernatural, so there's no telling what the rules are, but the more she contacts me, the more I get a sinking, nagging feeling she isn't okay. I'm not sure if it's because she communicating more frequently or if it's because each time I see her she looks more real, and more beautiful, and more...*I don't know.* Radiant, maybe. Iridescent, perhaps. *Angelic*...Yes. That word gives me pause though, because as beautiful as that notion may be, it also means mom isn't trapped in her car, somehow tapping into some ancient, deep-rooted mystical power. It means she's dead.

———

It takes us nearly an hour to check all of Mom's "spots." She had confided most of them to me, but Matt knew of a couple of other places I would have never guessed. It's amazing how inventive junkies can be when it comes to finding a safe place to get high.

"When was the last time you talked to this guy?" Matt asks as he pulls into a parking spot at the police station. "And what's his name again?"

"Jesse...Officer Jesse Dunbar," I add, since it suddenly occurs to me that Jesse had been one of many men who came *after* Matt had left, so he wouldn't know him. "And last night." I pop off my seatbelt. "He came over when I got back from Newburgh." I get out of the car and wait for Matt to catch up before I continue. "I'm sure he's already heard you're here."

Matt nods. "Probably. Small towns are funny that way..."

I look over at him and sigh. Matt was born and raised in the city, but when he graduated high school, his parents retired and bought a house in Middletown. Of course, Matt couldn't afford to stay down in the city by himself, so he moved up here and started going to a culinary school in Hyde Park. I'm not sure of all the details in between, but I do know he's never really cared for "small-town living." When he and my mother met one day at Rusty's and they started dating, he always told her he intended to move back home one day, and that he planned to take us with him. Of course, that was eons ago now, and while we've never left Middletown after Matt and mom went their separate ways, he had finally gotten on his feet enough to move back to his beloved city—minus us. Until now, that is.

I'm still not sure how I feel about that.

Until this afternoon, I had forgotten how cool Matt can be. In fact, the longer I stay around him the more I remember how sad it was that things hadn't worked out between him and Mom. He's a good guy, and no matter how ugly it's gotten between them, he's never let that come between his relationship with the girls. And he's a good father, and maybe the girls would be better off with him after I'm gone. I feel sad for even considering it, almost as if just the thought is a betrayal to my mother, but I know I wouldn't even have to seriously consider it if she hadn't disappeared. It's like she's left me no choice but to be the martyr who has to sacrifice my family's honor to save my sisters.

"Steam is practically coming off your head," Matt says as he pulls the door open for me.

I snicker at that despite myself, but it's funny to hear him use that turn of phrase. I used to get such a kick out of it when I was a kid.

"Care to share?" he asks, his voice dropping a notch as we make our way to the front desk.

I consider my best options but thankfully don't have to say anything because the officer at the desk motions us over. "Hey, Meg," he says as if he knows me.

I definitely don't recognize him, but I'm starting to figure out just how notorious my mother truly is. "Hi…" I glance at his nametag, "…Officer Paulson. I was wondering if Officer Dunbar had a minute?"

"Sure. I'll have him come up and get you when he's free." He motions to a row of chairs behind us and then reaches for the phone. "Just hang tight for a few."

Matt and I plop into two seats at the end of the row.

He leans over and whispers, "You know I'm here for you too."

I jerk at that and can't help but look over to meet his poignant gaze. After a second, though, I have to look away. "I can take care of myself." I don't mean for it to sound so harsh, so I shrug and sigh. "I mean…I'm not worried about me in all this. I just want to make sure the girls are okay and that they're able to stay together." I look at him again, this time with no reservations. "You will keep them together, won't you?"

A weird expression clouds his face. For the briefest moment, I register annoyance, but then his features soften and he smiles.

"I will take *all of you,*" he emphasizes, "because you're still a kid, Meghan. You're a very mature, very wise one, but a kid nonetheless, and even when you become an adult, I'll still be in your corner, on your side, helping you get through life." He places his hand over mine. "Because that's what parents do."

Tears well in my eyes and I'm just about to lose it when Jesse walks over and introduces himself to Matt. I take the moment to pull it together as Matt stands and extends his hand toward him.

"It's good to meet you," Matt says cordially even though I'm sure it's slightly awkward for both of them. "I'm Matt Johnson."

Jesse shakes his hand. "Hey, Matt. I heard you made it to town this morning. Glad to meet you, but very sorry for the circumstances."

Matt drops his hand to his side and sighs. "Right. Thanks. Hopefully, it's all just a misunderstanding we can all laugh about one day." He looks at me and gestures for me to get up. "I know you've been in touch with Meghan, but I'd love it if you can catch me up?"

"Of course," Jesse says as he motions toward a long hall-way. "I've got some new information to share as well."

That perks up my ears. "Oh, yeah?"

He nods but doesn't add anything while he leads us down a series of hallways to his very small office. After Matt and I get settled in the two chairs across from his desk, Jesse takes a seat and pulls a folder over. He opens it up and then looks at me. "I'm assuming you've gotten him all caught up?"

I nod.

"Great." He shifts his attention to Matt. "Well since then, I've been in touch with the officer in charge of Will's case."

"Okay," Matt says as he leans forward in his seat.

Jesse looks down at the folder. "The preliminary toxicology report has come in and it's…" He sits back in his seat and looks between Matt and me. "Well, it isn't very helpful at the moment."

"Meaning?" Matt probes.

"Listen, we can't assume anything, but the going consensus was that this guy passed away from an overdose because there was no evidence of foul play." Jesse lets that sink in for a moment. "The problem is his tox-screen is showing he definitely had some alcohol and marijuana in his system, but there aren't any lethal amounts of anything showing up."

My brows furrow as I consider that. "But his grandmother found him on the couch. Peacefully," I emphasize. "So that rules out all the gang-related stuff, right?"

"Not necessarily," Jesse says. "Just because there weren't any obvious signs of trauma doesn't mean he died of natural causes. At this point, we just can't rule anything out. Well, aside from the few results we've gotten back, but even then, more tests are being run as we speak."

"Well, there has to be something," Matt says, sounding just as confused as I feel. "I mean, it isn't exactly normal for a healthy guy to just sit down and die. Was he sick maybe? Did he have some kind of family medical problem or something?"

"As far as we can tell," Jesse says as he looks back down to the folder, "no. He was a relatively healthy person who didn't overdose on anything we've tested. *Yet.*" He looks back up at us. "Like I said, these are just the standard, preliminary tests, so we have to be patient. They'll do more testing as they work their way through the autopsy."

"And how long will that take?" I ask, looking between them.

Jesse sighs. "It could take months, Meghan, but at this point, I don't want you to stress too much over it because the important thing to take from all of this is that your mom wasn't anywhere around when he passed away. I even drove up there to check out the crime scene myself to be sure, but everything is checking out. This guy made it home alone."

My mouth drops open because I feel as though I need to say something to that, but I'm speechless, I guess in part because I don't know how to react. Mom hadn't gone back to Newburgh with him, which is good news—sort of—but that means she left the bar with him but then he dropped her off somewhere along the way. That's not good, because that leaves open a lot of possible scenarios, none of which have a happy ending.

"So what you're saying," Matt chimes in a melancholy tone that matches my somber mood to perfection, "is that we're still no closer to finding Maggie."

Jesse closes the folder and nods. "Unfortunately, no, but we're all still looking and we all still have faith she's going to turn up at any moment." He directs that last part to me.

I match his stoic gaze until he shifts uncomfortably in his chair, then I turn my attention to Matt. "Can we leave for New York first thing Saturday then?"

Matt, who's clearly thrown off by the question, shakes his head, but then he switches it to a nod. "Ah…yeah. Of course." He eyes me for a long moment. "Any special reason for the sudden change of heart?" he finally inquires.

A mental image of my mother's last heart-shaped message comes to mind, but I still don't feel comfortable telling anyone I'm receiving supernatural messages directing me to the Bowery Hotel. Not just yet, anyway—not until I can see why she wants me there in the first place.

Jesse leans forward in his seat and rests his elbows on his desk. "Meghan, is there something you aren't telling us?"

I shake my head firmly. "No…I just think it might be better to get out of here for a couple of days…"

Jesse and Matt both remain silent as they stare at me.

"Yet yesterday," Jesse counters, "you didn't even want Matt to know Maggie was missing."

A blush radiates across my cheeks as I toss a quick glance in Matt's direction. "Right…" I stretch out as I glare at Jesse. "But he's here now and this is all getting…intense."

They keep staring, and I don't blame them. Even to me, that sounds lame.

"So, you'll keep us posted then," Matt asks Jesse, thankfully breaking the silence *and* giving me a reprieve.

Jesse doesn't immediately take the bait. Instead, he keeps his eyes locked on mine. Sweat begins to bead my brow, but I force myself to stay focused, to not look away.

Amazingly, Jesse caves first. "Yeah. I'll touch base every day, just to make sure we're all on the same sheet of music."

That last part is naturally directed at me, but I somehow manage to ignore it. Instead, I get up and reach for the door. "Thanks, Jesse."

He just gives a slight nod of his head as an acknowledgement, so I hightail it out of there before he starts asking more questions. Matt quickly falls into step with me and is silent as we make our way out of the station. The moment we hit daylight, I expect him to bombard me with questions, but he doesn't. In fact, the entire car ride home is silent, so I can only hope he's too lost in his own thoughts to worry about mine.

15

WELCOME TO THE BOWERY

It's a picture-perfect Saturday morning as we near the Tappan Zee Bridge, the sun sparkling off the Hudson River like a thousand diamonds. It's a beautiful view, and as I let my eyes drift toward the Tarrytown skyline, my heart flutters a bit. I've always loved the drive down to the city, so today is the first time I've ever felt apprehensive about it. Granted, for as many times as I've visited, I've never been to the Bowery Hotel before. Usually, we take the bus straight into Port Authority and Matt picks us up. We'll spend most of our time just hanging around his apartment and going around the East Village, which is where he lives, but most times when I come down, he always takes us someplace cool and touristy. The Bowery has never made the list of places to go though, and I'm petrified to visit, especially because my mother has been eerily silent the past few days. *Will she finally reappear when I get there?*

"How much longer?" Misty asks from the backseat.

I glance back at her while resisting the temptation to roll my eyes. She has a really bad habit of regressing to an annoying five-year-old brat whenever Matt is around. Mom says it's best to just ignore it, so I don't answer her. Unfortunately, Matt does.

"It won't be too much longer until we make it to my friend's place," he offers.

I glance back at Misty just in time to catch *her* eye roll. She does not like sharing Matt with anyone. She tolerates us because we're her sisters, but she definitely doesn't appreciate anyone being his friend, especially when it's a female.

"She's not coming with us to your apartment, right?" Misty asks—for the billionth time.

"No, bud," Matt assures her in a calm tone. "She just lent me her car so I could drive up to hang out with you guys."

I can tell by her sour expression she doesn't believe him, but she thankfully doesn't say as much. Instead, she crosses her arms over her chest and shifts her attention outside.

For a moment, the tension in the car is so thick I think I may choke on it. I glance over at Matt, who's normally cool under pressure, but I can sense his dread and unease. It's coming off him in droves. I'm sure it's because as much as he's tried to make the past couple of days "fun" and "normal," we all know this isn't an ordinary weekend visit with Dad. This may be a permanent, life-altering change for everyone—especially Matt. So while he's tried to play calm and cool as he tells me not to worry even though all has been silent in Mom's search, I know he's stressed. Because really, at the end of the day, is anyone ever prepared to take on three daughters?

"What's her name?" Misty blurts out, her tone downright icy.

"Who?" Matt asks, feigning ignorance fairly well for an old guy.

"Your friend," she quips, not falling for it.

"Annabelle." He doesn't offer anything else, which cranks up the tension to a damn near suffocating level.

"So…" I say, hoping to diffuse the situation. "Have you ever seen a ghost at work?"

That definitely cuts through the tension, though it only clouds the air with confusion.

"Excuse me?" Matt asks as he glances over at me.

"The Bowery," I say. "I've been reading up on it. They say it's haunted—"

"The hotel is haunted?" Molly exclaims, finally jumping in on the conversation. She pops her head between the front seats. "Really?" She looks at Matt. "Have you seen a ghost there? Is that why you've never taken us?"

"No," he says, and then, as if to clarify, "I've never seen a ghost before. And I'm taking you to work with me tonight," he adds.

"Yeah, but that's only because it's Meg's birthday and she practically had to beg until you finally caved," Misty chimes in. "Does Annabelle work there or something? Is that why you've never taken us?"

Oof. This little kitten has claws. I glance back at her and I can actually see the hate vibes emanating off her. I look at Matt next. It's a fair question and one he'll confess to if he's smart.

"She used to," he offers to no one in particular. "Now she works at a restaurant in Harlem."

"*Hmm,*" is all Misty has to say about that.

"So the hotel is really haunted?" Molly asks me.

I nod, a little nervous to talk about it because I've been trying to keep it all hush-hush so Matt doesn't put two and two together that it's the reason I insisted on going to work with him tonight. I've guilted him into it, really, since today is my eighteenth birthday and it seemed like such a trivial request given that my mother is missing and my family is being uprooted.

"The hotel is actually one of the stops on a lot of the city's haunted tours," Matt offers conversationally. "They say guests have seen ghosts and that the elevator stops on random floors in the middle of the night—"

"Really! Have you seen one?" Molly asks, clearly excited about this newfound information. "Will *we* see one tonight?" She bounces a bit in her seat. "Can we ride the elevator?"

"I hate to burst your bubble, bud, but I've never seen or heard a peep, and I'm at the hotel pretty late at night—"

"But you aren't really *in* the hotel," Molly points out, which is true. Matt works at Gemma's, the restaurant next door to the Bowery.

"Have you been on the elevators?" Misty asks, her curiosity outweighing her anger. "What about any of your coworkers? Have they ever seen a ghost?"

Matt chuckles. "No, and no. I've never actually used the guest elevator before because the restaurant has its own entrance, and I don't personally know anyone who has seen a ghost. I've just heard about stuff." He glances back at the girls for a brief second before he looks back at the road. "If it isn't too crazy at work tonight then I'll see if I can take you guys into the main part of the hotel."

"Really!" Molly exclaims, her enthusiasm a bit contagious.

"Can you get us into one of the rooms?" Misty inquires. "Oh! Is there one that's really haunted?"

"I'm not sure," he says and then tosses a quick glance my way. "Maybe Meghan knows since she's been researching the hotel and she's suddenly developed a keen interest in coming to work with me."

Oh, crap. He's figured me out.

"Is there a special room, Meg?" Misty asks, completely oblivious to how loaded that question is.

My cheeks are blazing and I'm a little scared to speak because I'm sure my voice will give away my guilt.

"Is there, Meg?" Molly probes, both girls leaning forward to stare at me with wide-eyed curiosity.

"Um, no…" I clear my throat and avoid looking directly at anyone. "Not that I've read anyway. People just say they've seen a lady in white—"

The girls squeal and assault me with a barrage of rapid-fire questions I can't entirely piece together, given how they keep trying to out-talk each other.

"They've seen her in different rooms," I continue in hopes of calming them down. "And like Matt said, they claim the elevator is haunted. That it stops on random floors in the middle of the night and that sometimes…" I look at Matt, not sure of how much he's heard from the tours and not sure if I should even mention it to the girls now that I have a second to think about it.

"And?" Misty hedges.

I look back at the girls, who are figuratively chomping on the bit, and I sigh. What is it Mom always says? You can't put the genie back in the bottle. Yup. I already let the cat out of the bag, so I finish what I started. "And some people have said they've gotten on the elevator alone but somewhere in between getting on and making it to their floor…" *Man am I going to regret telling them this next part.*

"Tell us, Meg! What happens?" Molly asks, her eyes about to bug out of her head.

Matt sighs his disapproval and then shakes his head.

I reluctantly finish the tawdry and wildly inappropriate tale. "Another person will end up on the elevator with them."

They collectively gasp.

"Like he'll just appear?" Misty asks, her voice a horrified whisper now.

"Like right behind you?" Molly inquires, just as mortified.

Both seem petrified by the thought, which means I'm on

the road for lots of long nights with them both trying to squeeze onto my tiny twin-sized bed.

"It's just a story they tell people to attract customers," Matt says, trying to quell their fears. "All of that stuff is make-believe, girls, because ghosts aren't real." He looks over at me as he says that last part. "Even your mom was convinced it was fake."

My heart starts to race. "Mom knew about the hotel?"

He nods. "Oh, yeah. For a while, she was obsessed with it."

I contemplate that for a long moment. "So...she didn't believe it was haunted?"

"No, and she finally realized it was a waste of time trying to chase after something that wasn't really there..."

My heart skips a couple of beats as I match his gaze, and when he finally looks back to the road, I slump in my seat a bit. That was intense, and not because I get the feeling he was trying to convey he's on to me and he thinks I'm nuts. *No.* After that powerful moment, I almost would have welcomed that sentiment. Instead, in those few seconds of eye contact, I could tell exactly how he truly felt. That he's on to me, and that he's scared I might be right.

———

There are no amount of pictures online that can truly do the Bowery Hotel justice. There's just something breathtaking and beautiful and amazing about being here in person. The energy in the dark-paneled lobby is palpable. The only thing that can even remotely detract from the lobby's elegantly dramatic beauty is the red-headed bellhop who Matt just introduced us to. Spencer Walsh is at least six feet tall and he has a slim but muscular build. His red hair is cropped short and spiked high. His green eyes are soft, and the blush he's sporting almost perfectly matches the bright red vest that's part of his white-shirt-and-black-slacks Bowery uniform.

It's rare when my heart goes pitter-patter over a guy. Rarer still when the guy in question seems to reciprocate the sentiment.

Spencer greets my sisters with a goofy, nervous wave, and then he thrusts a trembling hand toward me. "It's nice to finally meet you, Meghan…" He shifts from foot to foot, not seeming to be able to keep still. "Matt's told me all about you."

It's my turn to blush. I shoot Matt a look—not a dirty one, naturally; it's more of utter disbelief since it's strange to have it confirmed that he does indeed acknowledge my existence even when I'm not around. In response, Matt motions toward Spencer's still out-stretched hand. *Oh, right!* I reach for it, but I only shake it for the briefest second because I don't want him to feel my palms sweating.

"It's nice to meet you too," I say, since Matt never mentioned him before, which he and I will definitely talk about later.

"I'm going to make the girls some dinner before it gets too busy," Matt says to Spencer as he starts herding the girls in the direction of the restaurant. "I was hoping that when you got a break at seven, you wouldn't mind taking them all for a quick tour."

"I'd love to," Spencer says, his eagerness causing my blush to deepen. He gazes at me for a moment longer then he looks at the girls and smiles. "I'll see you gals at seven then."

"Yeah, okay," I say sort of dreamily.

Thankfully, the girls choose that very moment to toss in their own enthusiast "we'll see you later!" so no one seems to notice my stupor, or at least I hope not. I watch Spencer as he hurries off to one of those fancy birdcage luggage carts, seeming none the wiser—

"Spencer and Meghan sitting in a tree," Molly coos.

Misty hops in on the chorus. "K-I-S-S-I-N-G!"

"Hush!" I whisper-snap, since it shouldn't surprise me that *they* noticed. I'm just grateful they have enough sense to keep their voices low.

"You like him!" Molly teases as we all head toward the restaurant.

"I don't even know him," I say nonchalantly.

"Doesn't matter," Misty counters. "That blush says it all."

I shake my head but I don't bother denying it. I'm like an open book when it comes to crushing on boys, so I would just be wasting my breath. Besides, I have a sinking feeling I'll need it later since I plan on picking Spencer's brain. I'm hoping he isn't only a pretty face to look at, but that he also knows all about this hotel and its haunted guests.

16

THE BELLHOP

At exactly seven o'clock, Spencer hurries into the restaurant. From my vantage point on the far end of the room, I have the perfect view to watch as he rushes toward the kitchen, probably because he doesn't see us all the way in the opposite corner—or maybe because he thinks it's polite or respectful to go to Matt first. Either way, he disappears behind the kitchen's swinging door, leaving me anxiously shifting my gaze between the two entrances that spill out from the kitchen into the dining room.

"She's like a dog with a bone," Molly coos, mimicking one of our mother's favorite phrases.

I look over at her just as she and Misty giggle.

"He is cute though," Misty offers between chuckles. "I would watch him too if I liked boys."

My eyes narrow as I shift my attention to her. "Well, boys are the devil," I reply, quoting another of our mother's favorites, "so keep it that way." I lean back in my seat and look between them. "Can you two behave yourselves while he gives us a tour? Or should I leave you here—"

"No, Meg!" Misty begs.

"We'll be good," Molly promises.

I intentionally allow time to pass before I reach for my spoon and start playing around with the remnants of my tiramisu. It's the best I've ever had, but with all the pasta I had eaten on top of all the nerves tying my stomach into knots, I can't bring myself to take another bite. "Okay," I finally say, "but please be on your best behavior, because I really want to hear what Spencer has to say about the hotel—"

"Us too," Molly cuts in to assure me.

I give her a stern look since she knows better. "Good. So don't interrupt him while he's speaking, and make sure you take turns asking questions."

As they nod, Spencer emerges from the kitchen alone. The restaurant is hopping tonight, so it doesn't surprise me that Matt isn't tagging along, but as Spencer turns and our gazes lock, I suddenly wish Matt was with him. Can I really handle a cute boy on my own while I'm trying to parent my two kid sisters *and* communicate with my missing mother? I don't think so, but as with everything else in my life, I've been left with no choice, so as Spencer approaches us, I try to calm my frenzied heart.

"Hey," he says when he arrives at the table.

"Hey," I say, smiling despite myself.

For some reason, that makes Spencer blush. "Hey…" he repeats, clearly stumbling over his words now. He hitches a very shaky thumb over his shoulder. "Matt says he's too busy to join, but when you guys are ready, I can give you a quick tour of the hotel."

"We're ready," Molly says with a smile.

"Totally," Misty confirms as she pushes her empty dessert dish to the middle of the table.

"Well, all right," Spencer says with a more relaxed smile now, "come on." He offers each girl a hand. "My name is Spencer Walsh and I'll be your tour guide."

The girls giggle as they grab onto his hands. I watch as he spins them around expertly and starts heading for the door. I hurry to catch up, but with the restaurant being so full, I fall behind until we get to the lobby. When we're all gathered around again, the girls release Spencer's hands and skip over to the fireplace. I watch them for a moment before I dare a glance in Spencer's direction. He's smiling.

"Thanks again for volunteering to take us around. Did you get a chance to eat?"

"Yeah," he assures me eagerly. "I always snack between customers, so I don't mind showing you gals around." His cheeks suddenly flush, and then he adds, "It's really my pleasure."

My cheeks catch on fire, so I look away and try to think of anything to say that won't make this already embarrassing moment worse. "Ah…you're really good with kids," I say, since it's true. He's a natural with the girls.

"I have three younger brothers."

"Three!" I can't help the reaction, but four boys! Goodness. His poor mother!

Spencer laughs. "Yeah. We're Irish Catholic…Dad kept wanting to try until Mom got her girl, but she wasn't willing to take the chance."

"I don't blame her," I say as I look at the girls again. "Listen, girls are pretty awesome, but I think four is a good number either way."

"Agreed," he says with a chuckle, seeming a bit more relaxed. "The boys were here last week for Spring Break in fact, so I got plenty of practice with tours."

"Cool," I say. "Matt mentioned you're going to school here. Where you guys from?"

"Jersey. Asbury Park."

"Cool," I repeat, feeling like a dork. Heat flushes my neck

and cheeks. "Jersey's pretty…we've been to Great Adventure a couple of times…"

"Me too," he says, his cheeks getting a bit rosy now as well. "Like every year for school trips, and a lot with my family…we get season passes…"

God. This is *so* awkward.

The girls pop back up at just the right time. "Have you seen a ghost since you've worked here?" Misty asks, thankfully breaking through the weird tension that keeps creeping up between me and Spencer.

"Do you ride the elevator a lot?" Molly inquires.

Spencer chuckles again as he shifts his attention to the girls. The way he changes when all of his attention is on them is like a magic trick. "Looks like someone has been doing their research. So tell me," he asks as he leans closer to them, "what do you know about the Bowery?"

That gets both the girls talking at a mile a minute. Spencer doesn't skip a beat as he guides them through the lobby, listening as they ramble on about what we had talked about earlier in the car and then gently adding correct or pertinent information through their banter when appropriate. I tag along, listening intently as he tells the girls all about the famous guests who have stayed at the hotel, and they eagerly eat up all of the Bowery trivia he tosses their way and then nearly lose their minds when he says that Selena Gomez sang a song about the hotel.

"Really?" they coo in unison.

"Yup," Spencer assures them.

The girls look up at me, their eyes wide and pleading. I give a slight nod of my head to let them know that as soon as we can, we'll find the song. Then I'm sure I'll have to listen to it a hundred times.

"Some people think the hotel is haunted because of the

cemetery next door," Spencer says as he loops us back to the restaurant.

"There's a cemetery too!" Misty exclaims. She looks at me accusingly. "Why didn't Dad tell us all this?" Her mouth pops open and then her eyes narrow. "Did you know about it?"

"I…" I catch sight of Spencer's pained expression. It's as if he knows exactly how I feel. "I read about it, but we kept getting sidetracked on other stuff when we were talking in the car…"

"Well, you know about it now," Spencer says cheerfully, "and I'm taking you there." He extends a hand toward each girl. "You gals up for waiting here with me while Meghan runs to tell Matt we're heading outside?"

"Yes!" they once again shout in unison.

Spencer looks at me and winks. My heart actually skips a beat. It's an amazingly uncomfortable and petrifying sensation, but it oddly, somehow, also feels good. I stagger backward toward the kitchen, my eyes still locked with his. "Yeah, okay. I'll go let Matt know."

"Behind!" one of the wait staff calls out, jerking me out of my hypnotic gaze.

I whip around just in time to avoid colliding with a very annoyed-looking waitress. "Sorry," I say as she whizzes by. I look back at Spencer and catch sight of my sisters giggling at my blunder. My cheeks ignite—for what feels like the billionth time, so I rush toward the kitchen, hoping the trip gives them enough time to cool down before I make it back.

As I push through the swinging door, I notice Matt prepping a dish of pasta. He notices me too.

"Hey," he says with a smile. "How's the tour going?"

"Good." I'm sure the blush is still evident, so I try to play it down a bit. "The girls are mad at us for not sharing all the gory details. I'm sure you'll hear all about it in the morning."

He chuckles. "Well, you can tell them I've never so much as heard a peep here, and I've been here for years now, so there's nothing to tell but a bunch of great stories that the Bowery's marketing team came up with to keep the customers coming."

I chuckle at that, but a part of me squirms because I hope he's wrong. "Do you mind if Spencer takes us to the cemetery?" I ask.

He looks up at the clock on the wall. "He only gets a thirty-minute break. I talked to the front desk manager and she's being lenient tonight, but don't keep him too long, okay?"

I nod. "Yeah, okay." I turn around to leave but he clears his throat in that annoying parental way. I spin around and my almost-cooled cheeks ignite again.

"Have you found what you were looking for?" he inquires, his voice soft enough so only I can hear the question over the clinks and clanks.

I avert my gaze and shake my head. "No…" I dare a glance at him again. "Not yet…"

His eyes narrow a bit, as if he's chewing on that, then he nods. "Okay."

I stand there for a moment longer, not sure if he's going to add anything else. When he doesn't, I take a few backward steps. "I'll send the girls in when we get back."

"Sounds good," he replies as he finishes garnishing the plate.

I leave him to it since he's running the pass and it's still really busy. I slip back into the dining room and weave my way to Spencer and the girls.

"Hey," Spencer says with a smile. "Everything okay with us to go?"

"Yeah." I motion for the exit. "He did mention that you don't have too much time though."

Spencer looks at his watch and shrugs. "We'll be okay," he

assures me, but then he turns and makes it outside in no time flat.

I follow behind as we round the corner of the block and start ahead.

"The cemetery's entrance is right down here?" Molly asks, pulling her hand out of Spencer's so she can point down the block.

"Yup," Spencer says. "You can't miss it."

"Okay!" Molly shifts to reach for Misty's hand. "Come on!"

"Hang on," I interject before they take off. I'm not entirely comfortable with them running off to a cemetery in the middle of Manhattan.

"It's okay," Misty assures me, mischief gleaming in her eyes.

"Yeah," Molly adds with a devious smile. "We're just going to walk a little ahead."

Oh. I get it now. I bite my lower lip and ask the "blush" gods and goddesses to have mercy on my cheeks. Thankfully, everyone lets it go and we walk along at a silent and swift pace.

"I didn't have the chance to wish you a happy birthday earlier," Spencer says. "So, happy birthday."

The gods and goddesses fail me. My cheeks ignite, so I'm forced to look down at my feet. "Thanks."

We walk a couple more steps in silence.

"If you're free…" he begins, "I'd love to take you to lunch tomorrow. I have to work at four, but maybe we can meet up here at two-ish?"

My heart, which has been on overdrive this entire time, practically beats itself out of my chest. With blazing cheeks and probably a noticeable full-body tremor, I look up at him and nod. "I'd love that," I manage to say with an amazingly sure voice.

He smiles, which wipes away what I finally notice was straight-up anxiety.

"Great. It's a date then." His eyes widen and a little bit of the trepidation resurfaces.

To reassure him, because, for some reason, I want to, I smile. "It's a date then."

He smiles again, the adorable expression somehow accentuating his gorgeous green eyes.

I feel my cheeks warming again but I make sure to keep smiling, which is easy enough to do because, for the first time in a long time, I actually feel like there's something worth smiling for.

17

GHOSTS IN THE WALLS

The New York Marble Cemetery isn't usually open to the public in the evenings. In fact, there aren't very many days and times of the year that a normal person like me can visit. Spencer says they only open the grounds to the general public one day every month, and only for a few hours, and only for certain months of the year, so it's usually impossible to get inside for a peek. Luckily for me and the girls, the cemetery hosts a ton of events for weddings and corporate purposes, and since the Bowery Hotel is literally next door, many of the guests of these said events are typically guests at the hotel. Spencer knows all about it because he usually helps these people up to their rooms, and he always gets them chatting on the way up—he says it helps with getting the best bang for his buck when it comes to tips.

I'll have to take his word on that.

Tonight, there's a modest-sized wedding reception going on. It isn't a super formal affair; otherwise, me and the girls would have stuck out like sore thumbs in our jeans and blouses. Thankfully, we had put some effort into our outfits this morning because we had known we were coming to the hotel for dinner. We even have on nice sandals, and this morning, I had taken the time to put the girls' hair into cute ponytails that have remarkably held up for the day, so they don't look like frizzed-out hot messes. My hair, which I had flat-ironed early this morning because I couldn't sleep, is hanging down the length of my back, and it's looking damn good too.

Fate, for once, seems to be on our sides, and as we walk into the cemetery with Spencer, no one questions our appearances. The fact that we seem to blend right in is a little trippy, so when we make it to the other side of the cemetery without so much as a second glance, it occurs to me the adults must think the girls and I are someone's kids being escorted to the party by the hotel staff. Not that I'm complaining. I want to hear all about the lore of the hotel and the cemetery, and anything that gives me extra time with Spencer seems like a bonus.

I dare a glance in his direction, taking in his easy-going smile as he says some cheesy thing to the girls about ghosts that makes my heart go pitter-patter. He glances my way just as I begin to admire his profile, which jerks me out of admiration mode and into a panicked frenzy. I whip around to look at one of the marble plaques mounted on a nearby wall and I somehow manage to trip over my own feet. Spencer reaches out to steady me, which only furthers my embarrassment, especially because the girls start giggling.

I turn my back on them and pretend I'm suddenly interested in the scenery. The rectangular space is beautifully decorated, the reception ironically leaning more toward a burlap-country theme, which seems out of place in the middle of the city, but it's lovely nonetheless, and the people seem to be in generally good spirits. It's nice to be around the happy vibes considering the blanket of stress, tension, and dread we've been trapped under all week.

When Spencer falls back into his tour-guide incarnation,

and I'm sure my cheeks have cooled, I dare a glance back in his direction. He's standing by another wall plaque a couple of feet away. The girls, who are ever mindful that we don't need any unnecessary attention directed our way, stand quietly as Spencer tells them about the history of the cemetery. I nonchalantly join back in on the conversation just as Spencer tells the girls people used to say the cemetery was located on 41½ Second Avenue.

"When I first heard that," he says, "I thought about Harry Potter."

My little sister's eyes get wide as saucers and she practically starts radiating light. "Like Platform 9¾!" she says so excitedly that I quickly look around to make sure she didn't draw too much attention.

"Exactly!" Spencer responds, his voice at a more level tone as he offers up his hand for a high-five.

Misty gladly jumps up to slap his hand. "I love Harry Potter!" she informs him, still excited, but she's thankfully contained. "Do you? What's your favorite book? Who's your favorite character?"

Spencer glances my way, and I can automatically sense he's both happy and horrified by Misty's enthusiasm. Happy because he's glad she understood his reference; horrified because she clearly knows more about the topic than he anticipated.

"She can go on and on about books," I interject, hoping to contain the situation before Misty explodes into an exuberant Harry Potter factoids and trivia hour that would leave even J.K.'s head spinning.

Misty looks up at me, eyes pleading. "I won't," she begs, meaning about the going-on-and-on part. "I promise! I'll just ask a couple of questions." She turns her attention back to Spencer. "Which was your favorite book? And who did you want Hermoine with?"

Spencer doesn't skip a beat. "The Sorcerer's Stone and Harry."

Misty smiles. "You're okay in my book, Spencer Walsh."

In response, Spencer actually blushes. "Well, you're A-okay in my book too," he says, offering up his hand for another high-five.

Misty happily complies, and when Spencer offers his hand to Molly, she slaps it too.

"So, what's *your* favorite thing to do?" he asks Molly.

Molly smiles proudly. "Singing." She looks around, and then her eyes finally settle on mine.

I give a slight shake of my head since I know that once she gets going, she gets way to into her routines. Granted, she's got a great voice, but I definitely don't want her outshining the bride.

Molly sighs.

"Maybe you can sing something on our way back to the hotel?" Spencer suggests.

That puts a smile back on her face. "Okay! Do you have a favorite song?" she inquires.

Spencer's face scrunches up a bit as he contemplates that. "Hmm…why don't you surprise me," he says after a long-suffering moment.

"Okay!" Molly repeats, then she turns to Misty and they start going over all of her best songs.

I listen to them go back and forth a moment, and just before I go to interject my opinion, Spencer steps closer to me. His proximity makes my heart skip a beat and when I look up to meet his gaze, a few butterflies flutter around in my belly.

"So…" He clears his throat nervously. "What's *your* favorite thing to do?"

"Oh…" I clear my throat too, and then I start nervously twirling a strand of hair. "I like to read…" Man, that sounds lame, but when you're poor, the library has a way of becoming your favorite place. "I'm not a big Harry Potter fan," I say, daring to assume by his earlier reaction that he isn't either.

He smiles and then chuckles. "Neither am I. Not that it's bad," he quickly adds, like some knee-jerk reaction—though, in his defense, I'm well aware of how dedicated and fanatical Harry Potter fans can be, "but with three little brothers, I've had to watch those movies *so* many times. On about the hundredth viewing, I developed a PTSD twitch that goes off every time Ron stutters something stupid, cowardly, or incomprehensible."

I chuckle and then make sure I'm out of Misty's earshot before I say, "Tell me about it. He gets under my skin too. *Oh, Harry,*" I mimic in a pretty decent British accent, "*I'm so s... s...cared!*"

Spencer laughs.

"Not that it's bad," I quickly add, following his politically correct stance, "but when I was her age I was way more into the spooky jump-scare stuff, like R. L. Stine."

"Me too! Though, if I'm being completely honest, I've never been a big reader. I'm more into movies. I love all the visuals and stuff."

"I get it. The girls are all about musicals, so sometimes it's nice to just sit back and watch, you know, without having to do all the heavy mental lifting."

"My mom is into musicals too. She used to force us to watch them because she wanted us to be *cultured*." He says that last part with a bit of a shrug. "I used to ask her to put Hairspray and West Side Story on all the time because I loved catching glimpses of Baltimore and New York."

"That's right," I say as I think about all the little bits of information I've gathered on him so far. "You're going to school to be an architect, right?"

"Yup," he says with a smile.

I inwardly cringe at his pride since I know next to nothing

about architecture. I mean. I know buildings and cities—though I guess in their most basic sense. Oh! And there's Ted Mosby too! But beyond those insignificant, and albeit fictional, aspects, I'm clueless. "I've never met an architect before." I finally admit. "How did you get into that?"

"You know," he says conversationally as if he's answered this question a billion times, "I don't know." He chuckles. "I tell Mom it was all those musicals. You know, like seeing all those cool, faraway places in the background." He snorts. "I even put that in my application essay for Cooper. But even after all this time, I can't really explain it, it's just..." He turns around and points at the Bowery.

I turn around too, and after sidestepping a bit to be closer to him, I say, "It's a beautiful building." I mean, that much isn't a lie, though saying it's pretty is about as far as my architectural knowledge goes.

"She is a beaut, isn't she?" he says as he very smoothly and very slyly slips his hand into mine.

My body tenses from the sudden contact, but as he sidesteps even closer and leans in to point at the building with his other hand, I force myself to relax. It isn't every day a boy wants to hold my hand. It's rarer still that it's something I'm thrilled about.

"It's just a basic postmodern sixteen-story high-rise," he says in an awestruck voice, "but in the short time of its existence, it's helped redefine this neighborhood and it's become part of American pop culture."

His excitement is a little infectious, but I definitely can't overlook how mature he sounds compared to the high school guys I'm used to hearing. Could I actually spend time with him without sounding like an idiot? Thankfully, I only have a second to reflect on that before he uses his hand as leverage to shift our position so he can point to the building next to the Bowery. He tells me a little about it and then he moves on down the line, sharing odd tidbits about the neighborhood until we make it all the way around the cemetery. Amazingly, the girls had stood quietly, listening as he went on about the entire block, but once he finally looks back at me, they skip off toward the dessert table. My kneejerk reaction is to follow them and tell them to leave the food alone. We aren't guests; we're wedding crashers, so it seems rude to eat on top of that, but I'm still too dazzled by the night, and the fact that Spencer is holding my hand, to go after them.

"Sorry," he says as he shifts so he can take my other hand into his. "I just get really excited about architecture. I've never really understood why, but when I look at landscapes or at a cityscape, I just...I don't know. I feel *something*. Like enchantment, you know. Like when you meet someone who just blows you away." He squeezes my hands and inches just a little bit closer to me. "It's like something inside you snaps, you know, and it just feels right."

My heart nearly explodes out of my chest and I suddenly worry about fainting. How mortifying would that be? I force myself to swallow even though my mouth is devoid of any fluids, and I smile up at him. That was seriously the nicest thing anyone has ever said to me, so I don't want to ruin the moment. To give myself a second to recover, I glance down at our joined hands before I look back up at him. "I understand," I say, not wanting to overdo it. "Everything about tonight has been amazing. Thanks for the tour." The sun had set about an hour ago, but even with the nearby street lights and the billion twinkling bulbs they had strung above the venue, I can clearly see the soft green hue of his eyes. They're seriously one of the most beautiful things I've ever seen before.

A woman carrying a box suddenly steps beside us, bursting the magical bubble we had cocooned ourselves in.

"Sparklers," she says with a smile, her arms extended so we can see that within the burlap-wrapped box, there are literally hundreds of fireworks. "For the sendoff," she adds, which I appreciate since this isn't technically my first wedding, but it's definitely the fanciest.

Spencer releases one of my hands and reaches into the box. He grabs a handful and thanks the woman. Clearly, even though he's in his uniform, he still feels more comfortable in this situation than I do.

"Girls?" he calls as he twirls us a bit so we have a good view of them.

I catch sight of them just as they take huge bites of their cupcakes. I gasp, mortified. Good grief! As I drag Spencer along with me, I count the discarded cupcake wrappers on the table behind them. Six! Six freaking cupcake wrappers!

"Great tour," Molly says to Spencer, then she quickly stuffs the last of the chocolate cupcake into her mouth.

Spencer chuckles. "Thanks! I didn't mean to bore you guys."

"It was good," Misty assures him, then she rams the last of her strawberry cupcake into her mouth. "The best," she adds with her mouth full.

Mortified, I quickly grab a plastic plate, sweep their wrappers onto it, and then I grab a ton of napkins. After stopping long enough to grab a bottle of water from the end of the table, I make it over to them and begin herding them away from the colorful confections.

"What happened to restraint?" I asked, being sure to keep the edge out of my tone for Spencer's sake. I hand them each a couple of napkins. They dutifully hold them out while I pour a dab of water onto them.

"Sorry," Molly offers after she wipes her mouth clean. "They're delicious though—"

"And there are so many flavors!" Misty adds.

"I understand that," I say as I hold the plate out in front of them so they can drop their soiled napkins, "but someone paid for these and it isn't polite to just hog them all up. Especially because we aren't invited guests."

"Here are some sparklers for the sendoff," Spencer says, cutting in with what I'm sure is an intentionally light tone. "Do you guys know how to use these?"

The girls all but forget about me as they reach for the fireworks. "Yes!" they respond in unison.

"We use them every year at our Uncle Rusty's house for the Fourth of July," Misty adds.

"Awesome! Well, have you guys ever done a wedding sendoff before?" he inquires.

They both shake their heads, so Spencer gleefully explains the procedure while he guides us toward the growing lines of people by the exit. From our spot among the crowd, we watch as the bride and groom have one last dance. As they sway along to Etta James's *At Last,* two women run along the line, lighting up the sparklers. The guests begin to shift then, almost hastily, so we can form two long, single-filed sparkler chains stretching out from the dance floor all the way to the exit. It all works out perfectly, and as the bride and groom hurry by us, waving and blowing kisses into the crowd, I'm awestruck and nearly moved to tears.

If I'm half as lucky one day, I'll have an equally beautiful wedding.

I look down at the girls as they squeal with glee, shouting their goodbyes to these complete strangers, and I smile. Then I look up at Spencer, who seems to have been looking at me all along. My heart skips a beat, and in an instant, I experience an entire spectrum of emotions emanating from him, like fear and embarrassment, but most importantly, love. It's magical, really, so while a part of me wants to shrink inside myself to hide, a bigger part of me just wants to enjoy the moment. I reach for his hand and smile when he eagerly takes it and squeezes it.

"Will you wait for me to get off work tonight?" he asks. "I'd love to walk you home."

I nod. "I'd loved that," I say even though I'm not sure if Matt will be okay with that, but even if it causes a rift or an argument, I realize I would do just about anything in my power to stay here with Spencer tonight.

18

THE UNINVITED GUEST

As we make our way back to the hotel, Molly sings Jimmie Allen's *Best Shot* while Misty covers the backup vocals. My sisters have very nice voices. I do too, but Molly definitely has the powerhouse voice. Right now, she's containing herself, so the song has a gritty, soulful quality to it that's beautiful in its own right, but if she wanted to, she'd be able to belt it out and probably have everyone on the sidewalk stopping for more.

Of course, as much as I'm always impressed with the girls' musical abilities, tonight, I'm once again distracted by Spencer. He's holding my hand as we keep up with the girls, and he seems genuinely impressed with my sister's singing abilities. As he watches Molly, I take time to admire him. He has a strong jaw, high cheekbones, and his nose is a bit crooked, almost as if it was broken at some point, which oddly enough, only adds to his charm. His red hair is still a trip to me. I would have never in a million years thought I'd fall for a ginger. I mean, I've always been attracted to white guys, but typically ones with dark hair and dark eyes. Spencer is like an anomaly, but now that I've met him and I've stared into his eyes, it's like I can't picture myself with anyone but him.

Man. This is turning out to be my weirdest birthday yet.

When Molly finishes the song, Spencer releases my hand long enough to clap, then we go back to walking hand in hand as the girls start on the Glee cover of *I Say a Little Prayer.* They finish up just as we make it back to the hotel entrance. Spencer pulls us to a halt so he can clap again, this time more enthusiastically.

"Wow! You girls are amazing!" he says as he steps over for high-fives. "I really mean that. My mom would love to join your group!"

"Really?" Molly squeals as she high-fives him.

"We can come over one day," Misty adds as she joins in on the high-five action.

"I would love that!" he adds as he stands tall to straighten his red vest. "Your sister and I will chat about the details later, but for now, I've got to head back to work."

"Okay!" they say in unison and then wave.

"Is it okay if we go in?" Molly asks me.

When I nod, they take each other's hands and head into the restaurant's main entrance.

"That really was impressive," Spencer says as he reaches for my hands, his expression genuinely surprised by their talent. "My mom would seriously die if she had two little girls to jam out to musicals with, so whenever you guys want to come to Jersey, let me know and I'll arrange it."

My heart frenzies at the invitation, but for the first time all night, I finally remember why we're here. The reminder of it deflates my good spirits, but thankfully not entirely. "I'm not sure how long we'll be here, but we'd love to go…"

He doesn't seem to notice, because his smile widens. "Great! We'll talk about it later? Right? When I get off?"

Jeez. That's another thing. "Yes," I say, sounding so sure even though Matt might prohibit it. "I'll meet you right here at midnight." I point to the main entrance.

"Okay," he says, then without any warning, he leans down and kisses my cheek. "See you then!"

Before I can get my wits about me, he's gone, the two doormen teasing him as he runs inside. I stand there a moment longer, still too stunned to move, but then I touch my cheek and smile. This is turning out to be the best night ever, and I don't want it to end, so I hurry into the restaurant and make my way to the kitchen. The girls are in the office, sitting around the computer, and Matt is garnishing a few dishes. He looks up just as I make it over.

"I hear you had fun," he says with a smile.

Most times it's annoying to have little humans sharing your life story with anyone willing to listen, but tonight, I'm oddly grateful for it. "Yeah. It's been…crazy," I say, not sure if that's the right word for it, but it's as close as I can get at the moment.

"Good crazy or bad crazy?"

"Good crazy," I confirm with a nod. "*Umm*…I was wondering if there was any way you'd be okay with me and the girls hanging out here tonight instead of taking a cab back to the apartment. Spencer offered to walk us home when he gets off…"

After cleaning off the rim of one of the plates, he looks at me. "Meg, this neighborhood has definitely gotten safer over the years, but I still wouldn't want you guys walking around at midnight alone." Before my heart has a chance to deflate, he adds, "I've already arranged to get off after the dinner rush, so I'll get the girls home, which means I'm okay if you wait *in* the hotel for Spencer to get off, but only if you guys are okay with taking a cab home."

I'm so excited all I can do is nod.

Matt winks before he goes back to fussing over the food. "If you can keep the girls occupied for the long haul though, that would be cool."

"Of course!" I say, already heading their way. "We'll just watch a movie until you're ready to go." I scoot out of a server's way just in time and then gallop the rest of the way to the office. I'm sure the girls are trying to find that Selena Gomez song, which is fine because once they're done searching, I'll find a full clip of *Hairspray* or *West Side Story* somewhere online so the girls can start practicing for our future dinner plans in Jersey.

————

It's a little after eleven when Matt and the girls leave. I walk them out and then watch their cab drive away into a sea of cars —the nightlife of this city never ceasing to amaze me. After another moment, I head back into the restaurant. Matt said I could kill time in the office until midnight, but without him here, it doesn't feel right to hang out in the kitchen, so instead, I go to the back and say goodnight to everyone, then I grab a couple of tabloids I had spotted earlier.

With the smut-rags in hand, I weave my way back into the dining room, which had thankfully quieted down, and I grab a seat at the little café table in the corner. After settling the magazines in front of me so it looks like I'm utterly engrossed in the latest celebrity gossip, I shift my attention outdoors. If I crane my neck at just the right angle, I can catch glimpses of people coming and going from the main hotel entrance, and if I'm lucky, *and* if Spencer has to run out to the curb to grab a guest's bags, I'll see him too.

"Pardon me," a lady says in an accent I can't place.

I look over my shoulder and stare up at her. The woman is very petite, her tiny frame clad in one of those old-fashioned, ruffled high-neck, long-sleeved shirts with lots of unnecessary buttons. Her skirt is equally vintage, the ankle-length get-up as puffy and ruffled as you'd expect a Victorian skirt to be, and she's sporting a huge quaff of hair that's pinned up in one of those old-fashioned pompadour buns. It occurs to me she's probably heading to some sort of time-period event—maybe the early 1900s or something, since picking out fashions of the times has never been my forte.

"Would you mind if I joined you?" she asks, and before I can even think of a response, she drops into the seat across from me. It was pulled out slightly, so it's easy enough for her to do, but instead of sitting to face me, she sits so she's looking outside. "Terribly sorry," she adds as she gazes out the window, "but I'm waiting on someone and this table has the best view of the street."

I know. "Oh...okay..." I fidget with the magazine that's open in front of me, unsure of how to proceed. I know this kind of thing is normal in the city, but in Middletown, people never just volunteer to share a table. It's something that, I'm quickly discovering, makes me uncomfortable, but I guess when you're in Rome...

"Are you waiting for someone?" the woman inquires as she continues to search outside.

"Oh. Um. Yes." In my head, the words "stranger danger" are blaring repeatedly, but I ignore them. I *am* eighteen now, and I *am* leaving for the military soon, so I'm going to have to get used to encountering new, strange people. "A friend," I finally offer.

The lady looks at me, which, for some reason sends a chill down my spine.

"Oh, a friend, you say?" she teases, her eyebrows going up and down in a comical way that I'm sure is meant to lighten the mood. She reaches across the table and offers her hand. "I'm Annie, by the way. Annie Moore."

Despite her light tone and seemingly pleasant introduction, there's something off about the lady. I force a smile even though I want to bolt, then I even more reluctantly shake her hand. It's stone-cold, so I have to keep myself from instantly recoiling. Slowly. Deliberately, I pull my hand back and smile. "Meghan," I offer, and then I add, "and, yes, a friend. He works here." I say that last part conversationally, but there's a method behind my madness. It's so the lady knows I'm not really here alone. "My stepdad works here too," I add. That's a half-truth, but it's just a little more security, even though I feel silly for overreacting to this little woman. She's probably my height, if that. And she's pretty—a little plain, but cute, so I don't understand the sinking feeling I keep getting when I look at her.

"So, it is a *he?*" she says, her attention back outside, almost like she knows that when she looks at me, I want to rip my eyes out. "It's always nice to have gentleman callers."

"Right," I say, still trying to place her accent. It isn't British. It's more like a New England accent, but with some kind of weird Midwest twist. It's still hard to tell, so I decide to toss the ball back in her court. "So the person you're waiting for is also a guy?"

She chuckles. "A guy?" she says, almost as though she's mimicking me now. "Your generation speaks so oddly."

My generation? She doesn't look much older than I do, but that statement suddenly helps to explain her accent. It isn't from a different region. It's from a different time-period. Like something you'd hear in one of those black-and-white movies. Man, this chick really is sticking to character. "So, where are you from?" I ask boldly, hoping to bother her enough that she leaves.

The lady swivels in her seat so she's facing me. After dropping her chin onto her palm, she looks me over.

I shiver.

"She's happy for you, you know," Annie says with a smile.

I shiver some more, and the hairs on the back of my neck start to stand on end. "Who is?" I ask, my voice actually cracking.

Annie sits back in her seat and crosses her arms over her chest.

That's when I notice how old-fashioned her ruffled shirt really is…and just how off she seems.

"When you're ready, she's waiting for you," Annie says quietly.

My heart sinks as I lean over the table, almost tempted to shake her. "Who is?" I ask, my voice trembling even though I try to contain it. "What are you talking about, lady?"

Annie looks at me for one long, eternal second, and in that instant, I feel as though she sees into my soul. Then she motions to something behind me. I whip around, scared that someone is right behind me, but there's no one. Instead, a waitress pushes her way through one of the swinging doors at that exact moment, her loaded tray lifted above her right shoulder.

A wisp of black smoke suddenly appears, as though lassoed out of thin air, and it stretches taunt just shy of the girl's ankles.

My heart races as I shoot out of my chair. "Look out!" I try to warn.

But it's too late.

The girl trips over the smoke, the tray flying toward a nearby table as the waitress falls forward. I wince as the plates of pasta splatter onto an unsuspecting couple and then I gasp when the waitress lands on the floor with a thud that carries all the way across the dining room. Glass shatters. People yell and swear. Then the room, for a moment, erupts into a panicked frenzy. When the last dish breaks though, and the people realize it was just an accident, they spring into action. One couple helps the poor waitress back onto her feet while another couple goes over to help clean up the spaghetti-laden patrons.

For a moment longer, I watch the chaos, but then I have the sense to turn back around, and just as I suspected, Annie Moore is gone.

19

THE LOBBY

When Spencer finds me, I'm sitting in one of the chairs by the fireplace. I had made my way over here to put some space between myself and the restaurant because I think I'm still in shock. *I saw a ghost.* I don't believe it—or, at least, I don't want to, but that seems to be the only logical explanation for what just happened in there.

"Hey," he says as he takes the seat next to mine, "I thought you were waiting for me in the restaurant."

When I look at him, his smile falters—not that I blame him. I probably look awful.

"Are you okay?" he inquires. "You look a little…" He's clearly at a loss, probably trying to find the right word that suits the situation without actually insulting me. "Oh! I know," he says, his tone going back to upbeat. "Were you in there when the waitress tripped? I heard she wiped out big time. Got a couple of customers a year's worth of vouchers for their troubles."

I nod my head before I fully understand why, but as my eyes lock onto his, I suddenly understand my innate reaction. I don't want him to think I'm nuts. I want him to like me.

Desperately. "Yeah," I say, forcing myself to pull it together. "I saw her trip. It was nuts…" *Yeah.* That seems like the right word for it.

"Was it as bad as everyone says?" he inquires.

I nod, my head still spinning a bit, but I suddenly get an idea. "It was pretty bad…but I missed most of it because I was distracted by one of the hotel guests…" I lean up in my seat. "Can you guys see who's staying here?"

That question definitely seems to catch him off guard. "Ah…yeah…well. Not *me,*" he points behind him, "but the people at the front desk can. Why? Everything okay?" His confused expression morphs into one of genuine concern. "Did someone mess with you?"

"No!" I say way too sharply. My cheeks, naturally, take the fall for my blunder, and the sudden temperature spike causes sweat to bead on my brow. "No one messed with me," I add in a more even tone. "There was just this woman who was sitting in the corner…" *Hmm.* I'm not sure where to go with this now. "Umm…we were chatting when it happened and I…"

Spencer's head tilts to the side, almost as if he's trying to physically follow that train of thought. "Oh. Well, we can go and ask about her." He points to the front desk again.

I get onto my feet, which seems to shock him. I know it shocks me. Thankfully, he gets up too and doesn't make too big of a deal of it while we head to the front desk. He does glance at me twice, and not in a good way, so my stomach starts to tie up in knots.

"Hey, Spence," a girl behind the front desk says as we approach. Her dark hair is spiked up in a cool, haphazard way and her makeup is dark but tasteful. Her nametag claims her as Michelle. She's older, maybe in her late twenties, and she's wearing a wedding band, which, even in this moment, I realize is something that's of the utmost importance to me. Granted, I get the feeling she isn't into guys, per se, but the thought of talking to a girl who may like the guy *I* like seems far worse an offense than trying to discover the identity of the possible ghost I was just talking to in the restaurant.

Man. This really is turning out to be a strange day.

"You must be Meghan!" she says to me exuberantly.

Michelle's excitement causes my stomach to sink to a depth I can't even describe, yet I somehow force a smile. "Yup. That's me."

"Matt talks about you all the time!" she exclaims.

"Oh…" Hearing that all day still hasn't made it any easier to respond to. "Yeah. He can be awesome like that," I add lamely.

"He can be!" Michelle agrees. "So, what can I help you with tonight? You need a cab?"

"Not yet!" Spencer interjects, which causes his cheeks to ignite.

Oddly enough, that eases nearly all my anxiety.

"She was looking for a guest she met in the restaurant," he adds, his voice a little squeaky.

"Oh," Michelle says quickly, like she feels bad for causing him such distress. She turns her attention to me and smiles. "I can help you with that for sure!"

My kneejerk reaction is to collapse into my shell, since I hate being thrusts into the spotlight, but I find courage from somewhere deep within me and say, "Awesome!" It even sounds genuine. "I think her name was Annie…Annie Moore?"

The girl starts to type on her computer but then jerks back and looks at me. I can't place her expression, not until she bursts out laughing.

Stunned by her reaction, I look up at Spencer for help.

He just shrugs.

"Oh, how clever!" the girl says to me. "Annie Moore! I almost fell for it!"

She goes into another round of high-pitch chortling while I stand there, completely unsure of what to say or do.

"Did your dad put you up to this?" she asks. "Oh, that little turd! He did, didn't he?"

When she looks right at me with tears welling in the corner of her eyes from laughing, I force a huge smile and a chuckle. "He did!" I say while pointing at her. "He totally put me up to it!" I add, so confused. So petrified. So baffled. So desperate to leave.

"That guy!" Michelle says, then she goes into another hearty round of laughter.

"I don't understand…?" Spencer says, chuckling too, but in that completely lost way. "Who's Annie Moore?"

Oh, thank god! Having him just as clueless as me is like a Christmas miracle.

"You know," Michelle says, still chuckling. "Annie Moore. The murdered prostitute who haunts the hotel."

"Ohhh…!" Spencer says. "Oh…so your Dad put you up to asking Michelle about Annie Moore so you could prank her…?" he hedges, clearly still lost.

"Right! A prank! Yes," I say, though I'm not sure how I manage it since I'm beyond shocked now. *Did she just say prostitute?* More importantly. Did she just imply the murdered prostitute haunts the hotel? Oh, gosh! That's what Annie had meant when she said gentleman caller. Gross!

"He's always teasing me," Michelle says, thankfully taking it upon herself to answer for me. "He thinks it's so silly that I believe in all of this stuff!"

"Me too," I add genuinely, and only because I realize an opportunity when it presents itself. "He says he's never seen anything, but I'm sure you have…?" I say, since this time it's my turn to hedge.

"I wish," Michelle says. "I've been here almost a year and nothing. Nada." She seems genuinely disappointed by that.

"But you tell your Dad I'm still a believer. Annie Moore. Man, he got me good," she says with a chuckle and then thankfully shifts over to help a real customer.

"That's funny," Spencer says, though he doesn't sound the least bit amused. "Your dad and Michelle *do* joke a lot…"

I look up at him, my stomach so tied up in knots I'm scared I'll puke if I open my mouth. The baffled expression on his face helps ease some of my tension though since I don't want to leave him hanging on such an awkward note.

"They do," I spit out. "I guess that's why he asked me to prank her…"

Whew. No vomit, for now anyway, but my stomach is still dangerously close to erupting.

"He was sure she'd fall for it," I add as I take a backward step. "Umm. Is there a ladies' room around, by chance?"

"Yeah." He still seems genuinely confused, but he smiles and points behind me. "Right there, actually. I have to go clock out, so I'll meet you back by the fireplace in about fifteen minutes?"

I nod. "Yeah. That sounds perfect." Hopefully, that will give me just enough time to get my head screwed back on right.

He waves and then hurries off toward the main entrance. I whip around and beeline to the bathroom. It's just as beautiful as the lobby, but I don't take the time to appreciate the décor. Instead, I go right into the stall and stand over the bowl. The week's events seem to crash down on me. Mom going missing. Us looking for her. Matt showing up. Us coming down here. Me meeting Spencer. I think it's more than anyone would be able to withstand, so it's not surprising my stomach is churning violently.

Breathe through it, Peanut, Mom's voice whispers in my head. *It'll pass.*

In that moment, I wish more than anything she could be with me, really rubbing my back to soothe my fears away.

"Where are you?" I whisper through tears I didn't even realize were falling.

In response, the hairs on the back of my neck stand on end.

Then I feel it—her hand on my back.

I can smell her too. Every person has a unique, individual scent, like an aromatic signature, and Mom's has always been a combination of Pert shampoo, Ivory soap, and cigarettes.

It's such a relief to hear from her again that I start to cry harder. It's been so difficult having her gone, but it's been even worse with the complete radio silence the past few days. Just then, as if to confirm she is indeed with me, the pressure on my back increases so that I feel one full rotation of a soothing back rub before I can tell she's gone. Not from the bathroom; just from the stall. The faucets squeak as they turn on, which I take as my cue to grab a handful of toilet paper. I roughly wipe my face and then blow my nose. After flushing the tissue down the toilet, I turn around and pull the stall door open.

Both faucets are running on full blast. The water hasn't heated up enough for the steam to build though, so I walk over and splash some of the water onto my cheeks, being mindful of the eyeshadow and mascara I had put on earlier. Even with all the craziness going on around me, I'm still fully aware of how disastrous mascara can be when not properly removed. By the time I'm done blotting my face dry, the steam has accumulated enough so Mom can leave her signature, heart-shaped message.

I reach for it and sigh. "I love you too, Mom." My heart aches in a way that makes it hard to breathe, but I muster on. "I'm here. At the Bowery. Just like you asked. Is there some-thing here I'm supposed to see?" I inquire. "Is there someone I'm supposed to find?" I ask that last part for Annie's sake.

Maybe that's why she had shown up earlier? Maybe she has another message for me, since, now that I'm sure she's a ghost, I realize she already delivered one. *She's happy for you.* I'm not sure exactly what Annie meant, but I think she was talking about my mom.

An eerie, almost nails-on-a-chalkboard sound fills the bathroom as the words "13th Floor" appear on the mirror. She finishes off that ominous-sounding message by enclosing a heart around it. Then the water shuts off, and I know she's gone again.

20

THE RULES

I'm not sure how I pull it off, but I actually beat Spencer to the fireplace. Glad for the reprieve, I try to figure out a way to get information out of him without making him think I'm crazy. I'm not sure if I can pull that off, but I'm willing to try, so I wrack my brain for some feasible ways to approach the topic. In the very short time I've known him, he seems genuinely interested in the hotel's lore, or he's at least learned enough to give a decent tour. He's also familiar with the cemetery's history, so I'm hoping all that translates into him knowing some more in-depth stuff about how to get onto the thirteenth floor.

I mean, I know it seems obvious. Just get on the elevator and go. The problem, of course, is that the Bowery Hotel, along with most of the other high-rise buildings in Manhattan, don't actually have a thirteenth floor. At some point, someone thought it was a good idea to just skip it—like pretending as though it isn't there somehow spares them the bad luck—so most buildings go from the twelfth floor to the fourteenth. They literally just mislabeled it, but that's what makes getting there so complicated.

Some have argued going to the fourteenth floor is adequate given that in reality it's really the thirteenth floor. Technically, I agree with that. Unfortunately, when it comes to the supernatural, the rules of logic rarely apply, so as much as I would love to just hop on the elevator and go up to the fourteenth floor, I don't think it'll be that easy. There's more to it, which I'm hoping Spencer can help me with.

While I wait for him though, I go over all the information I do know. From what I've read online, the hotel isn't *that* old. I wasn't reading to study for a test or anything, but I remember it was built in like the early 2000s, so the establishment itself hasn't been around for long, but the surrounding area has plenty of history. I do know the cemetery was incorporated in 1831. I'm only sure of that because I just read it on a plaque right before we left the wedding, but on one of the blogs I read the other day, the author claimed the haunted lore of the Bowery Hotel is related to all of the heartache and anguish this neighborhood has witnessed over the past century.

I know it's impossible to tell now, but once upon a time, Native Americans inhabited the Manhattan Island. In fact, a bit of trivia I picked up several years ago on one of our visits to Matt's has always stuck with me because I found it downright weird. The Native Americans who lived here used to call it Manna-hata because it was the place they gathered to collect wood for their bows. Apparently, back in the day, Manhattan was thriving with trees. It's hard to imagine now, given that it's such a concrete jungle, but the Native Americans who lived here swore by those bows, which definitely saw a lot of action. Even hundreds of years ago, humans were violent, and so this part of Manhattan witnessed its fair share of crime.

Of course, as the island became more heavily populated, the more this part of town caught the action. Phil loves the movie *Gangs of New York*, so I've learned all about Bill the Butcher and the Bowery Boys. There were plenty of bars, brothels, and shady businesses back then, so I'm sure there was plenty of despair. Annie Moore is a good example of that. And over the decades, New York, like the rest of the country, endured an onslaught of financial and political crises that undoubtedly culminated in a ton of tragedy. Unfortunately, I don't know enough about all the specifics, and even though I have some information to work with, I'm still not sure why the Bowery Hotel is haunted or how to bring up the sensitive topic of the thirteenth floor with Spencer.

I'm out of time though, because Spencer approaches me with a smile on his beautiful face.

"Sorry I'm late," he says as he pulls his arm from around his back and produces a beautiful bouquet of flowers.

I stare in shock at the combination of roses, tulips, and carnations nestled within a sea of deep greenery and mounds of baby's breath.

"I'm sorry for this being a little late…" he says as he steps closer, "but happy birthday, Meghan."

I look up at him to thank him, but I'm speechless. I've never gotten flowers from a guy before. I mean, Phil got me a corsage when we went to junior prom last year, but that doesn't count. That was out of obligation; this is just because…

When he offers them to me again, I take the flowers and smell them. Their scent is a little intoxicating and for a glorious moment, I forget why I'm really here. I have to get to the thirteenth floor. But I take another selfish second to admire them and relish the moment because I'm sure that for as long as I may live, this will always rank as one of my most memorable birthdays.

I shift the flowers aside so I can give him a hug. He definitely seems surprised by the gesture, but he immediately wraps an arm around me and gives me a good squeeze. I lean back to look up at him again. "Thank you, Spencer. They're beautiful." I sniff them again, adoring their scent.

"My pleasure." He drops his arm from around me but it's only so he can offer up his hand. "You up for a walk? I promised Matt I'd have you home by two, in a cab, but he's cool with us hanging right around the hotel and there's this great little bar called Phebe's down the street. They have some great food."

I take his hand and nod. "That sounds amazing."

We walk toward the front desk, where Michelle is busy with a guest. Even so, she glances our way and winks at me before she motions toward a vase at the end of the counter.

"Michelle helped me pick these out earlier today and she said she'd keep an eye on them while we went to grab a bite to eat," Spencer says as he reaches for the flowers.

"Oh. How nice of her," I say as I give her a little wave of thanks. When she smiles, I feel a little crummy for having thought such mean stuff about her when we first met.

"Phebe's has a little bit of everything and it's all good, but I especially love their chicken fajitas. You like Mexican?" he inquires as we head for the door.

"I do," I say, and as we make our way down the block, our conversation is just as lighthearted and easygoing. We talk favorite foods, movies, and music. Then we shift into a little heavier fare. High school war stories, past crushes, and crazy family members. As we're making our way back to the Bowery, I finally feel comfortable enough to bring up the elephant in the room. "So, did Matt mention why we were down here?" I ask.

Spencer glances down at me, an innocent look on his face as he shakes his head. "Not really. I figured you guys were just visiting for the weekend to celebrate your birthday."

I pull us to a halt at the corner and then shift to look up at the Bowery. It's imposing height makes my head spin a bit, since I'm not used to seeing any buildings higher than three-or-so stories, and also because there's a sense of foreboding that seems to cling to the entire structure like a fog. "We're here because…" But I can't bring myself to tell him about my mom just yet. "I wanted to see the hotel." I finally look back at him. "I've read some stuff online that I…" I swallow hard and search for the right words.

"You wanna see a ghost?" Spencer guesses, that sweet, gentle smile on his face, letting me know there's no judgment on his part.

"I…" I bite my lower lip for a moment then I shake my head. "Not necessarily a ghost," I add, and I mean it. Ghost implies death. I'm still holding onto the hope that this is still some weird mother-daughter psychic connection. *She's still alive,* I tell myself. Then I remind myself nothing or no one can hold Maggie May down, not even death. "I've heard stuff…you know, about the thirteenth floor."

"Ah," he says, still in that playful way of his. "Well, I can tell you I've worked here since last August, and I haven't technically seen a ghost…"

That piques my curiosity. "Technically?"

"Well," he says, sounding bashful. "I've had some weird dreams. Nothing, you know, sexual," he adds, his cheeks scorching now. "They're more like premonitions."

"Like seeing into the future?"

He nods. "Yeah…or at least I think so. Up until now though, I wasn't brave enough to play the game to be sure."

Play the game. Yes! Thankfully, he walked right into the conversation without me having to do much steering. "But you've heard of it? The elevator game?"

"Of course! Believe it or not, they actually tell us about it during orientation. I think just to take the mystery out of it so we don't mess around with the elevators."

My heart skips a few beats. "So they tell you the rules to play the game?"

"Yes. But, Meghan…" His smile falters and a dark cloud

seems to settle over his handsome features. "I'm told it can be dangerous, so if you're thinking of…what I mean is…would *you* do it? Is that why you want to know? Is that why you're here?"

His sudden mood change gives me pause. I mean, I was already nervous to try it, since they say the elevator game takes you to another dimension, but I'm leery to admit that to him given his reaction. "I…it's hard to explain," I finally admit. "I was kind of hoping you'd know a little about it though. Maybe even know someone who's tried it?"

"I know a lot of it," he says, that smile returning to his lips, "but the person you should talk to is Michelle. She knows like everything there is to know about this place. Come on," he says as he leads me back inside.

It's almost one in the morning, but the front desk is still busy, so Spencer and I take a seat in the corner of the lobby while we wait. In the meantime, Spencer tells me a little bit more about the hotel's lore—a lot of it the same as what I read online: like about the woman in white who randomly appears when people check into their rooms, and the mischievous guest at the bar who likes to toss drinks on people.

That story prompts me to ask about Annie Moore and the poor waitress incident earlier. Unfortunately, Spencer doesn't know anything about Annie aside from what Michelle shared with us, and when I ask him if there's a ghost that haunts the restaurant, he shakes his head. No one, as far as he knows, has ever seen a wisp of black smoke trip a waitress before.

Well, no one but me—though I don't share that part with him.

In hopes of changing the subject so he doesn't get suspicious, I ask him to describe the rules to me, since I read so many contradictory accounts of how the elevator game really works. Thankfully, he's more than happy to oblige.

"Online," he begins, "they say you have to get on the

elevator and then stop on certain floors in a certain order, which is true—to a point," he emphasizes that last part with the same theatrical flair as a magician performing their final, grand trick. "The truth is that you do have to go to certain floors in a certain order, but what you won't find online is that in order for the elevator game to work, you actually have to use the stairs."

It's his big a-ha moment, but I just feel dumbstruck. "Excuse me?" I ask.

He's clearly saddened that I wasn't impressed by his big reveal. "The staircase. That's where all the magic happened…" I think he can tell I only get more confused by that, so he tries again. "Okay, so there's a lot more to it than just going from floor to floor," he admits. "But I think we should wait for Michelle because she's really good at explaining it."

"Who me?" Michelle asks as she seems to suddenly appear before us, almost as if Spencer conjured her.

"Ta-dah!" Spencer says with a grand hand gesture, "right on time! Meghan, Michelle will be your tour guide for the remainder of the evening."

I look between them and start to get a sinking feeling they've either done this "tour guide" stuff before or that, at the very least, they conspired so her theatrical entrance was somehow planned. I mean, that last part seems silly and unnecessary, but what other reason would they have for such a cutesy routine.

Unless there's something more to all this—something nefarious.

I immediately realize I'm overreacting; that the day has just been extremely long and my week has been tragically emotional, so I'm just reading into things. Hotels aren't really haunted, and people are generally good. Hasn't Michelle already proven that? But when she motions her head toward the exit and signals for us to follow her outside, I begin to reconsider. Annie Moore seemed as real to me as they do and I had been wrong about her. So, what if I'm wrong about Michelle? Or worse yet, Spencer.

"Come on," she says as she starts walking out, "I'll tell you everything you need to know." And with that, she looks over her shoulder, winks at me, and then hurries outside.

As I watch her disappear into the darkness though, I realize that whether she's good or bad is irrelevant because as always, I've been thrust into a situation where I have no choice but to proceed. I have to find my mom. I have to get answers. So when Spencer stands and offers me a hand, I take it, but I make sure to proceed with caution.

21

THE SMOKE BREAK

Michelle is already halfway down the block. She's leaning against a small, red car, smoking a cigarette. Spencer and I wander over slowly, almost as if he's intentionally moving at a snail's pace so he can give her enough time to finish her cigarette before we join. Or maybe it's because we're once again walking hand in hand and he enjoys it as much as I do. I'd be totally okay with that.

As we join Michelle by the car, I take a moment to reevaluate the crazy emotional rollercoaster I've been on all week. It's seems nuts that, in the midst of everything I've lived through, I keep finding myself so enamored by Spencer, or how my feelings about what *is* and what *isn't* real keeps wavering. *Is Mom still alive?* I want her to be. But I can't shake the sense that all of the paranormal activity in the hotel is pointing toward another conclusion—one that I'm still determined to avoid.

"You're tied to it, aren't you?" Michelle inquires, then she takes a long drag of her cigarette. After exhaling a plume of smoke, she adds, "The hotel, I mean."

I consider playing stupid, but when I meet her piercing

brown eyes, I somehow know lying to her would be futile, so I nod.

She analyzes me for another moment, then she asks, "Who?"

My stomach sinks as I glance up at Spencer. Naturally, my cheeks light up, so I look at my feet. "My mom," I admit.

Michelle nods and then finishes her cigarette, the awkward silence between us palpable.

Finally, she drops the butt to the ground and steps on it. "How long ago did you lose her?"

My body jerks at that question, and I instinctively pull my hand out of Spencer's. "I didn't." I look between them and shake my head. "She's just missing," I say, my voice wavering a bit. "She isn't dead."

But as those words slip through my lips, the world seems to go still. Even the humdrum of the city fades to black. As I catch sight of the pity in Michelle's eyes though, my heart begins to shatter into a million pieces. *She isn't dead,* I repeat to myself, but the denial I've used as an adhesive to keep my heart from breaking is starting to fray, which I'm suddenly sure will result in a complete and utter breakdown on my part.

"I'm tied to it too," Michelle says, sort of conversationally.

I get the feeling it's her way of giving me a moment to pull it together, which I appreciate.

"I'm pretty sure it was Macy's mom… she was my ex-girl-friend…Macy was, I mean…" Michelle looks off into the distance and winces, as though just the mere mention of her former girlfriend is somehow painful. "It was her mom, Marigold, who started all this."

"What do you mean?" I dare to ask as I look between her and Spencer. "Like, you think one person is actually respon-sible for unleashing the ghosts in the hotel's restaurant and the bar?"

"There are ghosts everywhere," Michelle clarifies, but then

she points behind me. "In some places though, like here, there are more, because of the history of the location, and because of the cemeteries."

"So you think the hotel is haunted because the cemetery is right behind it?" I ask, needing clarification, especially since it's a great distraction from the earlier part of our conversation.

"Yes," she answers matter-of-factly, "but not entirely. You see, cemeteries always invite…" she falters for a moment, her gaze shifting back and forth between Spencer and me before she finally finishes with, "deities."

"Deities?" I repeat, unable to help myself, but that one word completely catches me off guard. "As in gods?"

"And goddesses," she adds brashly, like a reflexive compulsion that comes with being a raging feminist.

"Oh…" I stammer, suddenly feeling un-American. "Yes. Of course. *And* goddesses."

"Are you familiar with Norse mythology?" she inquires.

I'm once again caught off guard. "Ah…" I look up at Spencer. He just smiles and nods. I'm not sure what that means though, so I just look back at Michelle. "Not really…." I'm not sure why I suddenly feel guilty about that, especially because it isn't something schools rigidly go over—or at least mine didn't.

Michelle pulls a fancy cigarette case out of her pocket and lights another one up. "I didn't know much about it either," she admits as she shoves the cigarette case and lighter back into her pocket. Then she stands tall, stretches, and starts walking down the block, in the opposite direction of the hotel.

I'm not sure if we're supposed to follow, but when Spencer takes my hand and tugs me along to catch up, I reluctantly fall into step with her—cautiously—since this whole night just keeps getting stranger and stranger and I feel as though I keep falling farther down the rabbit hole.

"What I'm about to tell you hasn't been verified," she

states, once again in that matter-of-fact way of hers. She glances over at me. "But as someone who was, in a way, one of the last people intimately involved with the events, I'm probably closer to the truth than anyone has ever been."

I just nod, since I'm definitely not qualified to be judge or jury to that particular declaration.

"For shock value's sake, let's start at the beginning," she says, finally looking away. "Or at least to when the Native American started losing headway here, because that's when it started getting really violent. And see, violence has a way of effecting the environment. It's like it, I don't know, puts a strain on the supernatural veils that keep the realms separated." She looks at me again. "Does that make sense?"

I nod, since, I guess, in theory, I'm picking up what she's putting down.

"Right, so there's always been that," she continues, seemingly satisfied with my non-response, "but when they put the cemetery in, that caused a natural ripple in the veil—"

"Wait," I interject, and only because I really don't want to be taken for a ride, so being a skeptic seems like a good idea. "If that were true then there would be ripples like everywhere because there are cemeteries, like everywhere."

She smiles. "Exactly!" After flicking her cigarette butt into the street, she continues. "See, as much as people think life and death are two separate things, they really aren't. Our behaviors and beliefs affect how they interact, and since cemeteries are literally areas designated for the dead, it only makes sense that the veil is easier to manipulate there."

She seems proud of that proclamation. I'm just confused.

"Look," she says, "for the purposes of this lesson, don't worry about the technical stuff, because it's all like seriously mind-boggling. For now, just trust me when I say the New York Marble Cemetery has some powerful energy and some powerful occupants."

That statement is super ambiguous, so I try to clarify. "Do you mean the dead people?"

"No. The deities."

I nod since I had a feeling that's where she was going with this. "Okay, but I'm still not sure what that has to do with the hotel."

"Well, for a long time, it didn't." She looks over at me and seems amused by my confusion. "See, just having a cemetery in a neighborhood isn't enough to cause a ripple big enough to open the veil. It takes something big to do that, and it takes someone even bigger to make it stay open."

I stop short, which inadvertently jerks Spencer to a halt too. "Sorry," I say to him absently as I glare at Michelle. "What does that mean? It's like you're talking in riddles."

Michelle takes the stationary opportunity to light another cigarette. "You know, for most people, it's better to ease them into all of this." She motions to Spencer. "It took me about four months to get him to a place where I thought he could handle the truth."

Four months? It's another bombshell, so I can't help but glance at Spencer.

"In my defense," Spencer says, still in his light, cheerful tone, "we usually only have fifteen-minute breaks. And," he emphasizes, "with me, she wanted to show me all the stuff she's amassed over the years."

I look back at Michelle. "Stuff?"

"He means research. Mostly books and papers to support all of this," she clarifies, "and I have some pictures and interviews and other stuff too."

"Okay," I say, my mind reeling enough that I suddenly wish I were on the four-month plan. The problem, of course, is that I don't have four months. As usual, I have to work on a curve. "Well, can you give me the CliffsNotes version?"

Michelle inhales dramatically and then exhales with just as

much gusto. Then she sighs and shakes her head. "Yeah. Okay. But only because I know you're anxious to try and…"

I let a beat of time pass before I say, "And what?"

"It's just…look, Meghan, the only people I know who have had any success with seeing the paranormal in that hotel are people who…well, are people who are sick. You know, terminally, and you look pretty healthy, so I don't want you to get your hopes up."

I rub my forehead roughly, trying to make sense of all her gibberish since the sick thing is yet another curveball. "So on top of having to get upstairs in some crazy, random stairwell-elevator pattern, you also have to be terminally ill?" I drop my arms to my side and look at her.

"Well, I'm not sure if *everyone* has to be, but the people I know who have seen anything have all been." She flicks the cigarette butt into the street then reaches for my hands. "Did you see her? Annie Moore?"

I once again consider lying, but at this point, I know I don't have that luxury. "Yes."

"Are you terminally ill?"

I shake my head. "No."

"Well, then, Meghan, you may be the first healthy person I help up to the thirteenth floor," she says with a sense of wonder and amazement.

For some reason, I'm not surprised I'm the first, but I suddenly get the sinking feeling I'm going to be the last.

"I think you somehow already know this," Michelle says, "but the thirteenth floor of the Bowery Hotel is a tear in the veil—a very, very rare place in the world where the living can enter a hallway that leads into hell."

A million questions pop into my mind and the hairs on the back of my neck stand on end. I gulp and try to process it all, but I can't seem to focus on any one thing and the most pressing question of all just keeps taking center stage. "So you know why there's a hallway to hell in the middle of a hotel in Manhattan?" I ask her, my voice remarkably steady even though I'm pretty close to having a nervous breakdown.

Michelle nods, seeming to understand I need quick and easy answers.

"And you know how to get me up there?"

She nods again.

"How?" I ask pointedly since none of it makes sense so I need it spelled out for me—like really simply. "How can you help me get up there if you can't get up there yourself?"

"I've figured out all the steps," she says as she spins me around so we're walking back in the opposite direction.

"Where are we going?" I ask while glancing over my shoulder to make sure Spencer is keeping up.

"Back to my car. I think you need to see my research."

I jerk her to a halt, which causes her to look at me wide-eyed. "I believe you," I assure her. "I don't need paperwork to prove that. What I need is to get up there..." I glance at Spencer, who's stopped by us, then I look back at Michelle.

"I know..." she says, her expression morphing into confusion. "I mean I don't know, but I do." She looks at Spencer. "*I've* still never had an encounter—no ghost sightings or goosebumps or dreams, but this whole thing, right here, with you and Spence. I don't know..." She looks back at me. "I haven't seen or heard anything before, but I'm suddenly getting this gut feeling to help you, so maybe *this* is my first experience..." She looks off into the distance, her gaze bouncing left to right in an erratic way that makes it seem as though she's watching an invisible tennis match on fast forward, then she sets her sights on me again. "Come on!" she says as she starts dragging me along.

I look over at Spencer, who gives me a nod of reassurance. "So, you're onboard with all of this?" I ask him, suddenly curious about his motivations.

"I am," he says as he keeps pace with us.

I jerk Michelle to a halt and then turn to square off with him. "Why?"

He smiles that warm smile I've grown to love and says, "Because I know I'm supposed to help you."

"How?"

"Because I dreamt it."

And with that resounding declaration, Michelle jerks me ahead, presumably toward her car, and then toward Destination Unknown.

22

THE LADY AND THE LAKE

Michelle doesn't only have a binder full of research; she also has boxes and boxes of it piled high in the trunk of her car. For about fifteen minutes, I listen to her explain all the different sections of her color-coded system. She seems pretty precise and organized. Of course, there's only so much stuff I can glance at as she riffles through pages of information about a Norse Goddess of Death named Hel, who's also known as the Lady of the Underworld. She's apparently the reason why the thirteenth floor exists.

My head is spinning with information overload when Spencer waves his phone in front of my face, probably because I'm so fried from my impromptu Norse mythology lesson that I didn't hear him calling my name.

"Hey," he says gently, "I hate to be the bearer of bad news, but Matt just texted. He wanted to know if I had gotten you into a cab yet."

I glance at the time and moan. It's ten to two. My coach has finally turned back into a pumpkin.

"This could work in our favor," Michelle says as she hands over a binder. Not her big one; this one is smaller, though not by much. "Here. Take this with you and try to look it over as much as you can before you come back tomorrow."

I look down at the binder with my jaw unhinged.

"We're still on for lunch though, right?" Spencer inquires.

"Yeah." I peel my gaze off the book to look at him. "Tomorrow—or I guess it would be today, at two."

He smiles. "Yup. It's a date."

"It's a date," I repeat, always amazed that even in all the craziness, I can get swept off my feet.

"Well, I'll head inside so you two lovebirds can say good-night. I'll see you tomorrow, maybe around four-ish?"

I nod. "I'll be here."

She winks, then slams the trunk shut, and lights another cigarette. "*Hasta manana, chica,*" she says, her Spanish accent definitely on point.

I wave and watch her saunter toward the hotel for a moment before I finally look up at Spencer. "She's…"

He chuckles. "Yeah. She's a lot of things. I tend to find myself using the word quirky a lot when I talk about her."

"Quirky," I repeat like I'm trying the word out. "I like it."

He starts to say something but stops himself short. "Shoot!" he says as he reaches for my hand. "Your flowers!"

Before I can even register a response, Spencer drags me along. In our haste, I fumble the notebook, but I thankfully recover it just as we make it to the hotel's entrance. Thankfully, he stops long enough to ask one of the doormen to grab me a cab before he ducks inside alone. I get the binder situated and have just caught my breath when Spencer returns, my bouquet, which is still submerged in the vase, is in his hand. I have no idea how I'm going to manage it and the binder, but before I even get a chance to solve that mystery, the other doorman lets us know my cab is waiting. I turn around to see him holding open the door for me.

Spencer gently places his hand on the small of my back

and guides me ahead. I slide onto the backseat, place the binder beside me, and reach for the flowers. Spencer kneels beside the cab and hands them to me. Once I get them situated in my lap, I look down at him. It's a bit trippy, given how tall he is. "Thanks again for these," I say, my voice a bit shaky since I suddenly realize this is goodbye, which usually means a kiss.

"I'm glad you like them."

Time seems to stand still, yet my heart races so quickly I'm scared it's going to beat out of my chest. I focus on my breathing since the last thing I need is to pass out during my first real kiss. If it ever even happens. Will he kiss me? I mean, what if *he* thinks *I* think it's too soon? Or what if he thinks I'm not interested? I realize I can't let that happen, because I want to kiss him. It's a first since I've spent my entire life fighting against my emotions because I've never wanted to make my mother's mistakes. I've never wanted to end up broken and bitter like her, so I've avoided love entirely, but now that it has found me, I don't want to let it slip through my fingers, because that would also fall under the top five of my mother's gravest mistakes—missed opportunities.

So *I* kiss Spencer.

He's just as surprised as I am.

I lean back enough to look into his eyes, my heart racing so hard I can hear every single pulse rushing through my ears.

Spencer smiles that lopsided smile I'm quickly falling in love with and then he kisses me. Slowly. Deeply.

It takes my breath away.

When he leans back, it's my turn to smile.

"See you tomorrow?" he asks.

It's definitely a rhetorical question, but I nod anyway. In return, he smiles, then after playfully tapping my nose, he stands tall and gives the taxi driver Matt's address and a twenty. I sit there, feeling totally star struck. I watch as he closes the door and stands on the curb waving to me as we drive off. I wave back and then lean back in my seat and let out a long sigh. *Wow.* My lips tingle all the way to the apartment and I'm practically floating on cloud nine when I get upstairs.

That's when reality starts to sink back in. I had somehow managed to pin the binder against my body with my arm in a way that I could still carry the bouquet. With a doorman and an easy elbow-push elevator button, getting upstairs had been a breeze. Now, though, I need the keys out of my pocket. I go to set the vase on the floor but nearly drop them when Matt pulls the door open, startling me.

"Hey," he says, his expression morose; his voice grave.

As I take in the sadness etched onto his face, I instinctively take a step back. All my joy vanishes and dread replaces it. Fear starts coursing through my veins.

Matt reaches for the vase, almost as if he can tell my fingers have started to go numb. His movement causes the apartment door to slip open just enough for me to catch sight of him. Officer Jesse Dunbar. One of Middletown's finest here in New York City, at a little past two in the morning. His face is just as distraught as Matt's—a clear sign he isn't here on a social call.

The adhesive tape that's been holding my heart together rips.

I shove past Matt and push the door open the rest of the way. Phil and Grammy Anne are sitting on the couch, my sisters sandwiched between them. Tears are streaming down all of their faces.

No one says a word. No one has to.

They've found my mom, and she's dead.

————

The next few days go by in a blur, and I think the only reason I make it through each day is because of my sisters. I can't completely fall apart because they need me. The grief and anguish they both display are heart wrenching and sobering. Mom is gone. She's dead. She'll never set foot in our apartment again. She'll never try to make pancakes that she'll ultimately burn on the outside but are somehow raw on the inside. She'll never laugh again. She'll never yell at us for misbehaving.

Over the next couple of days, I watch as everyone goes through the motions of grieving. A part of me appreciates each instance because it gives me the opportunity to cry with them for a moment before I have to pull it together to pack boxes and sort through what goes to the Salvation Army versus into the trash. Uncle Rusty's been helping me go through the apartment and he's offered to store anything we want to keep. For now, I haven't been able to bring myself to go into my mother's room. I have a feeling most of that stuff will end up in storage though since I know I won't have the heart to get rid of it.

There's also a funeral to plan. Thankfully, I have Matt's help on that one, and Phil's grandmother has been pitching in with everything, even the costs since I've learned the hard way that funerals are very expensive. Naturally, my mother hadn't made any arrangements, so as in death as in life, Uncle Rusty volunteered to cover all the costs, but there are flowers and photos and mementos that are involved. Who knew there was so much to do in order to send someone off to the afterlife? So, I help where I can, like with picking out the best pictures to display at the wake, and by compiling her favorite playlist, but I leave the heavy lifting stuff to the adults because everyone wants me to just worry about the girls and packing.

Because we have to move.

Uncle Rusty volunteered to keep us until we finish the school year, which would have given Matt some more time to become adjusted to his role as a permanent, fulltime father, but Matt insists he's ready. He arranged to have the next ten days off from work and in that time, he plans to get us moved out and settled in our new lives in New York. I wanted more than anything to stay so I could graduate with my class. Granted, Phil is my only real friend, but the thought of leaving makes me feel sick to my stomach, which seems ironic given that all I've ever wanted is to get out of this one-horse town.

Despite that, for a second, I had even considered taking up Grammy Anne on her offer to stay with them, just long enough for me to graduate, but even though she also offered to keep the girls until the end of the school year too, Matt politely declined. He argued that the girls need stability right now, and he's right. So as much as I'd like to finally be selfish for once in my life, I can't be. They need me right now. They need our little family to remain as intact as much as it possibly can, because come July I'll also be gone.

Sergeant Hodges stopped by one day to pay her respects, and while she didn't stay long or get into anything specific, she did mention that everything could wait until me and the girls were settled. I got the impression there was a hidden message in there, but she didn't stick around long enough to explain and I have no intention of asking because I'm still going into the Air Force. I won't miss this opportunity no matter how much I would like to stay in Manhattan—because a huge part of me wants to stay now. I have so many reasons. But I can't. Because at some point after learning that my mother had been murdered and her body had been dumped in a lake, I've had one nagging, resounding thought. *Follow your dreams.* It makes no sense. I should be mourning. I should want to stay home now to protect my sisters. I should be too scared of the big, bad world, but somehow, now more than ever, I want to go.

Follow your dreams, Peanut. It's something my mom used to tell me all the time, and I can't shake the feeling she's still saying it even though I haven't "really" heard from her since our encounter in the lobby of the Bowery. Could finding her body have cut off our communication? I mean, I haven't heard a thing. Even the heart-shaped message in our bathroom is gone, but I'm sure she's still with me now—somehow. I think the key is for me to get back to the Bowery. Mom is there, on the thirteenth floor. I can feel it.

In between packing and taking care of the girls, I've been reading Michelle's book. It's a collection of the research she's compiled about the goddess Hel. A lot of it is academic stuff, but there's also a huge section of data that she's gathered from pagan websites and bloggers. There are spells, incantations, and invocations, and while I was initially hesitant to reach out to her and Spencer, once I did, and we got the awkward condolences out of the way, we've been back and forth. It's my first official group chat and given the circumstances, it's a bit overwhelming, especially because Michelle likes to send a lot of links. They're helpful, but it's hard for me to wrap my head around most of the history and the lore, because according to Michelle, what truly triggered the opening of the veil isn't written down anywhere. It's her firsthand account of the events and she refuses to send that information over text, and there's never a good time for her to call, so I have no choice but to wait until I get back to the city. Sunday seems impossibly far away.

In the meantime, I still spend a lot of time in the bathroom with the hot water running, hoping Mom reaches out with another message. The radio silence is killing me, and it always makes me go back to wondering if finding her has somehow interfered with the signal. Her body had been submerged in Harrison Lake. That thought always makes it feels as though a dagger has been plunged into my heart, but as much as I don't want to think of my mother's body being tossed into a lake, another part of me can't stop thinking about it. Maybe that's why she was able to use the steam to communicate?

Of course, it's a question I'm sure I won't get an answer to, and with the funeral only a day away, it's a theory I don't have time to indulge in. The girls are a wreck, so I can't stay holed up in the bathroom for long most times. Instead, I just go through the motions, reading Michelle's book when I can and trying to hold it together. The only thought that gets me through is that Mom is still with us. I can't prove it, and with every passing day it feels more and more like a pipe dream, but I won't lose hope—not until I get back to Manhattan and try to reach her at the Bowery. She's still there waiting for me. Or at least I hope so.

23

THE BIG APPLE

The Sunday after my mother's funeral, we arrive at Matt's apartment. It almost doesn't feel any different than the other times we've come down for a visit, so as I lug heavy suitcases through the hallway, I actually have to remind myself this is permanent. Mom is dead, and I'll probably only go back to Middletown once or twice to pick up paperwork from our schools and doctor's offices. Uncle Rusty, Grammy Anne, and Phil have assured me they'll help clean everything up for our apartment's final inspection, so no one expects me to rush back up there for anything. Manhattan is my home now, at least for the next couple of months, and it's where my little sisters will officially live.

They won't move out to join me after I'm done with my technical school. I know Matt won't let that happen, and the more I think about it, the more I realize they're going to be okay here. It's going to be a big adjustment, but after watching Matt with them this week and seeing how he's prepared, I'm not worried the way I used to be—with Mom.

If that isn't the saddest reflection I've ever had then I don't know what is.

Thankfully, the clamor inside the apartment distracts me from that depressing thought. It's good to hear the girls' laughter and it's even better to see them genuinely happy. Matt had pulled a rabbit out of his hat by having our bedroom transformed over the past week. If you ask me, I'd say it had Annabelle's name written all over it, but Matt won't admit that to me. Not that I asked. It was my way of letting him know I respect his privacy, and I'm hoping he returns the favor. I mean, he clearly knows that I'm still interested in visiting the Bowery, and he knows it isn't only to visit Spencer and Michelle, which is the story I've given the girls. They believe me. Matt does not, but he hasn't called me on anything, and when I asked if I could meet Spencer and Michelle this evening for dinner, he didn't object. Nor did he question me. He simply told me to be home by ten.

I had readily agreed because I didn't want to push my luck. We all have to be up early tomorrow since we have to go to our new schools. We don't start until Tuesday, but I'm still anxious. I've never been one on meeting new people, especially when I know it's bound to be awkward. No one transfers at practically the end of their senior year without a damn good reason, and once people find out why I have, I'm going to be the grand recipient of a lot of pity. It's definitely a new experience, but not one that's entirely different from the contempt I've received all my life. Both instances suck. I can't wait until I finally leave for the Air Force and only have to answer to people's attitudes for my own deeds, because it sure does suck to go through life always having to pay for someone else's sins.

As I help the girls unpack their belongings, I try not to think about the bad stuff from our past. Instead, I focus on all the good memories and the ones we're making every day. The new furniture Matt had gotten definitely helps. Before, the room had been a weird combination of a man cave and a guest bedroom. On one side, there had been a small entertainment center for a TV and gaming console, and an old futon Matt had lugged around for years that I used to sleep on whenever I came down with the girls. On the other side of the room, there had been a standard-issue Walmart-grade bunkbed for the girls. Now, the room had a fresh coat of lavender and soft yellow paint, the girls' favorite colors, and an entire corner of the room has been dedicated to an elaborate double loft-style bunkbed unit with desks underneath. It's seriously the most gorgeous piece of furniture I've ever seen and it's perfectly decorated—almost like something you'd see in the showroom or in some home-decorating magazine, with pretty, frilly comforters and throw pillows dressing the beds, and pictures of hazy, cheery-looking landscapes hanging on the walls. On the built-in shelves underneath the beds, there are cute knick-knacks that the girls are bound to fight over, and on each desk, there's a laptop. The home makeover is enough to cheer them right up and I think the fresh start has definitely set the mood for all the good things in store for them.

For me, Matt's beat-up futon has been replaced with a raised twin bed atop a couple of drawers. The piece of furniture is simple, but with the bunkbeds, it's a tight fit. I told Matt a blow-up mattress would have been fine, seeing as how I'm only going to be here a few months, but he assured me it's okay—and that he wanted me to feel just as at home. I don't think that's ever going to be possible. My mother wasn't the best mom in the world, but there's never been a time in my life I didn't live with her, and I'm starting to get the feeling no place will truly ever feel like home without her.

That resounding thought lingers as I help the girls hang their clothes in the closet. They're super excited about going down to the storage unit now to get the box with their shoes so they can use the cool, hanging shoe racks we discovered, so I let them go down with Matt so I can unpack my bags and take a moment to try to shake off the sadness. I can't seem to figure out the ebbs and flows of the waves of grief that over-come me and I wonder if it will ever go away. But do you ever truly recover from the loss of your parent, especially when they died in a horrific, violent way?

The words "blunt-force trauma" suddenly come to mind, and then the words "weighted down" ricochet through my brain like some kind of out-of-control ping-pong ball. They're words I overheard during the past week, whispers of conversa-tions I couldn't ignore—and now those words haunt me at the weirdest times, and they often cause the most awful mental images to surface. Like my mom wrapped up in some cheap blanket with weights tied around her ankles and neck. The police still haven't been able to determine how long she had been underwater, but it was long enough to warrant a closed-casket funeral. No one was allowed to see what was left of her so I had picked out my favorite picture of her and we had framed it so that it rested upon her casket. I walk over to my backpack now, since it had been one of the last things I had packed earlier today. My mom's picture.

I pull it out of my bag and study it for a long moment. Her blue eyes were sparkling that day, and her hair had been perfectly curled, and she was smiling that soft smile of hers. She had won the glamour shot one day at the mall and they had captured her natural, pure beauty perfectly. I know it wasn't the way she looked when they found her, but it's the way I wanted everyone to remember her. Happy. Smiling. Sweet. I run a finger over the picture, outlining her cheek, then I turn to look at the girls' new bunkbed unit. There's a corner drawer unit that's right between their desks, so I place the frame on one of the shelves. After adjusting it a bit so it's centered, I step back to look over my handiwork. It's perfect, and it somehow makes this place feel just a little bit more like home.

———

Even on a Sunday evening, the Bowery is hopping. I had expected it to be slow, or at least slow enough so we could grab a bite to eat at Gemma's without too much fear of anyone overhearing Michelle's huge revelation. Thankfully, she had known to prepare for a quieter place to gather, so I follow her and Spencer down to the basement with a bit of a bounce in my step. I'm equally excited *and* petrified to finally hear about the Bowery's haunted past.

Michelle leads us through a maze of hallways and into the shipping and receiving area. There's a ton of open space for people to maneuver pallets and such, but in the corner of the room, there's a small, enclosed office. From the shipping and receiving area, the office doesn't look that big, but upon arriving inside, I'm surprised to see there are four desks in each corner of the room, the nameplates indicating that one belongs to the shipping and receiving manager, another to the supervisor, and the other two for the clerks. In the center of the room is a long, narrow rectangular table with four chairs on either side and two others at each end of the table. Michelle makes her way to one of those chairs and motions for us to join. Spencer takes the seat to her left; I take the one to her right.

With each of us settled, Spencer, who's been carrying the bag with our meals, starts unpacking. We each had gotten huge take-out containers of pasta and an entire loaf of garlic bread to share. As Spencer hands out plasticware, Michelle passes around our drinks. I sit there, feeling bad that I didn't help with anything, though, in my defense, they clearly had all this planned.

"Did you bring the book?" Michelle asks as she pops off the lid of her take-out container.

I nod. "Yes." I shrug off my backpack, set it on the chair next to mine, and reach in for the binder. "Thank you for this.

It's exactly the way you gave it to me." I go to hand it to her, but she shakes her head.

"Hang onto that," she says just before stuffing her face with a mouthful of pasta. "You'll need it later," she adds, though I don't know how she manages it, given the amount of food she's chewing on.

I set the binder aside and take a moment to study Spencer. He's eating just as heartily and doesn't seem the least bit awkward about seeing me again. In fact, when I had first arrived, he'd greeted me at the door and given me a huge hug. It was nice, and Michelle's greeting had been just as warm. Neither had mentioned my mother or asked about the funeral, which I'm oddly grateful for. I mean, I'm sure it has a lot to do with the time crunch—the hotel is busy and they only get a thirty-minute break, but it helped ease my anxiety over seeing them again. Now, I'm just anxious to finally hear what Michelle has to say.

"I'm sorry about your mom," Michelle says. "I can't imagine what you're going through and I know all of this is only making it harder."

By "all of this" I'm sure she means the Bowery.

"Listen, I know firsthand how there's nothing you can say to someone during this time that doesn't get kind of awkward," Michelle continues, "so if you don't mind, I'd love to just jump right in and let you know what happened with Macy and Marigold."

I'm not sure why I look at Spencer first, but I do. He's still eating, but he's looking at me now. He gives a slight nod of his head, which I somehow know is his way of supporting and comforting me, so I look back to Michelle and nod, encouraging her to continue.

In response, she takes another huge bite of food. After washing it down with a healthy swig of sweet tea, she begins. "I've been trying to figure out the best way to tell you everything without confusing you." She takes a much smaller bite of her food now, her attention acutely focused on the pasta before her, almost as if she can't look at me as she recounts her tale. "I think the best way is to go all the way back to when Macy's dad was infected—"

"Infected?" I echo, since the word catches me completely off guard.

"Not infected," Michelle corrects quickly. "Sorry. I guess contracted would work better. He had a rare kidney disorder so he needed a transplant." She looks up at me then. "But this was back in the late eighties so he was lucky enough to find a donor. Unfortunately, he was one of the unlucky ones to get a tainted organ."

My heart sinks even though that thankfully doesn't happen anymore, but with my mom's propensity for sex, drugs, and rock n' roll, I'm well aware of the dangers of HIV and AIDS. Mom had a few close calls, and I remember the long weeks of waiting for results. It's one of the only times I wished someone could "fail," since, at least to me, it's ironic that being diagnosed as "negative" is a good thing.

"Sadly," Michelle continues, "with how frail his health had been before the transplant, it didn't take long for the doctors to figure out what had happened."

She seems to give me a moment to digest that.

"Unfortunately, between that diagnosis and his abrupt decline in health, he infected Marigold. Macy's mom."

My stomach clenches upon hearing that news. How awful.

"With his poor health, he didn't even make it two years." She spears a fork full of pasta, but she just stares at it. "Of course, I didn't know any of this when I met her in middle school, and by then, her mom was end-stage, you know, and she was..." Michelle shrugs. "It wasn't good. And it didn't help that she was just coming into her own and she didn't understand why, on top of everything, she was so different..."

From the bits and pieces she's mentioned before, I get the feeling Michelle means Macy was confused about her sexuality.

"I've always known what I am," Michelle says, confirming my suspicion between small bites of food, "and I was lucky enough to have my mom, who I think knew I was gay before I did and who supported me my entire life." She snickers at that for some reason. "So, at first I kind of thought it was fate that brought me and Macy together because I could tell she was struggling with her truths and I wanted to help."

While Michelle seems to reminisce on those memories, I finally unwrap my plasticware. I'm not the least bit hungry, but I don't want to rush her, not when this is clearly difficult for her to discuss.

"Anyway," Michelle says on a sigh, "as we got to know each other, one thing led to another, and we went from friends to —" She blushes. "Anyway," she repeats, and starts again, "during that time, her mom got sicker and sicker, and we had no idea what was going to happen to Macy because she had no family. I mean, she had her dad's side of the family, but he had died when she was only three. They had shunned her mother as if she was some sort of pariah, so she didn't want to go with them, but her mother had no family."

Michelle falls silent again so I go back to picking at my food while trying to make sense of everything. Her ex-girlfriend's story is a real tear-jerker, so I understand why it's so difficult for Michelle to share it, but I can't for the life of me figure out how this tragic tale has anything to do with the haunted thirteenth floor of the hotel.

"Then one day, out of the clear blue, Macy's uncle showed up," Michelle says.

I look up and our eyes meet for one intense second before I say, "But...I thought she had no other family?"

"Exactly," Michelle says. "Apparently no one knew about

him because Macy's grandfather had an affair decades earlier and it had taken the guy that long to find Marigold."

"I see," I say, even though I don't understand at all, but that all sounds eerily convenient.

Michelle drops her fork and pushes her plate aside. "Okay, so this is where I have to start filling in some blanks because this is the stuff I'm not entirely certain of." She sits back in her seat. "See, when we were kids, we just knew that her long-lost half-uncle shows up like some knight in shining armor because he's spent all his life looking for his family and he's just glad he found Macy's mom before she died."

"Okay…?" I say, desperately trying to follow.

"Her uncle, Wade, was loaded—had amassed a small fortune with an online start-up company, and of course, when he found Marigold, he offered to take Macy in."

She says that like it's a bad thing, but I see no dark clouds, just silver linings.

"Not that it wasn't great," Michelle adds after reading my confused expression, "because it was. I mean, my mom had offered to take her in but she couldn't really afford that, so even though I was heartbroken to see her go and super disappointed that she wouldn't move in with us, I was happy, 'cause it looked like everything was perfect now. I mean, her mom was at the end, you know, but her uncle seemed great and he had a huge place down in Philly, and so it was all really bittersweet."

When Michelle falls silent again, I look at Spencer.

He seems to understand my confusion, because he says, "Michelle was able to help Macy through the hard time of her mother's passing, and then she helped her pack up everything so she could move to Philly with her uncle."

I look between them. "That's…" *Well.* I don't know what that is. "So…was she okay? I mean, aside from her loss…"

"Yeah," Michelle says, finally finding her voice. "Or at least it seemed that way. I mean, we kept in touch for a while, but you know how it goes. She moved down there and came into her own and she blossomed." She shrugs. "I was happy for her, and everything seemed to be going great for her, so when we started to drift apart, I was okay with it, and after a while, you know, we lost touch. We just had two completely separate lives so aside from the occasional social media stuff, I didn't…"

I catch sight of the grief that passes across her delicate features and my stomach sinks again because I recognize that expression. It's the shadow of death. Once it touches you, it leaves an indelible mark on your soul that its other victims can spot from a thousand miles away. Without consciously registering it, I reach over and place my hand over hers.

In response, Michelle turns her hand to hold mine, but she keeps her eyes fixed on the half-eaten bowl before her. "Nearly ten years ago, Macy drove back to New York, made her way to the roof of the Bowery, and jumped."

My blood runs cold.

"I was having what I thought was a horrible day, so I was at some dive bar in the Bronx when I caught the story on the news." She snickers again, this time with a telltale sniffle. "The headline read, 'Girl from Philly Jumps to her Death.' And in that instant, I knew it was her. I just…felt it…" She looks off into the distance. "And then I went online and confirmed it. Macy had committed suicide and I didn't know why. I couldn't wrap my brain around it, not when everything had turned around for her. I mean, she was at a freaking Ivy League school! She had everything to live for, or at least I had thought so…"

Michelle drifts off into another bout of silence, so I look to Spencer, hoping he'll pick up where she left off again.

"She thinks that's the night the thirteenth floor appeared," he says softly. "The night that Macy died…"

I look between them, so beyond confused, but I'm also

glaringly aware of how distraught Michelle is over reliving these events. It's something that, up until a week ago, I wouldn't have understood, but now I do, so I sit and wait.

"Macy's mother made a deal with a devil," Michelle finally says, her voice devoid of emotion, her eyes shifting over empty spaces on the opposite wall like she's watching some invisible film. "Marigold sacrificed her soul to make sure Macy was taken care of, but something went wrong...something..." Tears spill onto her cheeks. "Macy somehow knew, and she could never shake the guilt of her mother spending an eternity in hell for her sake." Michelle swipes at the tears on her cheek, but they're only replaced by new ones. "So she did the one thing she thought would save her..."

"She jumped," I say, unable to hold back the reflexive response.

Michelle nods. "And when she did, she ripped such a big hole in the veil that it opened a doorway to hell."

24

ONWARD & UPWARD

When Michelle leaves to smoke a cigarette before she has to head back to work and Spencer excuses himself to use the restroom, I sit back in my seat and sigh. *Wow.* That was a lot to take in, so I'm having a hard time processing everything. The short of it is this: Macy somehow figured out her mother made a deal with the devil in order to make sure she was safe and taken care of after Marigold died. If you ask me, it's a noble deed, but I totally get why Macy would feel guilt-ridden for that. Would I be okay with my mother spending an eternity in hell for me? No, and now that the notion of that scenario exists, I can't help but wonder if that's something I need to worry about now too.

Is that why Mom is here? Had she made a deal with the devil for us? I mean, everything really has started to fall into place for us, which is exactly what happened to Macy...

At this point, there's only one way to find out for sure, and thankfully I know how. I reach for the binders that Michelle had left stacked on the table. With the time crunch, she hadn't been able to go through everything as much as I would have liked, but I at least know the story—or at least the version of it that Michelle has spent over a decade painstak-ingly compiling. As far as Michelle could tell, since she only had her memories of the events and a box of research and a diary she had found in Macy's bedroom after her funeral, she suspected that in her desperation, Marigold had started dabbling in stuff she didn't fully understand. With her time being short, though, she had resorted to trying anything and everything to make sure her daughter would be okay after she was gone.

According to Macy's diary, she vividly recalled the night her mom had come home from the Bowery. She had written it had been the first time she had seen her mother at peace, and after that night, no matter how sick she got, her mother's relief never dissipated. She kept telling Macy everything was going to be all right now, and when her Uncle Wade showed up, Marigold didn't seem at all surprised. It was almost as if she had been expecting him all along.

It was then that Macy began to suspect something, but it wasn't until years later, when she came back to New York for her senior class trip that she learned about the Bowery's haunted history. After that point, it became an obsession for her, and she had spent the next two years learning as much as she could about it. In her diary, she wrote of her visits to the hotel. She detailed her experiences as she attempted the elevator game. She chronicled her theories as they evolved with each new discovery. In the end, though, she was unable to crack the code, and it drove her mad. In her delicate frame of mind, the only solution was to prove the devil wrong—to show him that she hadn't lived happily ever after despite his best efforts—and what says that more than taking your own life? Happy people don't commit suicide, and so Macy jumped to her death, and it seems she was right. From that day on, the reports of apparition sightings and paranormal activity in the hotel spiked. Several unnatural deaths occurred, and several other people were able to cross the veil and come back to talk about it.

That's when Michelle had stepped in. She felt as though she had somehow failed Marigold and Macy, so she picked up where Macy had left off. She's spent the last ten years trying to figure it out and she's almost positive she's got it. She just needs to find someone willing to listen to her theory, and someone crazy enough to try it.

As I reach for the binder with the invocation to summon the goddess Hel, Spencer comes back into the office. "Hey," he says as he takes the seat next to mine. "Sorry about that. I just ran upstairs to ask if I could take a few extra minutes. I kind of thought maybe you had some more questions…" He shrugs. "I mean, I can't really answer too much stuff, but I know how overwhelming all of it is. And I'm sure it's even harder for you…"

I go back to leaning in my chair so I can really look him over. He's been so quiet today, and, really, for the entire time I've known him. He's always deferred to Michelle taking the lead, but he's like a dutiful puppy. "Why are you helping us so much?" I ask, realizing that he probably can't answer most of my questions, but he can shed some light on some of my deepest concerns.

Spencer sits back, almost as if he's been expecting this question all along. "I told you, I dreamt about this." He places his elbows on his knees and starts kneading his hands. "When I started working here in August, I started having these dreams…about you…"

He looks at me. Our gazes lock for a long moment, then I look away. I'm speechless.

"It was always the same dream," he continues. "Me and you on the Fourth of July. At first, I had them every couple of weeks, and I remember thinking it must have been from a movie I had seen but didn't remember, because it was like…

you know, in my mom's musicals—all romantic and kind of cheesy."

I dare a glance and see he's blushing. To help spare him some of the embarrassment, I try to steer the conversation in a better direction. "You said you saw us...on the Fourth of July?"

He nods. "Yeah. Always the same scene. Me and you at the Macy's fireworks celebration." He reaches for my hand.

I take it and squeeze, trying to reassure him that I don't think he's cheesy or crazy.

"After I got to know Michelle and she told me about the hotel's history, I started to think maybe those dreams of us weren't about some long-forgotten Hallmark movie, and then, right before you came down on your birthday, I started dreaming about another woman..." He squeezes my hand. "Well, not dreams...they were more like...nightmares." He peeks at me, but then quickly looks away. "And she was a bit... frantic. Like she knew she only had a few seconds in each of my dreams to communicate."

My heart skips several beats and the grief I've managed to ignore for the past few hours begins to creep back into my veins. "What did she say?"

"She just kept saying that when you got here to help you, and then when you left, to take care of you and the girls."

I wish I can control the tears that spring into my eyes.

"I'm sorry, Meg...at the time I didn't know what she meant, and I didn't immediately put you and her together. I mean, with us, in *our* dream, you're so happy. We're happy. It's beautiful, but with her..." He pulls his hand out of mine and roughly rubs his face. "But then after you left the hotel last week, I came back inside to grab my stuff and say goodnight... I went through my normal routine and when I went to the bathroom, she was in there."

I gasp as my heart skips a few painful beats. "By the sink?" I assume.

He nods. "And when I saw her there—like for real, in *real* life. At the hotel. I knew it was your mom. The resemblance was so obvious then, and when she repeated the message, it all finally made sense." He looks at me, tears in his eyes. "I swear I didn't know it was her before, and after I found out, I wanted to call you, but I didn't know what to say…"

For a moment, *I* don't know what to do or say. Then I reach for his hands. "It's okay."

"I'm sorry about your mom, Meg," he says solemnly.

I tear up at that, but I swallow over the lump in my throat. "Thank you."

"In my dreams, she always disappeared before I could respond, but when she was here, I had a chance to answer her, and I told her I would help you now and always."

The tears I've desperately tried to hold at bay spill over onto my cheeks.

"And she smiled," he whispers softly, then he pulls me in for a hug.

I collapse into his arms and for the first time since they found her, I cry. And while I hate breaking down in front of him, it's also oddly comforting. There's just something about Spencer that's familiar and calming, so even though I've only known him for a short time, and under such odd, horrific circumstances, I know there's no one else I'd rather be with in this moment. So, I cry, and then I sniffle, and finally, I just sit in the comfort of his embrace. A part of me wants to stay there forever, but I know time is of the essence. Mom is waiting for me, and I'm more than ready to find her now.

When I lean back, Spencer wipes my cheeks with his thumbs and then kisses my forehead. I smile up at him and excuse myself so I can go and clean up a bit. A nose-blowing is definitely in order, along with a hardy face-washing. After getting directions, I quickly make my way to the bathroom and attempt to straighten myself up. I blow my nose. I wash my face. I slide some Chapstick onto my lips. I rack my fingers through my hair, which I had parted down the middle and left loose. Then I step back to examine my handiwork. I look halfway decent. My face is still puffy, but only time can fix that, so I'm as cleaned up as I'm going to get. I smooth my hand over my hair one last time before I go, but then I realize the obvious. I'm in a bathroom *in* the Bowery Hotel. I reach for the hot water and let it run, the steam billowing quickly and fogging the mirror. I wait. And then I wait some more. No invisible fingerprints against the glass. No heart-shaped message forms.

"Mom?" I whisper as I search around the room. It isn't big. Just large enough for a handicap and single stall. I walk over to the smaller unit and push the door open. Nothing. Just a toilet. "Mom?" I call again. I shift over and push open the door on the handicap stall. It's just as empty. I turn back around, expecting her to be by the sink now, but she isn't. The bathroom is empty. The mirror has no message.

Disappointed, I walk over, turn off the water, then make my way back to the shipping and receiving area. As I near the office, Spencer pulls open the door.

"Oh, hey," he says, smiling, "I was just coming to check on you." He steps back and pulls the door open farther so I can slip by.

"Sorry, I just…" I stop to look up at him, trying to find the right words. "I…" But I stop short again, this time because Spencer's attention shifts to something behind me. His expression, though new and unfamiliar to me, seems to be the epitome of confusion.

"Can I help you, ma'am?" he asks the mystery person.

I turn around and then nearly fall over when I spot her. It's Annie Moore. She's standing across the room, by the loading dock, looking right at me with those fathomless, dark, beady eyes. I instinctively take a backward step and crash into Spencer. In turn, he grips both of my arms and holds me steady.

"It's Annie," I whisper to him, so he knows why I'm so frightened.

For her part, Annie adds to the creepy ambiance by not saying a word. Instead, she starts walking down the hallway, her image jerky and fading in and out of focus, like a proper ghost. My blood starts to run cold again and I shiver. In response, Spencer's grip tightens around my arms. I can feel him shaking. As scared as I am, though, I know I have to follow her, because she's here to help me. I turn and hurry into the office.

"What are you doing?" Spencer asks from the doorway.

I flip the appropriate binder open, scramble to the page, and then rip out the copy of the Invocation to Hela. "I have to follow her."

"But—"

"It's time," I say even though I wish it weren't. I'm scared, and the normal, rational part of my brain wants me to run in the opposite direction, but I can't. Mom is waiting. I glance down at the other binder. All Michelle's notes are in there, but I don't think I need anything else aside from the knowledge she shared, which I quickly go over again in my mind.

Marigold had snuck into the hotel through the shipping-and-receiving dock. She had used the stairs to avoid coming into contact with anyone so no one could question why she was here, but she had been sick—really sick—so she couldn't make it all the way up to the thirteenth floor on her own. Michelle thinks she made it as far as the second, then she used the elevator for the rest of the way. Naturally, there's no way to tell how the events actually unfolded, but Michelle is sure that, at some point, Marigold had read the invocation, because the original piece of paper is what had tipped Macy off all those years ago.

According to Macy's diary, Marigold had come home that night talking to her about the peace she had found at the Bowery. Macy had dismissed it all, sure it was just the ranting of her mother's fever-sick mind, but the next morning, when she was doing laundry, she discovered the crumpled up, bloodied sheet of paper in her pocket. For some reason, she had kept it, and when she came back to New York years later, she had it with her. The police had returned it to Macy's uncle the day after she died. The bag of her personal effects was placed in her room in Philadelphia, where Michelle found it after she had attended the funeral. She has the original safely tucked away in a sheet protector. I have a photocopy, which I'm hoping will be enough to get me where I need to be.

I turn to face Spencer. "Are you sure you want to do this? I promise I won't hold it against you if you want to leave."

He seems to consider that for exactly one second, then he holds his hand out to me. I ignore it, but only so I can walk over to hug him. He squeezes me just as tightly, my cheek pressed against his chest, my heart, while racing, also feeling oddly at peace. I revel in the moment for a second longer, then I back away from him. Our eyes lock, but neither of us says anything. Instead, he reaches for my free hand and we start walking down the hallway.

Annie is nearly to the other side of it by the time we make our way there. She blinks in and out of focus but seems to solidify when she stops to face the stairwell entrance. My heart races as I watch her head slowly pivot so she can set those beady eyes on me. She lifts her arm and points at the stairwell door.

I look up at Spencer. His skin has gone pale; his eyes practically bugging out of his head. A part of me wants to let go of his hand here; to spare him from the horrors I'm certain to face, but I know he won't let me proceed alone, and I don't want to, so I pull him along as I make my way to Annie. She watches me the entire time, the blank, faraway look in her eyes making my already upset stomach tie up in knots.

When we make it to her, she finally looks away, her attention on the stairwell door. With a slight hand gesture, the door blasts open, scaring me and Spencer so badly we both yelp. Annie, who remains expressionless the entire time, walks ahead. I can only assume she wants us to follow, so we do. She climbs the stairs at a slow but steady pace. We pass the first floor in silence, but as we round the flight of steps to the second floor, Spencer leans closer to me.

"This is where Michelle thinks Marigold stopped," he whispers. "Because it's the floor where sick people say they see the lady in white."

I glance up at him, grateful for the information—though, I have to say I don't like that he's back in tour-guide mode when we're probably on our way to hell.

Annie makes it to the landing first and turns to face us. Now, though, she's holding two vials in each hand. I study the murky dark liquid within the glass as we take the last few steps up.

"The Goddess will only respond to the infirmed," she says, her low, gravelly voice sending such a powerful chill through Spencer that I can feel it through our joined hands.

Annie holds a vial toward each of us.

Spencer takes his vial with his free hand.

I'm not as quick to oblige. "What is that?"

Naturally, Annie has nothing to add to her cryptic message, though in all fairness, Michelle's handy-dandy guide to all things Norse Mythology and Hel had prepared me for at least this much. Hel is the Ruler of the Underworld. She's the receiver of all those who die of sickness and old age, so the message isn't entirely cryptic—but the black yucky stuff in that vial sure is. Despite its mystery though, I release Spencer's hand and take the offering.

"Drink," she orders.

Spencer and I look at each other, and then, on a silent count to three, we both swallow down the amazingly sweet, fruity concoction. A second ticks by, us staring at each other, waiting for something to happen. Nothing does. I feel fine, aside from the racing pulse and adrenaline, then without warning, Spencer drops, his body collapsing onto the cement floor; the vial smashing as it crashes down the steps.

"Spencer!" I shout as I drop beside him. I tap his cheek. "Spencer!" When he doesn't respond, I look up at Annie. "What did you do to him?"

"This is as far as his journey will take him tonight," she says as she reaches for the invocation I had dropped. "You, on the other hand, must hurry."

I glance down at Spencer. "Will he be okay?"

"Yes." She walks over and holds the paper right in front of me. "But you will not be if you take too long."

"What's that—" I cough, more violently than I ever have in my life. The round of spasms sends jolts of pain up to my head and down to my toes. I heave in a huge breath in between fits, but it isn't enough oxygen. I nearly cough myself to death right there next to Spencer, the pain so intense that black spots dance before my eyes, and blood speckles the floor.

"What...did...you...do...to...me?" I somehow manage to ask.

Annie painfully grips onto my arm and pulls me onto my feet. I almost stumble over, but she pins me against the wall. "Cough into your hand," she orders.

I want to ask her what for, but I can't because the pain that's gripping my entire body is so intense that all I really want is to die—that's the only way I know the pain will go away.

"You are dying," Annie says in a stern voice, "your organs are all failing, so listen to me and listen good because I don't get my just desserts if you crook on me. Cough into your damn hand and then slap it onto this wall."

I do as I'm told, and I'm appalled to see the amount of blood that splatters onto my palm.

"Now read," she orders, holding the invocation in front of me.

I can barely see so I try to focus on the words, but I can't. My head is throbbing and my eyes are bleeding, the red haze a surefire sign of that.

"Read it!" Annie yells, the lightbulbs blowing out overhead for all her effort.

I start to cry. The simple act of it surprises me because it seems like such an odd reaction given my circumstances. Crying because I'm scared, when in reality, I'm dying, but that's what I start to do, and amazingly enough, it helps clear my vision. I see the words despite the darkness, and I feel the hope despite my despair. With a voice that defies my weakened state, I read the Invocation to Hela, each utterance and syllable causing the ground to quake beneath my feet. Yet, I never lose sight of the words or of my hold on the wall. I read the invocation to the end, and when I'm done and Annie drags me through the stairwell door leading into the second-floor hallway, I follow without a fight. I want to know if Spencer's okay, but I also know I'm running out of time. I can feel my body failing.

I stumble behind Annie toward Destination Unknown, sometimes falling, sometimes having to stop to cough. Each time, she lifts me up, and then after a few more unsteady steps, she resorts to carrying me. My head dangles and bobs, but my bloody eyes are still able to capture haunting images of what's happening in the rooms, each door wide open so I can see I'm not in the hotel anymore—I can't be, not with all the horribly strange, vile things I glimpse along the way.

"Here we are," Annie says, then a familiar dinging sound fills the air. "Elevator up to hell." She steps into the small space and sets me on the bench.

My head lolls to the side and I catch a glimpse of a lady in white standing in front of the control panel.

"Ganglöt will take it from here," Annie says as she kneels beside me. She gently tucks some hair behind my ear. "Your mother will be in the third room to the left. Don't go anywhere else, Meghan, do you understand?"

I nod, the hope of seeing my mother one last time the only thing holding me together.

"The longer you stay, the harder it is to leave, so get your message and come back, okay?" She actually smiles. "The girls and Spencer will be waiting for you, so don't linger." She stands and backs away, out of the elevator. "Third door to the left," she adds, and then the elevator doors slide closed.

25

THE THIRTEENTH FLOOR

The elevator ride up is quicker than I expect. I try to push myself into a seated position, but I can't. I'm too weak. Thankfully, once the door slides open to what looks like a normal hallway, Ganglöt turns to help me. She also looks normal, and beautiful, her Nordic features almost angelic, so it's hard to believe I'm about to step into the bowels of hell. She kneels beside the bench. "Third door to the left. Make it quick, okay?" Before I can figure out how to respond, Ganglöt touches my forehead.

The heaviness in my lungs begins to dissipate. The pain rippling through my body lulls. In a moment, I feel normal again—all my symptoms mercifully gone. I scramble off the bench seat and start wiggling parts of my body to make sure everything's in working order. All seems well, and I'm somehow all clean again—there's not so much as a trace of dirt or blood on me.

"Go!" Ganglöt orders. "Time is precious." She firmly but gently pushes me ahead.

When I'm in the hallway, I do a quick search of the area. It looks like a regular hotel hallway—like a real fancy one, with a plush red carpet and gold trim, and on the opposite end of the hallway, there are two golden double doors.

"Third door on the left," Ganglöt repeats. "Press the call button when you're ready."

I watch as she takes a backward step into the elevator and the doors slide closed. With her gone, I whip around and search the area again. It's still just a fancy hotel hallway, but I can't shake off the foreboding feeling that it really isn't as pristine as it seems, so I hurry ahead, instinctively heeding everyone's warnings. I make it to the third door on the left and reach for the knob since knocking seems pointless. I push the door open, which gives me a view of a standard room with a king-sized bed, and right smack in the middle of the space is my mom. She's pacing in front of the bed. When she turns to begin her approach my way, she spots me and stops short. In one instant, relief washes over her face; in the next, she begins to sob. She rushes over and crushes me in an embrace. And in that moment, I know it's really Mom. It's her. Her signature scent gives it away, letting me know she's really here.

She kisses my head a hundred times and squeezes me so hard I almost can't breathe again. Then she takes a step back and looks me over in that "mom" way of hers. "You made it. I knew you'd make it. Are you okay?"

I shake my head since I'm *so* not okay. "Mom..." I touch her face. Her beautiful, soft, smooth face. "You're..."

She smiles. It's her sad one. "I know, Peanut, and I'm sorry. I'm so sorry for everything I've put you and the girls through. I love you guys, so much. Please remind them of that every day."

"Is that why you did this, Mom?" I ask, suddenly angry with her. "Did you sacrifice your soul so we can live a better life?"

Mom looks away, ashamed. "No, Peanut, though if I had known that was an option before I died, I would have taken it." She looks back at me. "That seems so much nobler, but sadly, I didn't go out that way…" She takes my hand and pulls me toward the bed. "We don't have much time but I think I've figured out the best way to make this easier for both of us." She pushes me onto the mattress, then she reaches for the remote. "I'm going to show you how I died—"

"What?" I interject as I look up at her. "Mom—"

"Time is precious," she says as she looks at me with a great sadness in her eyes. "Please, Peanut. I only have a couple of minutes to spend with you and then you have to go. Forever. So please…" She sits beside me on the bed and pulls me into a tight embrace. "It was all my fault, so don't be angry with anyone. Don't let it consume you with hate. It was a simple accident of my own doing, so this one last time, I need you to help me clean up my mess." She leans back to look at me.

I shake my head as I search her eyes. "I don't understand."

With her arm still draped over my shoulders, she presses a button on the remote. The TV springs to life, with footage of the kitchen in Rusty's bar playing like something you'd see from the security camera's point of view. The angle of the shot is askew though, so I can only make out one corner of the kitchen and the bathroom. Both areas are empty, but I hear voices. One belongs to Uncle Rusty, for sure; the other belongs to a guy whose voice I don't recognize. They're arguing, shouting about the man not being allowed in the bar again, then I hear Mom. She yells some colorful stuff at Uncle Rusty about how he doesn't own her and how he can't tell her what she can do. It's an argument I've heard many times before— one where Uncle Rusty tries to intervene with wisdom and logic, but Mom just retaliates with bitterness and profanity. She usually only reacts that way when she's drunk or high—or both. From the sound of her slurred speech, I'm almost sure it's at least one of those things, and when she finally does stumble onto camera the evidence of that is glaringly obvious.

Mom staggers toward one of the cabinets…the one, I

suddenly realize, where we found her purse. Uncle Rusty moves into view and grabs her arm just before she can pull open the door. Mom rips her arm away just as a black guy comes into view and grabs Uncle Rusty's other arm and pulls him away from Mom. I lean closer and focus on the man. It's Will-i-am.

"Get your hands off her, fool!" Will.i.am says as he jerks Uncle Rusty off the screen.

The men's argument quickly escalates, and they begin to come in and out of view as they shove each other back and forth. Sadly. Again. This is not the first time I've seen this play out. Mom has a knack for pitting men against each other, and poor Uncle Rusty has been dragged into more fights than he can probably count. The shoving goes back and forth for a moment longer before Mom steps between them. Will.i.am tries to get a swipe in though, which Uncle Rusty evades with a quick right step. He accidentally crashes into Mom in the process, which, with his gigantic size, causes Mom to rebound backward from the impact.

She stumbles off camera.

A single, devastating clank resonates through the air.

Uncle Rusty and Will.i.am both stop to look at her, then Uncle Rusty moves off-camera. He says my mom's name once, then twice. Then he starts to panic. Will.i.am inches closer to them and repeatedly asks Uncle Rusty if Mom is okay. I'm so engrossed by the scene unfolding before me I actually flinch when Mom stops the replay.

I look at her. "What happened?"

With her free hand, she points to her head. "Caught my head in just the wrong spot on the corner of the bathroom sink."

My stomach churns and I shiver as I recall that horrific clanking sound. "But…"

Mom gives my shoulder a good squeeze. "No buts, Peanut.

It was quick and painless, and just an accident. Uncle Rusty didn't do it on purpose."

I look back at the TV, my mind racing with a million questions.

Mom forces me to look at her. "You know more than anybody that your Uncle Rusty is a good man."

I nod.

"He was trying to protect me, the way he always did, but when this happened, and Will was there, he didn't know what to do." Mom searches my eyes. "He got scared. Do you understand that, Peanut? He didn't want to go back to jail. He didn't want to lose everything he's worked so hard for."

She gives me a moment, and as everything begins to fall into place, I start to shake my head. "But he didn't really hurt you...you fell..." I say as I scramble off the bed, my heart racing, my brain short-circuiting. The cops had said they found her body in Harrison Lake, right down the street from Will's house—but if she had died at the bar, then how had she gotten to Newburgh? "Mom?" I look at her, my body shaking so badly I'm scared I'm going to fall over.

Mom stands and takes both my hands into hers. "Breathe through it, Peanut," she says softly, then she presses her forehead against mine. "Time is precious, so focus for me, okay? Just breathe through it while I talk."

I squeeze her hands and nod.

"Will threatened to call the cops. He said he was going to blame Rusty. He said he was going to tell them Rusty had pushed me, so Rusty just...*reacted*. His insulin was on the counter so he would remember to take it after we closed for the night, so he used it ..."

"He used it...?" I echo, my mind trying to wrap itself around that.

"He injected Will with a fatal dose of insulin," Mom adds softly. She releases one of my hands so she can tilt my chin, forcing me to look at her. "And he'll have to answer for that one day, Peanut, but everything he did afterward, to cover it up, including what he did to me—"

I jerk away from her as the final pieces of the puzzle fall into place. Uncle Rusty hadn't killed my mother, but he had killed Will…and then he had gone to great lengths to cover it up. Stunned and revolted at the realization, I look at Mom. "He…*he* put you in the lake?"

She reaches for my hands, but even though I try to pull away, she keeps ahold of them. "I need you to forgive him for that, okay?" I try to yank my hands out of hers but her grip tightens. "Meghan Marie. I need you to forgive him. Do you understand? After everything he's done for us; after everything he's worked for, he doesn't deserve to spend the rest of his days in a cage. It nearly killed him the first time and it'll destroy him now." She pulls me into an inescapable bear hug. "With everything that happened that night, he doesn't remember he accidentally held onto Will's key fob. He used the garage opener to get into the house, so he accidentally took the fob back to Middletown. It fell out of his pocket when he did laundry. It's in between the washer and—"

I shove out of her arms, completely and utterly enraged now. "You brought me here—to hell—to help you cover up *your* murder?"

I expect her to retaliate in her usual tantrum way, but she doesn't. Instead, she takes my hands again and shakes her head. "Accident, Peanut. It was just a horrible accident."

"But he killed Will!" It's not an accusation. It's just a fact.

She nods. "He did, and he'll have to answer for that, but not now, at least I hope not." She brushes a wisp of hair off my face and smiles. "You have to get going, Peanut, and I don't want you to leave angry. I wanted you to have peace in knowing it was an accident; that I went quickly and painlessly, and that I'm okay."

"You're not though!" I look around the hotel room, which seems a little more rundown than it did when I first arrived. "You're in hell, Mom!"

She nods. "It's where I belong, and I'm okay with that. I'm good. No one or nothing can hold Maggie May down, Peanut, not even hell itself, so don't worry about me, okay? You just enjoy your life. Follow your dreams. Be the role model for the girls I never was." She kisses the top of my head and then hugs me again.

I want to yell at her. I want to scream and punch and hit everything and everybody for all this, but I'm running out of time. I can feel it, almost as if some invisible rope is tied around my waist and is yanking me backward. So I hug her back. I squeeze her with all my might. I take in huge whiffs of her scent and I try to remember every moment of being in her arms because I know it's the last time I'll see her. It's the last time I'll be able to talk to her. "I love you, Mom."

"I love you, Peanut. To the edge of the universe and beyond." We embrace for a moment longer, then she steps back and takes my hand. "Come on. Let's get you out of here."

A part of me wants to stay because the thought of leaving her here alone eats at me, but that nagging feeling of being pulled back is beginning to get overwhelming too, so I follow her out the door and toward the elevator almost hypnotically.

"Tell your friend Michelle that Macy and Marigold are okay now, so she can start moving on too."

I look over at her and see that she's smiling. "But how…? I mean, I'm here, so wouldn't the veil have closed if Macy somehow broke the deal?"

Mom shrugs. "Some things are irreparable, Peanut." She pulls me to a halt by the elevator and motions toward the call button. "When the veil rips, regardless of the cause or the solution, the veil rips."

I press the button, that overwhelming feeling to return

beginning to reach an astronomical level now. The elevator door slides open and I have to keep myself from jumping in. I look at Mom instead. I try to remember every inch of her face. "I love you, Mom, and I promise I'll make you proud."

She cups my face in the palms of her hands and smiles. "You already have, Peanut. I love you. I love the girls. And I love Matt for taking care of you guys. You'll all be okay now, and I'll always be with you, okay?"

I hug her, squeezing her so tightly that if she were alive I would have crushed her. She kisses my head one more time, then she pushes me into the elevator. "I love you, M&M," she says and then holds her hands in a heart shape over her heart.

Tears begin to streak down my face as I hold my hands over my heart too. "I love you, M&M."

And the doors slide closed.

A sob escapes me, and then another, each one more painful than the last. Mom is gone now. Really. Forever. And it practically destroys me. I sink onto the bench, my body so wracked with sobs I don't notice the elevator is taking longer to get down than it had to get up. In fact, it isn't until the feeling of the elevator plummeting at a high-rate of speed overcomes me that I do notice anything is wrong at all. When I finally do, it's to find Ganglöt isn't at the wheel and the lights are blinking in and out. I look up, hoping to find an emergency hatch, but there isn't one, so I bolt out of my seat and make it to the key panel. All the floors are lit up and there's no emergency stop button.

I search around again, this time frantically, but there are no exits. No alternate strategies. I'm going to die, so Mom may not be alone for long. A screeching sound fills the small space, like metal against metal, and a burning smell begins to permeate the air. Smoke seeps in through the cracks between the doors and the lights finally flicker off for good. Thrust into complete darkness, I sink back onto the seat and await my fate.

The noise becomes deafening and the smoke chokes me, cutting off my air supply. I drop onto the floor, hoping to find one ounce of breathable air, but it's no use. Wheezing and alone, I finally succumb to the darkness.

———

"Meghan!" Spencer shouts, the desperation in his plea easy to register, given the decibel level at which he shouts my name. "Wake up!"

I moan and heave in a huge gulp of air, my lungs feeling as though they're about to explode. "I'm…"

"Oh, my god!" Spencer says. "Oh, my god! You're okay! Are you okay?" He shakes me. "Open your eyes!" he commands, and then he gives me another shake for good measure.

I blink, the movement taking a monumental effort, given that I'm more exhausted than I've ever been in my life. My body feels as though it weighs a thousand pounds.

"Meghan!" He grabs my cheeks and forces me to look up at him. "Look at me."

I try, but he's blurry.

"Say something," he orders.

"I'm…" Uttering that single word takes some major effort, and it doesn't help that he's holding my cheeks, so I tug my face out of his grip and try again. "I'm…okay…" I say, my throat sore, my voice barely a whisper.

Spencer pulls me into his embrace, and it's only then that notice I'm on the floor, in Spencer's arms. In the Bowery. As he practically squeezes the life out of me, my hazy tunnel vision dissipates so I can see the crowd gathering around us. I push back so Spencer knows to let me go. He helps me lean back a little. Then he pulls me onto his lap so I'm sitting up, but he doesn't let me go even though he's shaking, his entire body trembling so badly I consider switching places so I can hold him.

For a brief moment, I ignore the gathering crowd of hotel guests and gaze into his eyes. "I'm okay," I say, my voice still ragged. "Are you?"

He shakes his head, clearly not okay. He touches my face all over. I'm so worried and engrossed by his behavior that I actually jump when the elevator doors slide open behind us, the resounding ding sending a chill up my spine. I whip around and see Michelle and two doormen exiting the elevator.

"Are you guys okay?" Michelle asks, looking down at us incredulously.

As the other two doormen kneel beside us, Spencer, Michelle, and I exchange a knowing look.

"Are you okay, kid?" a nearby man asks. He's inched his way closer and seems genuinely concerned. So do the other hotel guests.

I nod since there's no way I can speak loudly enough for everyone, then I motion for Michelle to help me up. She takes my hands and very gingerly pulls me onto my feet. My legs are all wobbly, but Spencer gets onto his feet much more grace-fully and offers me some extra support.

"She's fine," he tells everyone. "Just a little tired after a long day."

The guests don't seem to buy it. Neither do the other two doormen, but Michelle shoos them away while Spencer helps me to the elevator. I have to admit I'm leery of getting on, but with the people hounding us from behind, I have no choice. As we cross the threshold, I shift closer to Spencer and can't help the tremor that rocks through me when I see we're on the fourteenth floor—or, in reality—the thirteenth floor.

He pulls me closer still and wraps his arms around me. "Is

it over?" he asks, his voice barely a whisper now too. "Did you see her?"

I press my cheek against his chest and nod.

"Are you okay?" he asks.

No. I'm not okay. I don't think I ever will be. So, even though all the phantom aches and pains are beginning to subside, I somehow know I'll never truly be okay again.

But I'll be all right.

I'll muster through.

And I'll try to make Mom proud.

STARS & STRIPES FOREVER

After nearly eight hours of waiting, the fireworks finally begin. The crowd isn't too bad in our little area at the South Street Seaport, which is exactly what Spencer was hoping for, because he's determined to find the exact spot he saw in his dream. "Is this it?" I ask for what feels like the millionth time after he pushes me another inch to the left.

He looks at me, then up at the skyline, then back at me. "It's pretty close," he says, and pulls me into his arms.

I smile. He smiles back. Then he kisses me.

When he leans back, he nods. "Oh, yeah. That was the spot."

Being in love is an awesome feeling, but *being* loved is even more spectacular.

"Eww!" Misty coos as she comes over to us. "They're kissing again!" she announces to everyone even though no one is remotely interested in us, given the amazing fireworks display.

Spencer releases me and turns around to pick her up. She pretends to fuss a bunch and then tries to squirm away when Spencer kisses the top of her head, but we all know she secretly loves it. The girls adore him and they're adjusting to New York better than I had ever hoped. It definitely helps that Matt has been great through all this and that I've finally come to terms with everything that's happened. I look over to Phil and Rebecca, who had come down from Middletown to celebrate the Fourth with us. I'm glad for it because Phil has been my rock, so while he didn't truly live any of those horrific moments with me, he's the only person in the world who really knows what happened, and without his support, I don't think I would have made it through.

Spencer sets Misty back on her feet and she drags us back to our little group—my new, crazy little hodgepodge family. There's Matt and Annabelle, though they're still under the guise of "friends" for Misty's sake. There's Michelle and her wife, Bernie. Phil and Rebecca are here too, and then there's me, the girls, and Spencer. As I huddle between them and look up at the fireworks, I smile. I love my new family and I'm grateful to my mom for bringing us together. After all, none of this would have been possible had it not been for her. And while a part of me will always resent her for asking me to do the unthinkable, I don't hate her for it. In fact, I think I love her more for it because in her own way, she finally did the right thing—or I guess as right as it could be given the circumstances.

For the moment though, I don't allow those thoughts to enter my mind. I can't change the past, no matter how much I dwell on it, but I can revel in *this* moment, in this place, with these people, so I do. We watch the fireworks and then we walk to a nearby restaurant and we eat unhealthy, greasy food. We laugh and we catch up about our week, and we discuss plans for the future. Spencer, and the girls and I, will be heading to Jersey for a couple of days to visit his family and then we're all meeting up again that next weekend for my big going away party. Basic training is right around the corner and while I never dreamed of having a big send-off, Annabelle suggested we have a gathering at the Bowery and it's just taken off from there.

Of course, my new hodgepodge family will be in attendance, along with Spencer's family and most of the staff from the Bowery, since I've gotten to know even more people since I moved down here and started working as a clerk part-time. I thought it would be hard, but it isn't. In fact, it somehow makes me feel closer to Mom, so it's been good. And to my surprise, quite a few people from Middletown are coming down too. Almost all my old Dollar Store coworkers are joining us, along with a couple of kids from school and Mrs. Jackson. I'm excited to see them.

Uncle Rusty is caravanning down with a couple of Mom's regulars. I've only seen him once since I got back from the thirteenth floor. It was when Spencer and I drove up a couple of days later, under the guise of me making a final pitstop to grab paperwork from our schools and stuff. I stopped in to see a lot of people that day, and I showed Spencer around town. I took him to our apartment and stopped by to see Mrs. Jackson. Then we met Uncle Rusty at his house. I had told him I couldn't bring myself to go to the bar, which is the truth. Accident or not, I don't ever want to see the inside of that place again. Thankfully, Uncle Rusty didn't question my choice, and so we met at his house for a late lunch. Introducing him to Spencer and then talking old times was a bit of a surreal experience. He even pulled out old photo albums and showed Spencer embarrassing pictures of me as a kid—like any loving uncle would do, and then he started to recount his favorite times with my mom.

It was then that I finally saw his suffering; his regret; and so I excused myself to the bathroom, but I stopped by the laundry room on my way. I grabbed Will.i.am's key fob from in between the washer and dryer and I've held onto it ever since. For weeks, I didn't know what to do with it. I've considered calling Jesse several times, but I knew that wasn't what Mom wanted, and so I've stewed on it some more—always trying to look at both sides of it. Then one day, out of the clear blue, Jesse called me. He claimed it was to just check in and see how we were doing, but then he started asking a lot of questions, and I knew he knew—or at least suspected that Uncle Rusty was somehow involved. But they couldn't prove it because the only evidence of his wrongdoing was in my pocket, and that's when I knew what I had to do.

For weeks after that though, I've continued to carry the fob with me everywhere. The time to get rid of it, up until now, hadn't been right, but when we're all ready to head back to our respective homes for the evening, Phil asks for a private moment to chat with me about something. We walk back to the pier in silence and I take a moment to overlook the East River.

"You sure?" he asks as he leans against the railing and looks down into the water.

I fish the fob out of my pocket, lean against the railing beside him, and dangle it by my fingertips. "Yeah…" I say, and only because I've thought it over so much. At the end of the day though, Will.i.am had no wife or children, and while I'm sure his family misses him in their own way, his grandmother is doing well. Phil knows that firsthand since he's gone up there a couple of times to check on her, and her nosy neighbors are always happy to see him. So while I don't think I have the right to pass judgment on anything or anyone, I can't bring myself to send Uncle Rusty back to prison for the rest of his life. It may not be the right choice, but Mom did say that at some point we'll all have to answer for what we do here, so our time will come—even mine. For now, though, I'm resolute in my decision, so I drop the fob into the East River, where hopefully it'll never see the light of day again.

Behind us, someone lights a Roman Candle, and the fireworks shine brightly just overhead. My mom used to love setting them off every year when we were at Uncle Rusty's, so it seems fitting, almost as if she had somehow managed to plan it herself. Not that it would surprise me. Nothing or no one can hold Maggie May Martin down, not even hell itself, so I hope she's still out there somewhere, doing crazy Maggie May things, because whether she's good or bad or right or wrong, she's my mom, and I love her.

———

Don't miss your next favorite book!
Join the Fire & Ice YA Books newsletter today!
www.fireandiceya.com/mail.html

THANK YOU FOR READING

Did you enjoy this book?

We invite you to leave a review at your favorite book site, such as Goodreads, Amazon, Barnes & Noble, etc.

DID YOU KNOW THAT LEAVING A REVIEW...

- Helps other readers find books they may enjoy.
- Gives you a chance to let your voice be heard.
- Gives authors recognition for their hard work.
- Doesn't have to be long. A sentence or two about why you liked the book will do.

ABOUT THE AUTHOR

Winter lives in the moment and loves nothing more than being surrounded by her family, her fur-babies, and a ton of great reads! When she doesn't have her nose stuck in a book, she's usually thinking up far away, fantastical worlds or she's cooking up a storm in the kitchen!

Because of her love for all things literary, Winter pursued a Master of Arts degree in English Literature and Creative Writing. Professionally, she is a manuscript editor, and in her spare time, she enjoys hosting author spotlights and posting book reviews.

In her private time, she is an avid reader of science fiction, fantasy, and paranormal romances, and one day she hopes to inspire young readers in the same way her favorite authors continue to inspire her today.

www.winterlawrence.com

 facebook.com/WinterBLawrence

 twitter.com/WinterBLawrence

 instagram.com/winter.b.lawrence

ALSO BY WINTER LAWRENCE
FROM FIRE & ICE YOUNG ADULT BOOKS

The Gamer Series

Eve 2.0: The Ultimate Gaming Experience

Eve 2.0: Night Terrors

www.ingramcontent.com/pod-product-compliance
Lightning Source LLC
Chambersburg PA
CBHW050730180626
46814CB00002B/684